AND THEN THEY WERE WED . . .

"I shall tell you exactly how to go on, madam, do not doubt it," Lord Edward declared. "Whether you like it or no, you are my wife, and shall behave accordingly."

"Indeed, my lord," Eliza replied. "I shall behave just as a marchioness should. I shall develop airs and graces and flirt with my fan. I shall also attend parties and routs and balls. In truth, my lord, I have decided that since our marriage is to be one of convenience, I shall take advantage of every convenience I can."

"As soon as you fulfill the terms of our agreement," Lord Edward said in an implacable voice.

This was Eliza's first inkling that marriage to the infamous Lord Edward Seaton might be fearfully more demanding than she thought. . . .

KATHERINE KINGSLEY was born in New York City and grew up there and in England. She is married to an Englishman and they live in the Colorado Mountains with their son.

A Natural Attachment

Katherine Kingsley

A SIGNET BOOK

To Sharon Albert, who understands about cows

And to Arthur *Amazona ochracephala auropalliata*, who is teaching me with a great deal of enthusiasm about the family *Psittaciformes*.

SIGNET
Published by the Penguin Group
Penguin Books USA Inc., 375 Hudson Street,
New York, New York, 10014, U.S.A.
Penguin Books Ltd, 27 Wrights Lane, London W8 5TZ, England
Penguin Books Australia Ltd, Ringwood, Victoria, Australia
Penguin Books Canada Ltd, 2801 John Street,
Markham, Ontario, Canada L3R 1B4
Penguin Books (N.Z.) Ltd, 182-190 Wairau Road,
Auckland 10, New Zealand

Penguin Books Ltd, Registered Offices:
Harmondsworth, Middlesex, England

First published by Signet, an imprint of Penguin Books USA Inc.

First Printing, August, 1990

10 9 8 7 6 5 4 3 2 1

Copyright© Julia Jay Kendall, 1990
All rights reserved

1

My sore throats are always worse than anyone's.

Jane Austen, *Persuasion*

Lord Seaton was not a happy man. He hadn't been particularly happy for most of his life, but that was neither here nor there: he didn't choose to dwell on his emotional state, considering it a wasteland with little chance of alteration. No, the cause of his unhappiness was more immediate, and he let his feelings be vented without inhibition.

"For God's sake, Black, must you be so heavy-handed?" He wiped the clammy sweat from where it had sprung anew on his brow, and looked down at the doctor, who was prodding the most intimate part of his person. There was no room for embarrassment: he was in far too much pain for that, not that embarrassment was a feeling with which he had any familiarity. But at this particular moment he was desperately concerned about his condition, which had sprung up very suddenly and without any apparent cause, leading him to think the worst had finally happened. He suppressed a strong wave of nausea, clamping his teeth down hard as the doctor's fingers continued to probe.

Dr. Black finally looked up from his examination and stepped back, indicating that he was finished. "I am truly very sorry, Lord Seaton. I know the pain must be severe. I do wish you had consulted me earlier. When did the fever begin?"

"I don't know, perhaps a week ago," Edward said irritably, dropping his nightshirt and gingerly getting back into bed. "I thought nothing of it. You know how easy it is to contract a fever in this damnable climate. Now, tell me what in hell has happened to my blasted testicles! They're three times the size they should be, and feel as if a mule just kicked them square on.''

"Was your throat sore and swollen with the onset of this fever?"

"Yes," Edward said shortly, wishing the doctor would get down to the diagnosis. "But that was over a week ago, and it cleared up before this happened. I can't see what one has to do with the other."

"I'm afraid one has a great deal to do with the other, my lord. Aren't you aware that there has been an epidemic of mumps raging through Jamaica recently?"

"No. I've been away. But I can't see what mumps has to with my problem."

"It appears that you have a full-blown case, my lord."

Edward's brow snapped down. "Mumps? Don't be absurd, man. Mumps are for children. Anyway, I've never heard of a case of the mumps lodging in such a spot."

"It is a complication that sometimes occurs when a mature male contracts the illness. I assume you never had mumps as a child?"

"No, not that I recall," said Edward, raking a hand through his hair and trying to scan his memory. His childhood was not a time he often brought out for rumination. "No, I'm quite sure I didn't."

"Well, my lord, unfortunately you have them now. There is nothing for it except to treat the fever and wait for the illness to run its course."

Edward grinned broadly as a flood of relief swept through him and the absurdity of the situation struck him. A laugh escaped, but he stifled it quickly as a stab of pain sent a fire raging through his groin. "Mumps," he said weakly when he'd recovered. "I'll be damned. It must have been that puling little Porphyry boy who came to visit with his vile mother last month. I thought he looked more bacon-faced than usual. Well, I feel absurd, being a man of four-and-thirty with a child's illness, but it's far better news than I thought you were going to deliver. I didn't fancy living with a flaming case of syphilis and ending up like my mad cousin. They had to export him to Australia,

God save the Australians. So, when is this blessed nuisance going to disappear, may I ask?''

"Another week should see you on your way, my lord, if you follow my directions and observe complete confinement in bed.''

Edward snorted. "I'm hardly going anywhere in this condition. And can I expect to return to all my, ah, previous activities without any unpleasant consequences?''

Dr. Black managed a tight smile. The Marquess of Seaton was renowned in Jamaica for his philandering. A more attractive rake could not exist, with his fine figure, dark hair, and flashing blue eyes, but he was, nevertheless, a rake, and Dr. Black took care to see that his daughters were even more carefully chaperoned than usual when Lord Seaton was in residence. He certainly didn't want the crescent-shaped birthmark that Lord Seaton sported low on his hip exposed to their tender gazes, as it reportedly had been to much of the island's female population. He had in truth been curious to see if the infamous birthmark was fact or rumor, and when Lord Seaton had raised his nightshirt, the fact had sadly been confirmed.

Dr. Black considered it a fortunate thing that Lord Seaton was the owner of a number of sugar plantations that were conveniently—for the parents of unmarried daughters—scattered far afield. It was also a fortunate thing that Lord Seaton was so involved in his business concerns that he was often not in residence. But Dr. Black was now in the unfortunate position of having to deal Lord Seaton a bad piece of news regarding the long-term disposition of those concerns, and he didn't relish breaking the news. Lord Seaton's temper was legendary.

"Well?'' Edward demanded, slightly alarmed at the way the old sawbones was regarding him. "I will make a full recovery, will I not?''

"Yes, my lord, I have every expectation that you will. However, there is one matter I feel I must mention.'' He cleared his throat and assumed his most professional expression.

"Oh, for God's sake, get on with it,'' Edward said impatiently. Now that he knew he wasn't suffering from an unmentionable and incurable disease, he wanted the doctor away as quickly as possible. Doctors were most decidedly not his idea of amusement. "And you might remove that melancholy ex-

pression from your face while you're at it. What is it, Black?''
he said more slowly as he perceived the doctor was struggling
for words. Seaton's chest suddenly tightened as his initial alarm
returned. ''Perhaps you did not understand me correctly. I was
asking if I'll be able to conduct myself as a man. In other words,
you dolt,'' he said as the doctor still did not reply, ''I will be
able to have sexual intercourse, will I not?''

The large green bird sitting on a perch near the bed had been
watching the proceedings with a sharp eye. ''Go stuff yourself,''
he said quite clearly.

''Oh, stubble it, Archie, or I'll stuff you and eat your infernal
tongue for breakfast. Well, Doctor?''

Dr. Black blinked twice and ran his finger around his collar.
He decided to couch his message in the most highbrow medical
terms he could, not only to soften the blow, but hoping that
perhaps Lord Seaton would not completely understand him. Self-
preservation was high on his list of priorities.

''I will be able, will I not?'' Edward repeated dangerously.

''Yes, I believe you will, my lord,'' the doctor croaked, and
then braced himself. ''But it is the outcome of that activity that
is in grave question. Over the many years of my practice I have
repeatedly observed that in cases of mumps in the adult male,
bilateral swelling of the testes unfortunately results in the
inability to promulgate.''

There was a long pause as Edward absorbed this piece of
information without any discernible expression, and Dr. Black
thought that he might have escaped more easily than he'd
anticipated. But in this assessment he was badly mistaken.
Edward was merely trying to recover from the shock the
doctor's words had caused. He fixed the doctor with a dangerous
eye. ''Do you mean to tell me I'm going to be bleeding sterile?''
Edward bit out each word from between his teeth until the last
exploded into the air with a great shout.

''Not to put too fine a point on it, I'm afraid that is the case,
my lord.'' Dr. Black winced, then his eyes widened as he saw
Lord Seaton reach for the pitcher of water next to his bed. He
just managed to make it through the door before the pitcher hit
the wall with a great crash. He was lucky to escape with only
a slight drenching. After all, it could have gone much worse.
No man likes to be told he has become sterile, and Lord Seaton
would like it less than most.

"Bleeding carbuncle," squawked the parrot through the door, and the doctor scurried off before anything else could happen, hoping his services wouldn't be needed again.

The remainder of the year continued to go just as badly for Edward, as did the following. He lost a ship to a typhoon, a ship that had been carrying a small fortune in sugar and rum and from which he had stood to make a large profit. Instead, he suffered a setback and had to work twice as hard to make it up. He had recovered from his absurd case of mumps, and as the fool of the doctor had promised, he was in no way sexually impaired, a point he had hastened to prove to himself at the very first opportunity.

But the question of sterility nagged at him constantly, as it did again this morning. He had concluded a pleasant-enough evening with Rosamunde Bradley, a most attractive and willing widow, but he still felt empty and dissatisfied. He had never questioned his ability to father children and had always intended to marry and produce an heir and a spare, for the marquessate was an ancient one and he did not believe in neglecting his responsibilities. Now there would be no heir and on his death the title and the entailment would go to his mad syphilitic cousin in Australia, if by some miracle he managed to outlive Edward, which was highly unlikely. Failing that, there was no one else. The tenth Marquess of Seaton would be the last. It was a damned shame.

Indeed, although it was foolishness of the highest order, he had been taking no precautions against impregnating the women he chose to disport himself with, hoping one of them would take with child: Edward would have been perfectly content to marry whichever one did. But pregnancy did not occur in any of them, and at the end of the year he regretfully concluded that Dr. Black had been correct in his assessment. It bothered him a great deal more than he had ever thought such a thing would. In his more honest moments, which only came when he wasn't paying close attention, he was forced to admit to himself that knowing he could not sire children made him feel less of a man.

But he discussed this with no one, not even his greatest friend, Peter Frazier, who knew about everything else in his life. There had been times he had been tempted to tell him the truth, times that Peter had asked him what was worrying him, and he had almost spoken of it, but somehow the words would not come out. The truth was simply too humiliating.

Edward pushed away the cargo invoices he'd been trying to study with little success, wiped his mouth, and stood, taking his coffeecup with him. He went over to the veranda railing and leaned on it, looking out over the lawn to the indigo sea, the white spume of waves rolling gently in on the long strip of sand below. He loved the sea and spent as much time as he could on it. There was nothing like the sight of the wind catching in the sheets of the sails above, the feeling of the ship quickening, the creaking of the masts in the still of the night.

He sighed heavily, suddenly nostalgic for a long sail. But there was far too much to be done before he could indulge himself in a voyage. Scowling, he went back to the table where his work awaited him. Jamaica was in the midst of the rainy season and it was hot and extremely humid, which always made Edward ill-tempered. He never failed to ask himself why he chose to live in such a climate at this time of year, when England would be cool, the countryside soon magnificently autumnal. He had been telling himself that it had been far too long since he had returned to England—five years, in fact. All of his more recent voyages had been to South America or the Carolinas. Peter was the partner who went back to England to conduct any business. Perhaps it was time for him to make the journey himself. It might alleviate the *ennui* that had fallen upon him these past months, and he supposed he really ought to see that Seaton was running smoothly, as much as he disliked the place.

He looked up to see Hamlish standing there, slightly pink in the face, a most unusual state for the man, who usually anticipated his master's needs before his master did. "Well?" Edward demanded.

"Lord Seaton, there is a woman who insists on seeing you immediately. She's a native woman, my lord. I told her you weren't in, but she says she has business with you. She refuses to go away, my lord."

Edward regarded his butler with a bored expression. "Then have her taken away, Hamlish. Or pay her off, if you must. But don't disturb me with her problems. I'm busy." His attention returned to his invoices, but he shortly realized that Hamlish had not budged. "I thought I'd dismissed you," he said irritably. "Would you like to explain why you're still standing there looking like a globefish?"

Hamlish shifted uncomfortably. "The woman has a child with her, my lord." He colored even more deeply. "She says it belongs to you." He was completely taken aback when, instead of hearing the expected roar his lordship was so good at producing, no sound came at all. His lordship simply stared at him as if he'd lost his mind, which he thought he'd might well have done, having had the temerity to deliver such a piece of news.

"A child?" Edward finally said, his voice cool. "What sort of child are you referring to, Hamlish? Are you insinuating I have fathered a child on this hapless native woman? If so, you may consider yourself unemployed."

"It is a very small child, my lord, all wrapped up in blankets, looking close to suffocation in this temperature. I only saw its face briefly, but I believe it was quite English in appearance."

Edward's mouth twitched. Hamlish looked as if he wished to sink through the floor. The unfortunate man couldn't possibly know how ludicrous the situation was. It had been well over a year since his attack of the mumps. But he thought it wouldn't hurt to put a good face on things. "I see," he said, his eyes returning to the sheaf of papers. "And how old is this babe I'm supposed to have spawned?"

"It is fast asleep, my lord, and as I said, bundled up, but judging by its size, I would put its age at something in the vicinity of two years."

Edward's eyes shot up again, suddenly very alert. "Are you quite sure, Hamlish?"

"Well, my lord, I haven't any children of my own, but my sister has quite a brood." He was quite puzzled by his lordship's sudden interest. "What would you have me do, my lord?"

"I'd have you cease to ask me asinine questions. Bring the woman in, Hamlish. She had better bring the child as well."

Hamlish bowed, then turned and walked out of the room, mustering around him as much of his dignity as he had left. He was beginning to think Lord Seaton had gone from being merely cantankerous to completely insane.

Edward had not lost his reason, nor anything close to it. He was not prepared for an instant to accept that the child was his own. More than likely this was some foolish attempt at blackmail, and not the first time that such a thing had happened to him. He ran a hand over his eyes. Really, why he was even considering the interview was beyond him.

He stood as the veranda door opened and a very round, dark-skinned woman appeared in it. She wore a scarf wrapped around her head, and she clutched her bundle tightly to her chest.

"Mrs. Mavis Bugle," Hamlish intoned with only the slightest raise of an eyebrow, then backed away, softly closing the door behind him.

"Please sit down," Edward said, indicating a chair, but the woman stood her ground, looking him up and down. "Shall I turn around so that you might examine my backside as well?" Edward asked curtly.

"Humph," Mavis said. "I reckon your backside's just as pretty as the front, or my mistress would never have been so taken in." Her voice was deep and warm, the accent southern, not the Jamaican patois he'd expected.

"Your mistress?" Edward leaned his hip against the railing, crossing his arms across his chest, and regarded the woman wryly.

"That's right, my mistress, and I done buried her last month, no thanks to you. She died of a broken heart, sir, although the sorry state of her lungs hastened her along to her maker."

"As I understand from my man, you're claiming the child you're holding is mine, Mrs. Bugle. Perhaps you would be so good to tell me the name of your mistress?"

"I'm not surprised your kind would forget so easily. Martha Medford was her name, bless her soul, of the Charleston Medfords, until you brought ruin down upon her sweet head."

Edward looked at Mavis more closely, a faint bell going off in his head. Martha Medford. Yes, he vaguely remembered her, a pretty, vivacious young blond woman. Had she been married? No—not married. He remembered now: she had been a departure from his usual fare. He had been surprised and not pleased to discover slightly too late that she was a virgin. Virgins were not to his liking for a number of reasons, the least of them being physical inexperience. Virgins had a tedious habit of imagining themselves in love. Virgins also had a habit of expecting marriage immediately upon their deflowering. In short, virgins were a bore. He ought to have stopped it right there, fool that he was. She had been engaged to be married, though, so he'd thought himself safe enough, and after all, the deed had been done. They'd had a few most enjoyable nights together, warm nights lightly scented with magnolia blossom and azaleas . . . When? When had it been? His mind sped. The last trip to South Carolina had been two and a half—no, three years before. Take nine months away for a pregnancy and you'd have a child into his second year. "Good God," he said involuntarily.

"If God was as good as I'd hoped, sir, he'd have mowed you down right where you stand. Miss Martha waited and waited for you to come to her. She just knew you was coming back, and that's why she never did tell her family who the father of her unborn baby was. Sent her away in disgrace, they did, with only me to look after her. They said they'd take her back after the baby was born if she'd give the poor mite up, but my Miss Martha wouldn't think of such a thing. 'Edward will come and find me, Mavis,' she said time and time again. But you never had any intention of coming for her, no, sir. I knew it, too, and told her so, but my mistress wouldn't believe me. It was only when her lungs started tearing up on her that she finally gave up and said we'd go to you ourselves. We started the journey, but she died only a week later. 'Promise you'll take my baby to his father when I'm gone, Mavis," she said, crying her eyes out, and I did, with the last of her money—"

"That," said Edward, cutting her off, "is the biggest pile of sentimental claptrap I've ever heard. If you've been trying to appeal to my finer sentiments, you might as well know I haven't any. And if there's one word of truth in what you've said, which I very much doubt, then your mistress might have written me at any time. Naturally I would have done the honorable thing."

"Honorable," Mavis said with scorn. "If you'd had an honorable bone in your body, you never would have bedded her, and once you had, you might have thought to ask her to marry you. It was all the poor child ever wanted. But if there was one thing Miss Martha had, despite her lack of common sense, it was her pride. She never would have gone crawling to you."

"I promised her nothing," Edward said coldly. "What she chose to make of our encounter after the fact had nothing to do with me."

"No? She sure didn't make this child all on her lonesome. I don't see as she had much choice at all, once you took advantage of her. It was fine for you to go sashaying off into the sunset without another thought cast in her direction. But she had plenty left to think about, and none of it was very sweet," Mavis replied tartly.

Edward picked up a pen and fingered it. "There is absolutely no evidence that I am this child's father, Mrs. Bugle. If your mistress gave me her favors with so little a struggle, she might have given them to anyone else after me, including her fiancé."

Mavis shook her head. "Oh, no, sir, you ruined that chance for her, too. Mr. Kincaid knew the child couldn't be his, not that Miss Martha would have tried to pretend it was. Mr. Kincaid was a good southern gentleman. He would never have taken the mistress to his bed before the wedding, unlike certain English lords who don't have no more manners than a strutting cock."

The pen snapped and Edward fought to retain his control. No one had ever had the nerve to talk to him in such a fashion. "If you're thinking I'm quite such a paper skull as to take your word on this flimsy set of circumstances alone, then you're quite mistaken. I can imagine that you thought it would be easy enough to fob the child off on me, but I won't be had. You have absolutely no proof—all you have is the word of a desperate girl."

Mavis glared at him. "Just so's you's not thinking to disclaim the child, your mighty lordship, sir, my mistress told me to show something to you if you had any doubts. She never thought you'd think your own child anything other than that. You was the only man she ever laid with, that she swore to me. 'Mavis,' she said, 'I loved that man with all of my heart.' It just goes to show how easily we're taken in, now don't it." She marched over, and before Edward had a chance to react, she placed the heavy bundle in his arms. "I think it's high time you took a good look at your son."

"My—my son?" Edward said in a daze. It hadn't even occurred to him to consider the sex of the child.

"You heard me. Your son. You's all he has left to him, God

help the poor boy. Only twenty-six months old and look what he's come to in life.''

Edward juggled the baby awkwardly and finally managed to free a hand. He carefully started to pull the blanket away from the baby's face, wondering what on earth he was going to see. Perhaps it would have a harelip, or its nose would be squashed. He almost held his breath.

Wide blue eyes fluttered and opened. Alarmed, the baby stared into Edward's own blue eyes for a moment, obviously didn't like what he saw, scrunched up his face, and howled for all he was worth. With alarm, Edward thrust the child back into Mavis' arms. "For God's sake, quiet him, will you?"

"I can see you's got all the makings of a natural-born father," Mavis said with disgust.

"I see nothing that indicates I'm anything of the sort. He has blue eyes. All babies have blue eyes," Edward said, thoroughly rattled.

"It wasn't his face the mistress had in mind as proof, although any fool could see the child takes more after you than his own mother. And if you knew anything at all, you'd know that babies' eyes settle into all sorts of different colors by the time they have three months to call their own. It's this right here my mistress meant, not that she should've known about it in the first place." Mavis pulled the rest of the blanket away and raised the struggling child's little gown. There, low on his small, plump hip, was a dark birthmark in the shape of a crescent moon, the twin to Edward's own.

"What do you say now, sir?" Mavis demanded.

Edward felt quite ill. A number of March males had carried a mark exactly like it for generations. He sank into a chair and put his forehead into his hand, trying hard to recover himself. "I think we had better talk at length," he finally managed to say, surprised that his voice came out evenly.

"I think we'd better do just that," Mavis said firmly.

An hour later, Edward climbed the stairs to his room, feeling unexpectedly exhausted. In the space of minutes, he had been presented not only with a child, but a son at that. At first he had been unable to think of anything good about the situation at all. But then, after his brain had started to function again, he began to see that there might be a saving grace. For close to two years he had been certain that he would never have a child. Well, he certainly wouldn't have in the future, that much was clear, but it had never occurred to him to consider the past. A son . . . Suddenly his sterility did not seem such an onus, for there was a way to turn the child's existence into an advantage. Now no one need ever know of his condition, but better yet, why could he not continue the Seaton name and title? Perhaps it need not die with him, after all. Awful old Justin Brixtose in Australia could hardly kick up a fuss; he could barely remember his own name as it was. The only thing standing in the way was the fact that the boy—Matthew: he'd have to remember to think of him as Matthew—was illegitimate. He slammed into his bedroom. How did one get around illegitimacy?

Edward threw a cursory glance at Archie, who was in the middle of a grooming session, pulled off his jacket, cravat, and shirt, and poured himself a large measure of brandy. He then went to the window and threw it open to the muggy day. It bloody well looked as if it was going to rain again, he decided, although the continuous downpour was the least of his problems. Matthew, the small boy with the crescent moon on his hip, who now resided in a back bedroom along with his outspoken nanny—now *there* was a proper problem. He took a long drink from the snifter.

Archie distracted him by sidling along his perch, leaning as far forward as he could, and peering hopefully at Edward's glass. Edward smiled. "You're a lush, my friend," he said, holding the glass out. Archie plunged his head into it, took a long swallow, then shook his beak and chirped, swung upside down for good measure, and dived back into the glass again.

"Enough," Edward said, pulling the snifter away. "Next thing I know you'll be singing drunken ditties loud enough to wake the dead." His unfortunate choice of words brought Martha Medford to mind, and he spun around on his heel and threw the glass against the wall. "Damn," he spat. "Bloody hell!"

He sat down abruptly, his hands running through his hair. If only the girl had had an iota of sense, she'd have applied to him as soon as she'd discovered her condition. Now she was dead, leaving her child motherless, and illegitimate as well. It was only the fact that she knew she was dying from advanced consumption that had started her on her way to hand the child over to him. He supposed she must have intended a quick wedding and then expected immediately thereafter to swoon away into the afterworld. Well, her timing had been slightly off, he thought belligerently. If she'd only moved a little faster, two years faster, he would have had a legitimate heir, for he'd have married her in a flash, silly woman. Still, an illegitimate son was better than none at all, if he could only think of a way to turn the situation around with no one the wiser. Adoption was useless, and in any case, he might as well announce his problems to the entire world.

An unholy smile suddenly lit his face as an idea struck, and he threw his arms over his head with a shout.

Archie looked at him inquisitively, and Edward smiled wickedly. "Well, bird. How would you like for us to acquire a wife?"

Archie picked up a foot and scratched his head vigorously, then delicately cleaned the dust off his toenails.

Edward laughed. "Exactly how I feel, my fine feathered friend. Exactly how I feel. Of course it will require a trip to England in order to find someone suitable for my purposes, but that should be no problem. I've had it in mind in any case, and I'm sure you'll enjoy the voyage, won't you, Archie? Just think about being back on the good old salty sea. We'll have to drag young Matthew and the shrew Mavis along with us, but that is necessary, I'm afraid, if I'm to accomplish my end. I have every confidence that things will work out." He smiled again, his blue eyes alive with deviltry. "Indeed, every confidence in the world. After all, I'm a matrimonial prize."

2

I do not want people to be very agreeable,
as it saves me the trouble of liking them a
great deal.

Jane Austen, *Letters* December 24, 1798

E dward sighed heavily as he looked around the crowded
room. He was inexpressibly bored. London held no more
fascination for him than it had five years before, and it
seemed that with the exception of the usual new crop of
ingenues, nothing had changed. But worse, far worse, was that
he had not found anyone suitable to take as a wife. He frowned
and resolved to leave as abruptly as he'd entered, deciding that
the evening was yet again a waste of time.

"Lord Seaton?"

Edward turned to see a vapid but pretty female looking up
at him rather mistily, a tremulous smile on her lips. "Yes?"
he replied coolly, having had his fill of insipid misses. He
seemed to remember that this one was particularly stupid.
However, since he doubted that a woman of true intelligence
existed, and since he was hardly in a position to be overly
choosy, he realized that he could really not make an issue out
of it.

"Do you not remember me? We met in Jamaica three years
ago last summer. I am Pamela Chandler."

"Ah. Yes, of course, Miss Chandler. How very nice." He
began to move away when he felt her hand on his sleeve and
looked down at it with a raise of his eyebrow.

"I was so hoping to see you here this evening. I had heard

that you had returned, but we have only just come from Lincoln-shire ourselves. My parents and myself, that is. Perhaps you remember that I was on my way to join them in British Honduras? My father was fortunately recalled recently. It is such a relief to be back in England, don't you find? The tropical heat does affect one so."

"Does it?" Edward said, briefly considering Pamela Chandler as a candidate for a wife and then discarding her. She could not possibly have borne his child twenty-nine months ago if she'd been in British Honduras under the watchful eye of her parents. Better he keep his eye on someone older, someone willing to trade the lie for wealth and position. It was proving to be an impossible task. His eyes returned to scanning the crowd as if the answer might lie there.

"Oh, don't you find the constant heat a burden, my lord?" Pamela said, fluttering her lashes, and Edward looked at her with slight disbelief. She surely had to be twenty or twenty-one by now. He would have thought she'd outgrown such coyness.

"Occasionally, Miss Chandler. However, one adapts."

"Indeed, it must be so, although some people are never bothered by the heat. Why, my companion, Miss Austerleigh, was positively stoic. She would walk out with enthusiasm in the middle of the day, can you imagine? I could never bring myself to stir before the late afternoon. But then, Eliza always was a peculiar girl, didn't you think? I found I could not miss her overmuch when she left me, not long after we arrived in British Honduras. In truth, it was a relief."

"Oh, yes, Miss Austerleigh," Edward said with a vague memory of the strange girl, tall and angular, with red hair, a face full of freckles, and an introverted demeanor.

"Yes, indeed," Pamela continued with a little pout. "She was not amusing company in the least, always going on about underbrush and snakes and scribbling in her journals." She giggled. "In fact, I stole a peek every now and again, just to be sure she wasn't saying anything nasty about me—and you'll never guess, but your name occurred more than once, Lord Seaton."

Edward, thinking that someone should take Miss Chandler over his knee and give her a good spanking, looked down at her, his eyes lidded so she could not read his distaste. "Oh?" he said. "I cannot think Miss Austerleigh meant for her thoughts to be read."

"Do you scold, my lord? You are quite right if you do, for I know it was very naughty of me, but quite irresistible, you know. Eliza's jottings were most nonsensical, and to think she included you . . . Well! Isn't that the most absurd thing you ever heard?"

Edward's eyes narrowed dangerously. "Absurd, Miss Chandler?"

"Oh, I don't mean that you are not worthy of having every woman in polite society setting her cap at you, but Eliza . . . Well, she is only just on the fringes, you know, and if it hadn't been for Lady Westerfield dying two years ago and leaving her Sackville, she would still be penniless, not that she's well to go now. I understand she is struggling dreadfully to keep the horrid old place. I cannot think what her ladyship was about, even if Eliza was some sort of relative. As it was, she was only about in society because she was my paid companion. She'd had a Season, naturally, but that was before her stepfather died and left her quite destitute. So, really, she had a great deal to thank me for, and I thought her most ungrateful when she just picked up and left me with hardly a word and went back to England with Hermione Ludlupe. I don't suppose you saw them again? They wintered in Jamaica, you know. But Eliza would have had no entrée, for Mrs. Ludlupe was not well and so not able to go about. Eliza could not do so on her own, not that she'd be capable. I heard poor Mrs. Ludlupe died shortly after arriving back in England, no doubt from the boredom of having to put up with Eliza and her lack of conversation on the journey. It seems to be the effect Eliza has on people. It is a tedious sail from Jamaica to England, do you not find, my lord? I made it myself only some three months ago."

"Actually, Miss Chandler, I quite enjoy it."

"Oh, well, if one is accustomed to the sea . . . My health is delicate, and so sailing does not suit. Eliza was always very insensitive to the fact, but I suppose lack of breeding shows in such cases. Her mother came from Yorkshire stock."

Edward wished to God she'd stop babbling. He wondered what sort of jealousy drove Pamela Chandler to speak so poorly of her companion, who could hardly have been a threat with her uninspiring appearance and lack of conversation. And then something stirred inside of Edward's head, the faintest thread of an idea that began to pull into a tighter weave by the second. Why not? he thought as he sped over the possibilities. He had nothing to lose.

"Actually, I did know," he said, wondering what he was getting himself into. "I knew Lady Westerfield quite well. Sackville marches with Seaton, you see, and it was quite intentional that Eliza should be there. And I do believe the Westerfield connection came through Yorkshire landowners on the maternal side. I don't immediately recollect the name, but they were well-respected and certainly received. Eliza may have been unfortunate through no fault of her own, but she is definitely of good family."

"Oh! I—I had no idea. You speak as if you know Eliza better than I had realized."

"Yes, Miss Chandler. I do know Eliza a great deal better than you had realized. Please excuse me. Your servant." He bowed, leaving Pamela staring at him openmouthed, and quickly made his way through the room, saying a brief farewell to his hosts.

"Grigson," he commanded his butler as he strode through his front door. "See that the traveling carriage is ready for me at seven tomorrow morning. I plan to retire to Seaton. I do not know how long I shall be gone, but keep the house in readiness for my return."

"Yes, my lord. And the child and his nurse, my lord? Will they be going with you?"

"No, they will not, Grigson. They also shall await my return. I will give Mrs. Bugle my orders."

Grigson only bowed. The entire staff had been buzzing about the small boy who bore a remarkable likeness to his lordship, not to mention the boy's alarmingly forthright, dark-skinned nurse, and his lordship's reasons for bringing them to England, for he had said nothing by way of explanation.

Edward gave him a long look, but saw nothing he could take exception to. He went up the stairs and down the right-hand corridor to the room next to his son's and rapped sharply on the door.

Mavis' sleepy head appeared, a huge white kerchief covering her head and a voluminous dressing gown wrapped around her ample body. "Now, what can you be wanting at this hour, sir, may I ask?" she demanded, tying her sash. "I sure can't think you've suddenly been taken with a pain, and I know you won't be wanting to visit with Master Matthew, 'cause you haven't once laid eyes on the child since we came off that boat."

"Impertinence, Mavis Bugle, will gain you nothing but unemployment, and then who will Matthew have to look after him? I have come to tell you that I am going to the country tomorrow. I am going to find Matthew a mother, and I will remind you once again to say nothing to anyone about the original circumstances that brought you both here, not if you wish for Matthew to have an inheritance and yourself to keep your neck on your shoulders."

"I won't say nothing, sir. I already gave my word on poor Miss Martha's grave that I'd see the best for her little boy, so you don't need to go reminding me, not that what I think you're doing is sinful. But it's for God to decide how he'll deal with you, not me, so's you can rest easy on that matter."

"It would behoove you, Mavis, to try to limit yourself to 'Yes, my lord' and 'no, my lord.' I am not in need of a speech every time I wish to address you." He turned on his heel and walked away, and Mavis softly shut her door, but she muttered a string of invective as she waddled back to her bed.

Eliza Austerleigh was not much accustomed to men. In fact, she wasn't at all sure she even liked them. In her twenty-eight years she had experienced nothing but misery at their hands. First there had been her father, who drank himself into an early grave; then her stepfather . . . But she preferred not to think about him at all. She had felt no grief when either of them had died. There had been the various young bucks whom she'd met during her one and only Season, a humiliating experience in itself. And then there had been the gentlemen who had flocked around Pamela Chandler during their progress through America and the Caribbean, while she stood by and watched. They had paid Eliza lip service, but no more. She understood, naturally: she had nothing to offer them. She was not in any way what gentlemen might consider attractive, she was painfully shy, she had no money to call her own—at least she hadn't had until two years before, when a distant cousin had died and unexpectedly left her a house and a small competence. But the worst humiliation she'd suffered at the hands of the male sex had been dealt her by the Marquess of Seaton.

Why, then, was he standing at her front door, asking her if she was receiving visitors?

"Miss Austerleigh?" he repeated.

"I beg your pardon, Lord Seaton. I am merely surprised to see you. I had not realized you had returned to England." Eliza knew that her face had gone quite red, and she bristled at the thorough, rather insulting inspection he was giving her. A surge of hot anger surged up in her, and she had to swallow against the bile that had unexpectedly risen in her throat. He clearly hadn't changed. But she would not allow him to make a fool of her, not here on her own doorstep. Her hands clenched into fists at her sides as she struggled to maintain her equilibrium, and she only just managed dimly to make out what he was saying through the mist in her head.

"I returned only recently and I've just today come up to Seaton from London," he said as if entirely unaware of her discomfort. "But perhaps we might be more comfortable inside rather than holding this conversation in your doorway."

"Oh . . ."

"Is that an imposition, Miss Austerleigh?"

"No—I mean, if you'd like, then, of course, you must." She untied her apron with shaking fingers as she spoke and stepped to one side. "I'm afraid that Lady Westerfield is not here, however. She died over two years ago. Perhaps—"

"I did not come to call upon Lady Westerfield, Miss Austerleigh. It was you I came to see."

"Me? Why? And how did you know I was now living here?"

Edward took an inward breath and prayed for patience as he ducked his head through the low-slung door of the front parlor and took in the dingy furnishings. "I merely thought I'd renew our acquaintance, Miss Austerleigh," he said, taking the chair she indicated. "It has been so long since I have been in England that I find I have lost touch with many people. You, however, I met only a few years ago in Kingston, and since you are now my neighbor, it seemed a logical thing to look you up. Do you object?" He crossed one leg over the other and regarded her neutrally.

"Certainly not, Lord Seaton. You have every right to call upon whom you please. I am merely curious that you chose to call upon me, given that we exchanged hardly a word the entire time I was in Jamaica. I hadn't realized that you had any interest in my conversation, Lord Seaton. Or perhaps you've come out of curiosity to discover if I have any at all. Sherry?''

Edward gave her an incisive look, wondering if Miss Austerleigh might have an iota of intelligence inside her head. But he dismissed the idea as ridiculous as he took the proferred glass. "Won't you join me?" he said as she sat down empty-handed.

"No, thank you, Lord Seaton. I have a full afternoon's work yet to do. I have been cleaning, as you can probably see; you'll have to excuse my appearance and that of the house. I'm afraid we're both in the same state of disorder—dusty and disheveled.''

"Have you no servants?'' he asked with surprise, thinking the situation was worse than he'd first anticipated.

"Certainly I have servants. One or two, that is,'' Eliza amended, perfectly willing to tell him the truth. Far be it from her to disappoint him. "I have a cook and a housekeeper. And there are men for the outdoors, which is far more important.'' She didn't find it necessary to add that the men were upstairs helping Annie to rehang the upstairs draperies, which had been carefully cleaned and mended, instead of in the greenhouse, from which she ran a small but mildly profitable flower business.

Eliza looked down at her toes. The situation seemed completely ridiculous to her, almost farcical. Here she was closeted in the musty front parlor with the incredibly self-satisfied, extremely sophisticated Marquess of Seaton, as handsome as a god, as well he knew. He was wearing beautifully cut country clothes in the latest fashion, which served only to emphasize his muscular, well-conditioned figure. His boots were polished to a high shine and his neckcloth was of the snowiest white linen. She had a mobcap on her head, from which her hair was escaping in every direction, and she was wearing the oldest, most ill-fitting of her dresses, not that she had any that were becoming. There had never been any extra money for that.

Eliza smothered an urge to laugh as it crossed her mind that maybe he had come for a bit of sport, the countryside being temporarily empty of beautiful young women. But to come to her? That really was laughable. The reprobate Lord Seaton must have fallen on desperate times.

"Miss Austerleigh, I have the most extraordinary feeling you haven't been paying the least attention to what I've been saying.''

''I—I beg your pardon.'' Eliza managed to look up and meet his very blue eyes with her own brown eyes opened wide. She saw most definite annoyance in them, which pleased her enormously. Oh, she'd give him exactly what he expected of her, and more besides. ''I do try to attend,'' she said doubtfully, ''but it's hard keeping two thoughts in the same place. I was just wondering if I had anything in the house to offer you in the way of food. I think there might be some bread and butter, but I cannot think where Cook is. I can make something myself, if you'd like,'' she said, brightening.

''Please, don't trouble yourself. I'm not in the least hungry.''

''Very well.'' She folded her hands in her lap primly.

''As I was saying, I was most surprised to learn that you were living just down the road from Seaton. I saw Miss Chandler when I was in town, and she informed me that you were no longer companion to her. I understand Lady Westerfield was a relative of yours and left you this house.''

''Lady Westerfield was my mother's cousin. It was very good of her to leave me her house. As Miss Chandler probably also told you, before Sackville I had no home.''

''I see. And do you live here alone?''

''I hope you do not find it scandalous that I do, Lord Seaton, but in truth I have had my fill of companionship.''

''Really? Have you no other family?''

''None, my lord, but I hope that the fact that I am alone in the world does not move you to tears. I should be most distraught, and really, I am not in need of sympathy, I assure you, for I manage quite well.''

''I have no intention of offering you anything close to sympathy. Sympathy is not an emotion in which I tend to indulge myself or others.''

''That comes as no surprise, my lord,'' Eliza said, and was rewarded with a frown. ''I meant only that it takes a certain kind of person to be genuinely sympathetic, or empathetic, for that matter.''

''And are you saying that you believe I have no empathetic qualities, Miss Austerleigh?''

''I am saying, my lord, that the capacity does exist in some people, but it is a quality I have found to be quite rare. I do not know you well enough to judge, but empathy has not been the foremost quality I have heard mentioned when your name has come up in conversation.''

"Oh? I hardly think my name can have come up often.''

"Hardly, my lord.''

"And when it has?''

"Oh . . . do you not know yourself well enough to know what others might think, my lord?'' Eliza asked innocently.

"I know myself very well, I believe, and I care little for the opinions of others.''

"Then why do you ask me, my lord, when surely you would care less for my opinion than the opinion of someone you might hold in greater regard?''

"Are you fencing with me, Miss Austerleigh?'' Edward asked.

"Indeed not, my lord. I have not the first notion of fencing. I believed it to be a sport confined to gentlemen. Perhaps I was wrong?''

"I meant verbal fencing,'' Edward said impatiently. "Never mind, Miss Austerleigh. It is an expression that means one is parrying one's wit against another's.''

"Oh, no, my lord. I have not enough skill or even wit to attempt any such thing. I am rather stupid, you see, and so I am well-suited to my isolation, where I will not offend others with my lack of thought. I find it distresses me not in the least, but others do not find me quite so tolerable.''

Edward was silent for a moment. "Yes, I can see that isolation might suit you,'' he finally ventured. "And do you enjoy your life in the country?''

"Yes, I do. I'm very fond of my chickens. They produce nicely and are undemanding company. And what brings you to England? I was given to understand that you cared very little for your birthplace.''

"I have no particular fondness for it, no, but I have affairs to put in order. I have been away overlong.''

"And how long do you plan on staying, now that you are here?''

"That depends entirely on how long it takes me to accomplish my objective, Miss Austerleigh.''

"Your objective, my lord? And what would that be?''

"It would be premature of me to state that now, although, Miss Austerleigh, it is entirely possible that you might play a large part in helping me achieve it."

Eliza was taken aback. "How—how do you mean, my lord? I cannot see how I could possibly have any part in your plans."

"Ah, but the future is often a surprise, Miss Austerleigh. Have you never found it so?"

"Constantly, my lord. But I might as well forewarn you. Whatever objective you might have in mind, I can be no part of it. I am not adept at scheming, for it requires concentration, and that I have in short supply. It is best to be honest about such things, do you not think? One's faults, I mean."

"Certainly," Edward said, feeling as if he'd just spent fifteen minutes in Bedlam. His eyes fell on the writing desk and he viewed what it held with interest. "Ah," he said, rising and picking up a slim, leather-bound volume, "I see you have Mr. Babcock's excellent book about Jamaica. I am most curious it should be in your possession. Did you enjoy the island so much that you would want to read about it?" His voice held a note of real surprise.

Eliza flushed. "I enjoyed it very much, my lord."

"I am delighted. Naturally I have a great fondness for the place myself." His finger idly stroked the leather spine. "Miss Chandler told me that you returned to Jamaica on your way back to England. I was surprised, as I did not see you. When was it you returned?"

"It was only four months after we'd departed, my lord. We stayed from January until June, as Mrs. Ludlupe was ill for some time and thus confined, and then we had trouble booking passage. But I was quite content, as the winter and spring seasons are most attractive. The climate is finer than the summer and autumn, but I found them to have their own charm; I cannot help but enjoy the violence of the elements. There is something unfettered—"

She stopped abruptly as she realized that she'd said too much. She would give nothing of her inner thoughts to this arrogant man who expected every woman to drop at his feet and worship at the altar of his charm. "But of course England is so much tamer, and chickens really are happier in a contained environment, I feel. I cannot think it is good for them to run about wild as they do in Jamaica, every which way so that one cannot help but wonder where to step. Surely it is not good for laying. But I did enjoy the pictures. In Mr. Babcock's book, I mean. They brought back very fond memories, and I thought the colors so attractive. I'm afraid the pen-and-ink sketches I found rather dull, did you not also?''

"Not at all," Edward said despondently, having again thought for just a moment that he had caught the slightest glimmer of intelligence, only to have the illusion shattered. "I particularly enjoyed them. But don't let me keep you. I can see you are impatient to continue with your chores. Perhaps I might call again sometime when you are less preoccupied. No, no. Please, don't bother. I'll see myself out.''

As soon as she heard the door close, Eliza leaned back in her chair. Now that he was gone, her entire body began to tremble from head to foot. She sat like that for a few minutes, and then, before she could begin to start pondering the real reason for Lord Seaton's visit, she went to get bucket and mop to begin the process of scouring the front hall. Hard work was the perfect antidote to Edward March.

That evening, after her solitary meal, Eliza donned her cloak and went out to the barn to check on the animals and see that they were safely shut up for the night, a chore she much enjoyed. The horses were somehow comforting, the cows her friends. The barn was warm with the heat radiating from the beasts, and she petted each one and called it by name. "Here, Buttercup,'' she crooned to the youngest of the milking cows, who had only recently arrived and was still a trifle skittish. "Settle down, now.'' She gave her a good scratch behind the ear and Buttercup gave a soft blow of satisfaction and rubbed her head against the front of Eliza's worn cloak. "Good girl," she said gently, and moved away, well-pleased. She then gave the final dose of medication to Clementine, who suffered it without complaint, and softly closing the door behind her, she took her lantern and walked back to the house, pausing for a moment to enjoy the sight of it from the knoll.

Sackville was a simple manor house, not grand or imposing, but it was her home and she loved it dearly. She ran her eye fondly over the graceful gables and the mullioned windows, now sparkling clean, as were the draperies inside hanging at their sides. It was an enormous improvement over the sight that had greeted her on her arrival. Lady Westerfield had not lived at Sackville for some time before her death, and the house and the grounds had fallen into a deplorable state of disrepair.

Eliza had quickly discovered that she had a gift for estate management, if one could call Sackville an estate. It boasted only fifty acres, dwarfed by the thousands of acres that were attached to Seaton House. But she'd put those fifty acres to good use, planting as many of them as she could, using the others for grazing. She had yet to make a profit, and she worried constantly that she would lose Sackville if she didn't turn it around quickly, but she was determined to do so, for she knew she had the talent. Now it was just a matter of fending off the creditors, but she could hardly complain. She loved her work, and running an estate was certainly far more interesting and entertaining than being paid companion to Pamela Chandler, who had had an alarming capacity for silliness as well as a talent for being difficult.

Eliza hadn't realized how demanding she'd found the position of companion until she'd been released from it. After her mother had died, she'd really had no choice. She'd had very little money and no one to take her in. Lady Westerfield had been good enough to stand her the one Season she'd had, but she hadn't taken, and Lady Westerfield had become infirm, so the only alternative had been to become a lady's companion. She'd been employed by a succession of elderly women, and when Pamela had undertaken her journey to British Honduras and asked Eliza to go with her, she had leapt at the opportunity. But in many ways she had come to regret her impulsive acceptance of the post.

For the two years that she and Pamela had traveled, she had never had time to call her own. Pamela was extremely demanding and had never missed an opportunity to let her know that she was a servant, there to do Pamela's bidding. Eliza, being of a solitary nature, took great pleasure in reading and in writing. But it was only when she received the news that she'd come into Sackville and had left Pamela with her parents in British Honduras to journey back to England that she had been free to indulge herself in these simple pleasures. She had thoroughly enjoyed the voyage, traveling with Mrs. Ludlupe, who made no demands on her at all. When they had stayed over in Jamaica, Eliza had finally been able to see the sights without the constant comments of Pamela to cloud her impressions.

She did like that part of the world very much. There was nothing quite like the Caribbean Sea, with its azure waters and coral reefs and the astonishing variety of sea life. She'd been sad to leave it behind for the choppy gray waters of the Atlantic Ocean, but nevertheless she delighted in the sail. Poor Mrs. Ludlupe had suffered badly from *mal de mer*, an affliction that fortunately had not been visited upon Eliza, and she'd spent her time heavily bundled up against the cold, reading and writing to her heart's content.

Eliza pushed through the heavy front door and cast her eye around the front hall with pleasure. They had scoured the floor and relaid the thick Persian rugs. It was a definite improvement. Next she was going to tackle the parlor. Poor Lord Seaton had looked quite taken aback by its dusty condition, but he could hardly know that it hadn't been used in a very long time, and all her energy and money had gone into buying livestock and starting up the greenhouse.

"I'm off to bed, if you don't need me for anything else, miss," said Annie, poking her head out of the back hallway. "Everything right and tight with the beasts?"

"Everyone's bedded down for the night. It looks as if Clementine's eye has cleared up, thank goodness. That salve seems to have done the trick."

"That's good news, miss. She's a good breeder, that cow, worth every penny you paid for her."

"I certainly got a bargain, discovering she was with calf after I bought her. Mr. McGillicutty must have been kicking himself when he heard, although I wish she wasn't due in the middle of the winter."

"Those winter calves do freeze more easily, miss, but Clementine will be in the barn, so it should be fine. Two for the price of one, and you can't complain about that."

"No, I can't. Off you go then, and leave the candles. I'll put them out when I go up."

"Right, miss." Annie's head disappeared back into the hallway and Eliza grinned. She was very lucky in her small staff. They were hard workers and very loyal, and they never begrudged her anything. She never would have been able to come this far without them. Even now it was touch and go, and she didn't look forward to the coming winter, for she'd already experienced two of them at Sackville and knew how difficult they could be. But she still had a month or two before the real cold took hold, providing it stayed a mild autumn, and she could only pray that the temperature would not drop too low. Fuel would be in short supply as it was. On that thought, she blew out the candles and climbed the stairs to bed, intending to read the next chapter of her book on agricultural science.

But the book went unread, for as Eliza settled down among the pillows, her mind strayed back to the unexpected visitor she'd had that afternoon. It made no sense at all that Lord Seaton had called on her. None. She didn't believe for one moment he'd been paying a neighborly visit, nor that he had come to further their acquaintance when he'd wanted absolutely nothing to do with her in Jamaica. Then what did he want?

That he was after something was obvious. The situation had very much resembled that of the spider and the fly, only she had been the fly in her own parlor. She thrust her chin into her hand and thought. And then it came to her, and she sat bolt upright in bed, the book sliding off her lap and landing on the floor with a thud.

"Oh, dear God," she whispered. "Perhaps he wants Sackville."

Edward cursed as he flipped through the account book. He'd been at it all morning, and the steward's face had grown more and more florid as Edward shot a series of questions at him. It was becoming painfully clear to Edward that Seaton had been badly mismanaged since he'd been there last, and the accountings he regularly received in Jamaica did not match with either the books or what he saw around him. He had spent two days at the task: Edward was nothing if not a responsible land-owner, and his Caribbean properties ran like clockwork. He might have no liking for Seaton, which he had left fifteen years before, but he could not bear to see land go to waste. Nor did he much care for being cheated. He had only himself to blame, for it was he who had left Nash in charge, he who had not bothered to return, content to leave the estate's affairs in Nash's hands, which were obviously as corrupt a pair as he might have found. He finally slammed the book shut and looked up.

"I suppose you have an explanation for all this at the ready, Nash?"

"Yes, my lord. You see, last year we changed our accounting system—"

"Leave it!" Edward rose from behind the desk and leaned across it in a highly menacing manner. "You have let the land go to waste, Nash. You have channeled funds into your own pockets. You have taken what should have been a prosperous property and run it halfway into the ground. There is no excuse, none whatsoever, for this kind of criminal mismanagement. By God, I have half a mind to prosecute, but I'd rather never have to see your face again. Pack, Nash, and be off. Do not think to darken my doorstep again, or I swear I shall do you bodily harm."

He waited until Mr. Nash had scurried out the door, then threw his pen down on the desk with a muttered oath. It would take months to sort out the mess Nash had made of his affairs, damn him. Damn him! It was worse than mismanagement and thievery; it was a breach of trust. It was unforgivable. Absolutely unforgivable. But then Seaton had a history of that sort of thing. Unfaithfulness, betrayal, abuse—he'd often wondered if it was imbued in the very stones of the place.

And now he was forced to install a wife, and it looked as if addlepated Eliza Austerleigh was the only appropriate candidate. Providence had seen fit to put her not only three miles down the road, but also in Jamaica at exactly the right time for his needs. Furthermore, she had no family to kick up a fuss when the marriage was announced. She would no doubt be so grateful to him for offering her a title and wealth that she'd jump at the opportunity to marry him, no matter what she had to do or say for the privilege. But why did providence have to choose Eliza Austerleigh? Chickens? He moaned and put his head in his hands for a moment, then sighed heavily. Ah, well, who was he to argue with fate? He supposed he'd better start setting up the situation to appear believable. He suddenly realized he was freezing. The house had always been very cold.

"Wyatt," he roared, and the elderly butler appeared in the door. "Get a fire started in here, and be sharp about it. Tell that damned Pringle woman I expect to have a fire in the library day in and day out whether she thinks I need it or not. Better yet, send her to me and I'll tell her myself. And Wyatt, stand up, man. I cannot abide slouching or shuffling." He threw himself back into his chair and tried to make a beginning at sorting out the ledger.

"There, there, you mustn't upset yourself so, Mrs. Pringle," Wyatt said, holding out a large handkerchief to the sobbing woman. "It's his lordship's nature. I never did know such a temperamental man, save for his father before him. Couldn't say I was sorry when he turned up his toes. No one was. No one was sorry when his present lordship took himself off to foreign parts, neither, right after the fact. Barely stayed for the funeral, he did. But he always was a difficult child, was his lordship, and hasn't changed his ways, not a bit."

"I cannot tolerate it anymore, Mr. Wyatt, this continual shouting, showing up where he doesn't belong and upsetting the servants—no, please, no, thank you, nothing but temper and demands." She wiped her face all over and looked up at the butler with red and swollen eyes. "My heart just won't take it."

"You have to be understanding, Mrs. Pringle. I've been here over thirty-five years now. It's never been a happy house. His lordship before, the ninth marquess—now, he was a mean one. He beat his wife till she was black and blue all over, he beat his boy, he never had a kind thing to say. It was no wonder her ladyship picked up one night and ran away. She couldn't take any more of his mistreatment and harsh tongue. She went out the window because he'd taken the handle from her door."

"Ran away with an Italian count, I heard," Mrs. Pringle said with a heavy sigh, "and never came back again."

"No, she didn't, and it didn't improve his lordship any. She was a nice woman, kind and all that, but not very sharp up top, you know. It used to anger the old marquess terribly when she didn't get things right. I don't think he much liked women. And then there was the little lord, Lord Glouston as he was then. He was only a small lad when his mother left. He never said anything when he was told, just went white as a sheet. I'll never forget it. He was fond of her, you know."

"It's sad, a lad losing his mother so young."

"Seven he was. It was then that he became impossible. That tutor of his didn't do him any good, either. Strange sort, all tall and skinny, with a clammy face and nasty eyes."

"Lordy," Mrs. Pringle said, leaning forward, her distress

temporarily forgotten in the excitement of the moment. Mr. Wyatt had never discussed the family before like this, not in any detail.

"He had some habits I heard rumored at," Mr. Wyatt said, caught up in his narrative. "Nothing a God-fearing Christian would condone, if you take my meaning."

"Goodness!" Mrs. Pringle's hand went to her bosom.

"It was a hard time for the little lord, it was. He was forever running away and being brought back, beaten and locked in his room without food for two or three days on end."

"Oh, it's not right. It's just not right."

"No, but what were we to do? His lordship would have had our heads if we'd interfered. I think"—and here he lowered his voice to a whisper—"there were some unnatural goings-on between that tutor Dweebs and the old marquess."

Mrs. Pringle looked about to faint.

"It wasn't easy for his lordship growing up, not that it makes it right to behave as he does now. But who are we to complain? He's hardly here, although I wish the house had some attention given to it. It's a sad waste to be butler here with no direction, no one to care."

"Don't I know, Mr. Wyatt, don't I know? It's not easy on me, but I've never been one to complain. But I cannot put up with his lordship much longer, I want you to know, hardships or not. It's too much on me, expected to make everything as he wants it, with no staff and no money to spend to put it right."

"He'll be gone soon enough and take that disgusting bird with him, I hope."

"Oh, that bird," Mrs. Pringle moaned. "It will be my undoing!"

"Your undoing? You do not have to serve at table with it sitting on the back of a chair, flinging food in every direction. You'd think seed would be good enough for it, but curries and caviar? It's all I can do to get the stains out of the Aubusson carpet. And the language!"

Mrs. Pringle clapped her hands to her ears. "Say no more! Fancy losing Molly and then Fred, all because the bird couldn't keep a decent tongue in its head, and Fred thinking that it was a moral outrage for his Molly to hear such things, which it is, but we are short-staffed enough without that parrot getting people worked up. I want to go live with my sister, that's all

I want, and I'll do it the first chance I get. I'm not taking any more.''

"But we couldn't manage without you," Mr. Wyatt said soothingly. "Have another cup of tea. His lordship will be soon be gone for another five years, and life will be back to normal.''

"I hope you're right, Mr. Wyatt, for my heart won't take much more of this.'' She sipped her tea gloomily.

3

The sooner every party breaks up, the better.
                                    Jane Austen, *Emma*

Life was so unfair, Eliza thought with annoyance as Annie pulled her dinner dress into place with a final twitch. As if it wasn't bad enough that Lord Seaton had appeared and was living just down the road from her, as if it wasn't bad enough that she had to hear his name dropped from every lip, now on top of everything she had to go to this dinner party when Marguerite knew perfectly well she had a complete terror of social functions. It really was too bad.

"Very nice, miss," Annie said. "It's a pity you've worn it so often, but it can't be helped.''

"No, it can't, and I'd far rather spend the money on the animals. Lord and Lady Clarke can hardly mind seeing it once again, and Lady Clarke assured me that the company will not be large this evening.''

"And right nice of Lady Clarke to ask you. I daresay she's not so bad for a Frenchie, downright kind sometimes.'' Annie stood back and looked at her mistress's wild red hair with a frown. She knew something ought to be done about it, but she didn't know exactly what, and even if she had known, she wouldn't know how to go about doing it. She twisted it up as usual on top of Eliza's head and skewered some pins into it.

"Yes, she's very kind, Annie. Lady Clarke was the only person to welcome me to Oxfordshire with open arms. I realize, of course, that things might have gone more easily had I chosen to live with a respectable companion, but I truly couldn't bear the idea. I'd rather live with social censure, thank you."

"Well, you have Lady Clarke to keep you from the worst of the wagging tongues. It's not as if I don't live here with you, miss, not that any one of the toffs would call me respectable." She chuckled.

"More respectable than most of them, I would wager," Eliza retorted. "But nevertheless I do owe Lady Clarke a debt of thanks for her open-minded attitude, although I fear that the only reason she is so insistent in including me in her entertainments is because she nurses a fond desire in her bosom to see a romance blossom between me and some unfortunate squire."

Annie grinned. "Not a thing wrong with romance, miss. I wouldn't mind a spot of it myself. Too bad my Harold, bless his soul, had to go and make a hero out of himself at Waterloo. I was spoiled, I was, by the love of a good man. You go find yourself a good man, miss. Mayhaps one'll show up at Lady Clarke's tonight."

Eliza smiled. "Now, what man is going to put up with a woman who smells of the barn, Annie?"

Annie sniffed. "Can't say I smell a thing but lavender on you, miss. Who's going to know unless you tell him?" She handed Eliza her wrap.

Eliza took one last look at herself in the glass and sighed. The yellow silk, a cast-off of Pamela's, had never suited her, the color doing nothing for her skin. She had altered it to fit her taller, slimmer figure, but it had never looked quite right to her. But then clothes and she had never been a good match. Her hair looked as unruly as ever, red tresses threatening to escape every which way, which no doubt they later would. Altogether it was not a pleasing picture; her stepfather had warned her often enough not to imagine herself anything but homely. But there were other things in life than beauty, she told herself, standing up straight and squaring her shoulders. If nothing else, she had good posture. She simply wouldn't think about her freckles and the disastrous color of her hair. She certainly wouldn't think about the way her nose turned up or about the dent in her chin. If she felt uncomfortable, she would think about her cows. Nodding firmly, Eliza marched downstairs to the waiting landau.

It was a chilly night and Keble Park was ten miles away. Eliza's little nose was completely numb by the time she arrived. The house was ablaze with light but small enough to appear friendly. While companion to Pamela, Eliza had stayed at some houses that had been daunting. She herself had grown up in a modest residence, not much larger than Sackville, a property belonging to her mother that her father had largely ignored and her stepfather had finally gambled away shortly before his death. She liked the lines of Keble House, square and simple, with long windows fronting all three floors. Eliza took a deep breath, summoning up her bravery, which threatened to desert her completely. These occasions were torture, but she could not let her good friend down. Marguerite was so full of charm and good humor that it was impossible to refuse her anything. Eliza skewered an escaping pin back into her hair and walked up the low steps to the front door, handing her cloak to the footman.

She was just resisting a temptation to snatch it back again and run straight out the door when Lady Clarke appeared in the foyer and spotted her.

"My darling Eliza," Marguerite exclaimed in her enchanting French accent. "I thought you would never arrive. Come, my delightful friend, and meet our guests. We have such entertaining company this evening. Look, George, dearest, Eliza has arrived." She took Eliza by the elbow and steered her toward the drawing room. "In fact, your neighbor is here. Have you met Lord Seaton, Eliza? He has spent most of the past years in the Caribbean."

Eliza's heart nearly stopped in her chest as she absorbed Marguerite's words at the same time that her eyes took in the alarming sight of the Marquess of Seaton standing off to one side, surrounded by a group of people. His dark glossy head was bent in attention as he listened to some comment, and his stance was relaxed, one strongly muscled leg slightly bent, his elbow resting on the mantelpiece beside him. He was tall enough to top the heads of the other guests, which only made him appear more forbidding. He looked up suddenly and his eyes met hers. A cool smile appeared on his lips. Eliza felt quite sick as he excused himself from the group and came toward her, putting his glass down on a passing tray as he went. She swallowed her dread, wishing her knees weren't knocking. Why did all of her poise desert her in a crowd? She had handled him well enough when they had been alone, but now she felt quite stupid, as if her brain were filled with cotton wool. And then she remembered that as far as he was concerned, she was quite stupid, so it was all to the good.

"Eliza," Marguerite said with delight at the warmly interested look in Edward's eyes. "Allow me to present the Marquess of Seaton. Edward, Miss Eliza Austerleigh, who now lives at Sackville—"

"I know Miss Austerleigh," he said rather abruptly. "Good evening. I trust your chickens are in good health?"

"Chickens?" Marguerite said faintly. "Have you chickens, Eliza, darling?"

For some reason the absurdity of this remark had the effect of steadying Eliza. "I have," she said. "They are well, thank you, Lord Seaton. And yours?"

Edward's mouth twitched. "I am not aware of the state of my chickens' health, but if I have any, I assume they are also well and multiplying nicely."

"Actually, my lord, it has been my experience that chickens do not necessarily multiply as easily as one might wish. They do not respond well to autocratic demands."

"Oh, and what do they respond to, Miss Austerleigh? Tender persuasion? I cannot in truth see myself crooning words of love to a hen."

"I cannot see you in that position at all, my lord," Eliza responded, and then blushed furiously as she realized what she had said. "Excuse me, Lord Seaton, Marguerite. I see someone I must speak with." She hurried away, and Marguerite looked after her with astonishment. Edward looked after her with something very different, and Marquerite glanced over at him to explain that Eliza did not usually behave in such a manner. But her words were arrested by Edward's concentrated gaze, and she decided to say nothing at all.

Eliza was not at all pleased when Lord Seaton joined herself and Major and Mrs. Moreland, who were telling a very boring tale of their daughter's come-out. She was less pleased when he claimed acquaintanceship of long standing. "Oh, indeed," he said to them, "Miss Austerleigh and I enjoyed a very pleasant friendship when she came to Jamaica with Miss Chandler—the Sussex Chandlers, you know. It is always so refreshing to meet people from the motherland. New blood does wonders for those of us who are subjected to the limited society of island life.''

"I think you are doing it a bit too brown, my lord," Eliza said quietly. "We were but the briefest of acquaintances. I was merely there in my capacity as companion."

"But such a very good companion, were you not?" Edward said with the barest hint of a chuckle, and Eliza had a sudden desire to slap him. It did not surprise her that he would be so cruel as to poke this kind of fun at her, but he could hardly know how deeply he had hurt her in Jamaica.

"Are you still with us, Miss Austerleigh? You seem to be pondering the question overlong."

She bit the inside of her lip, summoning her dignity. "Miss Chandler was most easy to companion," she said as forcefully as she could. "Indeed, it was she who had to suffer me, for I can be very trying. I feel I was most fortunate to be offered the opportunity to travel. . . ."

She babbled on, hardly knowing what she was saying, but whatever it was, she knew she wasn't making much sense.

Edward, rather than becoming bored and wandering away, stayed at her elbow as if she were the most fascinating creature on earth. The next thing she knew, he insisted on partnering her into dinner, much to the surprise of the rest of the company, not the least of whom was Eliza.

Throughout the rest of the evening Eliza felt as if she were trapped in a nightmare from which there was no awakening. Lord Seaton sat at her right, and instead of leaving her in peace, he kept up a steady flow of conversation to which she was forced to reply.

"The duck is superb, is it not, Miss Austerleigh? Did you partake of the jerked pork while you were visiting our fair isle? It is heavy with spices, but quite a favorite of the natives and also myself. . . ."

This went on for remove after remove, Lord Seaton engaging others in conversation but always coming back to her. She was miserably aware of his strong body next to hers, of his well-shaped hands, still slightly brown from the strong tropical sun, aware of his sharply drawn bone structure, his penetrating eyes, such a deep, vital blue, eyes that regarded her lazily but persistently, and she wanted to cringe under his regard, knowing what he was seeing and what he thought about it.

"Tell me, Miss Austerleigh," he said, interrupting her thoughts, "are you wool-gathering again? You seem to have a tendency in that direction. Or is my conversation not lively enough for you? Perhaps I should address your immediate interests. Sackville seems to keep your hands very full. You have a tidy acreage, have you not? It must be very difficult for you to manage. I understand you have no bailiff and that Lady Westerfield had left the property in disorder for a number of years. Have you let the fields remain fallow? It is a pity, for the soil is good. But I suppose an influx of funds is what is needed to see Sackville produce as it should."

Eliza had done her very best to cope with the situation, but when he started in on her beloved Sackville, a hot surge of anger welled up inside of her. She'd be damned if she let him take Sackville from her, no matter what his price. She couldn't think why he needed it with the amount of acreage he already had; the only logical conclusion she'd been able to draw was that her land ran briefly with his, and he might have reason to expand his border.

"Miss Austerleigh? Have I lost you? Or perhaps you have no interest in the land itself and prefer to concentrate on your poultry."

Her shyness forgotten, she turned in her chair and regarded him with flashing eyes. "Actually, Lord Seaton," she said bitingly, "the fields have been harvested and replanted for winter crops. No doubt that is why the land looks fallow to you. I have also left some fields free for grazing. I have a herd of dairy cows, you see."

"Indeed?" Lord Seaton wiped his mouth with his napkin, his eyes filled with amusement, an expression she had not seen there before. "How very enterprising."

Eliza gripped her hands together in her lap and spoke in a furious undertone. "I realize that such enterprise might well give you a disgust of me, my lord, but I don't think it will be the first time. And it is hardly my affair what you think or feel. Sackville is my only concern, and I'd thank you to turn your interest in other directions."

Lord Seaton looked at her assessingly for a moment, and then, much to her surprise, he burst into laughter, drawing the attention of everyone at the table who hadn't already been listening. But he declined to explain himself, saying only that, as always, he found Miss Austerleigh refreshingly original.

Eliza was exceedingly grateful when Marguerite gave the signal to retire, and Eliza took her leave shortly thereafter, before the men could return from the dining room. She seethed all the way home, stung that she had been goaded into tipping her hand, and vowed she would never let Lord Seaton goad her again.

After that Eliza seemed to see Lord Seaton everywhere she went. Whether she chose to ride early in the morning or late in the afternoon, making her daily inspection of her property, he almost always happened to be out riding at the same time. She could hardly object that he chose to exercise his horse on his own land, nor could she quibble that he chose the rolling hills that overlooked the Sackville acres, which was admittedly good ground for giving a horse its head. He never did more than raise his hat when he saw her, but it had the effect of ruining her day nonetheless. She concluded that he spent all of his time on his horse, looking over Sackville land and plotting how to take it from her. She toyed with the idea of planting hedgerows to make the boundary more explicit, but discarded the idea as a waste of time and money. And to keep Lord Seaton and his plans out of her mind, she threw herself even more deeply into her estate work, visiting tenant farmers and asking for their ideas on livestock management and drainage, planning for the following spring. Preparing for the future gave her a feeling of permanence that Lord Seaton's presence continually robbed her of.

A week after the disastrous dinner party, Eliza made an excursion to town to do some shopping. She was just coming out of the bookstore with a new book on the management of illness in cattle, and she was completely absorbed in her thoughts when she caught something unsettling out of the corner of her eye. Bringing her focus to it, she discerned the odious figure of Lord Seaton, and he was coming across the street. Lowering her eyes, she moved quickly away, hoping he would not see her, but he paused in front of her with a smile, raising his hat politely. "Good morning, Miss Austerleigh."

"Lord Seaton."

"A fine autumn morning, is it not?"

"Indeed." She realized that they were drawing attention and tried to move past him, glancing up as she realized he was deliberately blocking her way. "Excuse me, please."

"Certainly, Miss Austerleigh. Chilly but not without promise."

Her eyes flew back to his in confusion. "I beg your pardon?"

"The morning," he said blithely. "Chilly, but not without promise. I believe the afternoon might be warmer."

"I see. I expect you are correct in all things, Lord Seaton, and so I will take your word on the weather. I am not very accomplished in reading the sky myself, although I seem to have an uncanny nose for detecting rain or snow."

"I have always found your nose to be of great interest, Miss Austerleigh. Really, it is quite charming."

"You, Lord Seaton, are well-deserving of your reputation," Eliza said tightly, thinking what a pleasure it would be to put her hands around his throat and choke him.

"And what aspect of my reputation might that be, Miss Austerleigh?"

"Why, your reputation for a glib tongue, Lord Seaton. Has no one ever mentioned it to you before?"

"Not in quite such terms, no. However, I will take your words as a compliment."

"Oh, please do not, my lord. I am no hand at compliments. I wish I could be, but I find it difficult thinking up flattery, for one never knows what might flatter one person and insult the next."

"And so you speak whatever comes into your mind?"

"I do, my lord, although usually that is not very much. But I have sometimes thought it a blessing, for then one does not worry overmuch, nor have to care what other people think. I imagine someone with such intelligence as yours must worry all the time."

Edward cocked his head and looked at her assessingly. "If you had not told me differently, Miss Austerleigh, I would think you had a very clever way with an insult."

Eliza's gloved hand flew to her mouth and she gasped. "Oh, no! You see, I have gone and done it again. Do forgive me, my lord, for although I do not know what it is I have said to offend, I can see that I have indeed done so. There. Now you understand why it is better that I keep to myself and practice no conversation at all. You will forgive me, my lord, but my horses grow cold.''

He bowed. ''I wouldn't dream of delaying you. No doubt you have fields to plow and chickens to feed. Good day.''

Eliza drew her mantle more closely around herself and walked off as quickly as she could. She could feel Lord Seaton's eyes on her back until she turned the corner, and she had an absurd impulse to run to her carriage.

''Really, Eliza, do you not realize how eligible the marquess is?'' Marguerite said over tea two days later as Eliza told her of her encounter with him. ''You do not seem to take the least notice of Lord Seaton, and he pays you such attention! It is the talk of the county, my dinner party and how the marquess favored you. And now you tell me how you cut him on the high street.'' She nibbled daintily on a sweetmeat.

''There is nothing to take notice of that I can see,'' Eliza said tartly. ''And I'm too busy with Sackville to bother with Lord Seaton's eligibility or where he chooses to walk in town. And I did not give him the cut, I merely had things to do.''

''I think you are going to work yourself into the ground, Eliza. Why can you not take up a more practical pursuit such as finding a husband? Then he could provide the money you so badly need, and you could have a more enjoyable life.''

''I like my life, Marguerite. You really mustn't feel sorry for me just because you have found such happiness with George. I am perfectly content, and I really don't think I am suited to marriage.''

''Nonsense, Eliza. Every woman is suited to marriage. Your mistake is thinking you are too old and no man would want you. I am sure that is not true. It only means making more of an effort, it is that simple. I could introduce you to many an eligible man if you would only let me try. You would be surprised what delights a husband can bring.''

Eliza blushed to the roots of her hair.

''Oh, forgive me, Eliza,'' Marguerite said quickly. ''I am a Frenchwoman and I sometimes forget myself when it comes to matters like these. But nevertheless it is true. And then there are the children, a great joy, and you are one who would make a wonderful mother. It would only take a husband for you to have a family of your own."

"I think not," Eliza said quietly. The fact that she would most likely never marry rankled only when she thought of the children she would never have. Children she would have liked very much. "And even if I did want it, I cannot think it is possible. Please, Marguerite, let us discuss something else. The subject causes me acute discomfort."

"Very well, Eliza," Marguerite said, smiling quite happily.

"Marguerite, what are you planning now?" Eliza said suspiciously. "I know that look, and I want you to know now that I will have no part of your schemes."

Marguerite gave a fatalistic little shrug. "I cannot convince you of something you refuse to believe. But one day you will look back and laugh at yourself, for I can see what you cannot."

"Marguerite, you have been a very good friend, but I fear your French blood compels you to see melodrama and romance where there is none."

"Bah! I know what I see. And I also see Lord Seaton. Look at the way you avoid him. It is only a woman who is afraid her heart will be lost who runs as you do. And he follows, does he not?"

Eliza looked away, thinking that Marguerite had the marquess's motives quite confused. "I cannot prevent him from crossing my path, Marguerite. He is practically on my doorstep, after all."

"Precisely. It is very interesting, this. We shall see what comes to pass. Thank you for the tea, my dear. I shall send a footman for the flowers. Your blooms so enliven my house. I have just had your sketches framed and I hung them this morning. They look very nice. You must come and see them soon."

She kissed Eliza's cheek and squeezed her hand, then put her hat, a charming Coburg bonnet, on top of her chestnut curls, tied the sash into a large bow under her chin, then tucked her hand into the crook of Eliza's arm as they walked to the front door. "I am so terribly glad you've come. I cannot credit that it has been over two years. Having you here has quite alleviated my boredom. What other woman can I talk to about botany and history and all those other forbidden subjects? Now we need to find you a husband who is also able to converse with you.''

With a mischievous smile she went out the door, leaving Eliza to ponder her last statement.

4

One half of the world cannot understand
the pleasures of the other.

Jane Austen, *Emma*

It seemed there was to be no peace from Lord Seaton's campaign, Eliza thought heavily three days later as the blasted man came striding across her front lawn. He was, as usual, immaculately turned out in creaseless buff pantaloons and a bottle-green coat. She was, as usual, shabbily attired in her work dress of worn blue muslin, covered by a thick shawl. She'd been happily planting ornamental bulbs when she'd heard the hoofbeats and had slowly straightened to see him bearing down her carriageway. Oh, there was no doubt that he cut a fine figure, that he and a horse looked as if they'd been born to show each other to advantage. And there was also no doubt that the very sight of him caused a bitter loathing to rise in her breast. He swung off his mount with graceful ease, indeed, but that did not mean that her eyes had any more reason to be pleased at his unwelcome appearance.

"Good afternoon, Miss Austerleigh," he said in his rich, mellow voice. "I trust I have not intruded? Your stance is not the most welcoming I have ever seen." He raised a finely etched eyebrow at the hands planted on her hips.

"Good afternoon, Lord Seaton. And quite frankly, you have intruded. Although you might consider yourself quite above it all, I do wish you'd behave the way the rest of polite society does and leave your card at the door."

"But with whom would I leave it, Miss Austerleigh? Your cowman or your cook? I thought it might be easier to approach you directly, rather than attempt to track either of them down in their respective domains. In the case of the former, I fear I would sadly muddy my boots, and in the case of the latter, I would fear for my coat. Flour is not considered an appropriate covering for superfine, never mind what might happen to my card in either instance. I merely thought you safer than the other alternatives."

"You were mistaken, my lord. I do not enjoy constantly being surprised by you, nor do I enjoy being found in such a state of undress. And if you thought to charm or amuse me, I am neither charmed nor amused easily. I haven't an appreciation for such things. Spare yourself the effort."

Edward's eyebrow rose another fraction of an inch. "Miss Austerleigh, I cannot help but think I have somehow done something to cause you offense, but as much as I have racked my brains, I cannot think what it was. Perhaps, given what you have just said, it was appearing on your doorstep a fortnight ago when you were unprepared for visitors? I beg your most humble pardon if that was the case, but having lived in the islands for so many years, I have forgotten how to stand on ceremony."

"It is not ceremony I require, Lord Seaton. As I said, it is simple courtesy."

"Ah. I was not aware that I had in any instance been discourteous. It was certainly not my intent. Perhaps you would care to further enlighten me as to my faults so that I might make reparation."

"No, my lord, I am not interested in reparation, nor in enumerating your faults. It all sounds far too complicated and taxing. I only want to continue with my work. As you have no doubt gathered, I take a great interest in my property and very little interest in you."

Edward tapped his crop against his boot, and Eliza thought he most probably was longing to apply it to her backside, if the expression on his face was anything to go by. "I see," he finally said. "That is a shame, as I have come to speak to you on a matter that is of very great import to both of us."

"Nothing, my lord, that you have to say to me could be of any possible import." Eliza wiped her hands together and pushed a strand of hair from her face, leaving a streak of dirt behind. "I know I am quite hopeless in making myself understood, but I really do not know how to make myself any clearer."

But still he stood there, now regarding her with an unfathomable expression. She suddenly felt very tired. Men had never been her strong suit, and this man was quickly becoming the worst of the lot. "My lord, I think this interview is at an end."

"I think not, ma'am. I will be very happy to leave you in peace as soon as I state my business, for it is on business that I have come, despite what you may be thinking. Plain-speaking seems to be the only thing you understand, and so I shall be as plain as possible, although I had hoped to conduct this conversation inside in a more suitable setting. I have a proposition, Miss Austerleigh, that will make you a very wealthy woman and give me something I need quite badly."

"I would not accept a farthing from you, my lord, nor have I any intention of giving you anything at all. Despite what you might think, I do have some pride."

Edward frowned. "I assure you, I will see to it that the arrangement is entirely equitable—"

"No! I'm afraid any arrangement is completely out of the question," Eliza said. "You may think me a complete fool, Lord Seaton, as well I might be, but nevertheless almost from your first appearance I have been aware of what you wanted."

"You have?" he said blankly, and she could see that she'd thrown him completely off balance, a fact that gave her a measure of satisfaction.

"I have. I am not interested in your proposal. I would thank you not to mention it again."

"But, Miss Austerleigh, how could you possibly turn down such an opportunity? Please, allow me to explain the circumstances—"

"Lord Seaton, do you never desist? I have told you, most definitely, that I am not interested. It is an end to the matter."

Edward regarded her for a moment, then slapped his crop hard against his boot. "Very well, Miss Austerleigh. I am not so foolish as to stay where I am not wanted. It is a pity, but I can't expect to have my way at every turn, can I?"

"I'm pleased you choose to take that approach, my lord. I had thought you might attempt to coerce me."

"Coerce you? I confess, Miss Austerleigh, you surprise me; I cannot quite make you out. Your character seems to have alarming twists and turns to it. But to show you I have taken no offense at your refusal, please accept an invitation to attend a ball I am holding at Seaton in a sennight. I would take it most ill if you denied me this small favor, for then I would know you were holding hard feelings against me, and that would make me most unhappy."

"I somehow doubt that, my lord."

"But it is quite true. I feel that I have been boorish in the extreme. It is an aspect of my nature that I often have cause to regret, and I should not have allowed my impatience to get the better of me. I had hoped for more than you were willing to give, and I have rushed you in the extreme into making a decision. Please allow me this one small request. Otherwise I feel I shall have to dog your doorstep until I am convinced you have forgiven me for my ill manners."

Eliza considered. As much as she loathed both balls and him, and the two in combination were almost unthinkable, he had put her in an untenable position. Better to suffer a ball than to have to deal with him on a daily basis, for she had no doubt he meant what he said.

"Miss Austerleigh? You look quite confounded. I truly do apologize."

"Oh, very well, then. Thank you, Lord Seaton. I accept. Now please—"

"I am most gratified," Edward said with a slight bow. "I cannot say that I take defeat easily, and so I warn you that I am going to persist in my suit. Good day, Miss Austerleigh." Edward turned and walked off without another word.

The next week went by in a bustle of activity as Seaton House prepared for the ball. Everyone was in a foul mood, but Edward's topped everything, for the servants had to contend only with preparing the house, which was in no condition for that sort of entertainment. Edward's mood was directly attributable to Eliza, whom he considered a stubborn, ungrateful miss with no manners.

"The girl has an overinflated sense of her own importance," Edward muttered as Hamlish dressed him the evening of the ball. "She wouldn't even hear me out. Imagine turning me down out of hand. You'd think I'd picked her from all the women in the world because I found her more attractive, more beautiful, more intelligent . . . Intelligent! Ha! She has a brain that resembles Swiss cheese, so full of holes that one cannot deal with her with any sort of rationality.''

"Yes, my lord," Hamlish murmured obediently.

"Blasted girl. She does nothing but make my life difficult. But I shall win the battle and I shall also win the war, Hamlish. Tonight when she sees how it is to mix with the cream of society—only a very small portion, mind you, but nevertheless, cream—she will change her tune. I will dance attendance on her, and we shall see what society makes of my choice in wives." His eyes danced wickedly as Hamlish helped him into his black, swallowtail coat. "I am setting the cat among the pigeons, only in this case I am setting the pigeon among the cats."

"Yes, my lord," Hamlish murmured again, feeling heartily sorry for Miss Austerleigh. He stood back. "You are ready, my lord."

"Naturally I'm ready, you fool. I've been ready for a week, ever since the girl had the temerity to refuse me."

"I meant that I have finished, my lord."

"Ah," Edward said. "Very well. I go to do battle, bearing charm, wit, and determination as my weapons. And remember, Hamlish, you are not to say a word to anyone, or I shall grind your bones to dust."

"Naturally not, my lord. I am as loyal as the day is long. I shall express my pleasure at seeing Lady Seaton when you indicate that the time is right."

"Exactly so, Hamlish, exactly so. You shall live long and well on the stipend you'll receive."

"Perhaps, my lord, but only when I am ready to retire. You would never be able to keep another valet, and I cannot desert you to that fate."

Edward gave Hamlish a filthy look. "Don't you think to blackmail me, man."

"Certainly not, my lord. May I wish you luck?"

"You may, although I'm sure I'll manage very well on my own." Edward strode out the door.

Eliza entered the hall with Marguerite and George, who had

been kind enough to collect her and bring her in their carriage. She looked around, curious, for she had heard descriptions of Seaton House and its magnificence. The hall was teeming with people dressed in the height of fashion, and alive not only with a riot of colorful silks, satins, and velvets, but also with hundreds of torches. The marble floor gleamed sparkling white, pillars rising from it to climb past four stories to a ceiling painted with frescoes. The wide stairway mounted past portraits and more portraits, presumably deceased members of the March family. Lord Seaton bore a strong resemblance to many of them. His haughtiness appeared to have come from generations of in-breeding, for they all wore varying degrees of the arrogant expression Eliza had seen so often on the face of the present marquess. Eliza's eyes traveled back down the rich red carpet than ran down the stairs and settled back on the milling crowd.

But as full of people as the house was, as loud the conver-sation, as bright the lights, Seaton House still struck her as feeling empty. It was odd that something could seem so full and empty at the same time. Not only did it feel empty, it also seemed to be slightly shabby if one looked very closely, as if the Holland covers had just been whisked off and would just as soon be whisked back on again.

Eliza had long ago learned to compensate for her shyness by spending her time observing, and she was so busy observing while trying to appear unnoticed behind Marguerite that she completely missed Lord Seaton's approach, and she jumped half out of her skin as she heard his voice behind her.

"Miss Austerleigh," he murmured as she spun around. He took her hand and lightly kissed its back. "I was wondering when you would choose to grace us with your presence. Good evening, Marguerite, George."

Eliza flushed and pulled her hand away, uncomfortably aware of his uninvited nearness. It took her a moment to regain her composure, and Marguerite stepped into the breach.

"It is entirely our fault that we are late, Edward. As usual, it took me longer to prepare myself than I had allowed time for, and my dear George was pushed to the limits of his patience." A charming dimple appeared in her cheek as her eyes danced. "I often wonder that George is as good to me as he is when I cause him to be late for nearly everything. I kept poor Eliza waiting as well. I am sure she despaired we would ever arrive to collect her, did you not, Eliza?"

"No . . . I . . . not at all," she managed to croak. "I had no idea, Lord Seaton, that you had been watching for us." She was horribly conscious of the miserable spectacle she presented. The dress just didn't fit as she'd hoped, the color was all wrong; she felt as awkward as a newborn calf, all angles and wobbly knees.

Lord Seaton smiled easily. "But naturally I have been watching for you. Why would you think otherwise? I thought I had made it very clear to you that your attendance meant a great deal to me. Come, Eliza, let us cease this formality. There are many people to whom I would introduce you; I gather you have not been about much since leaving Jamaica, and I would like to remedy the situation if you will but let me." He slid a hand through her elbow.

Eliza's dark eyes went to his in bewilderment. If he was playing at a game, it was none she had ever encountered before. He seemed so sincere, and anyone watching or listening, as many seemed to be, would think they were good friends. It was there in the warm way his eyes held hers, the firm grip on her arm, the smile on his mouth that spoke of intimacy. Intimacy? Of all the nerve!

"Lord Seaton," she hissed, her head bent, "I cannot imagine what you are trying to accomplish with this absurd pretense. I warn you, I will not change my mind."

"Absurd pretense?" Edward replied lightly, delighted that Eliza was playing so easily into his hands. "But I pretend nothing. You should know better than that."

"You presume too much," Eliza replied darkly.

"Do I? A thousand pardons, but I do not see the harm in such a small presumption."

"One can never be too careful, Lord Seaton. Presumptions can be very dangerous: one never knows when something unforeseen will happen and upset the best-laid plans."

"No," Edward agreed equitably. "One never can foresee such things. However, I have found that in such cases, it is what one makes of the situation after the fact that is important to recouping one's losses." He turned to an approaching couple just as she was about to aim a barbed rejoinder at him. "Have

you met Lord and Lady Poindexter, Eliza? They are old friends.
May I present Miss Eliza Austerleigh? I believe you know Lord
and Lady Clarke . . .''

And so it went. Eliza wanted to shrivel up and die from
misery. Lord Seaton pursued her everywhere. Every time she
tried to disappear into a corner, he was there, pulling her out
again. She did not know how he managed it, for he did not
appear to ignore his other guests and danced with many an
attractive young woman. But without being overly obvious, he
still contrived to give the impression that it was she who held
his attention. She could not work out why he was so intent on
making fools of them both, but knowing him to be callous and
diabolical, she finally decided that if he made them appear to
be on the most satisfactory terms, then people would auto-
matically assume she had willingly sold her land to him, if he
should manage to find some underhanded way to wrest it from
her.

This truly galled, and when Marguerite came up and tapped
her on the shoulder with her fan with a meaningful look
accompanied by a wide smile, she was more than ready to kick
Lord Seaton's shins. When a moment later Lord Seaton himself
came up and asked her for the next waltz, she very nearly did.

"Eliza?" he inquired at her look of mutiny. "Surely you
waltz?"

"I wish you would not call me Eliza."

"No?"

"No."

"Perhaps you would rather I call you something more
endearing? I would have no objections." He flashed her one
of his devastating smiles.

Eliza's brown eyes went black with suppressed fury, but she
smiled up at him for all of the world to see. "My lord, I do
not know why it is you have singled me out, but I can only
suspect you of the darkest motives."

"In truth?" he replied, still smiling. "It is amusing. In the
past I have been guilty of the very darkest of motives, but I
assure you, my dear Eliza, in this instance, my motives could
not be purer. I thought I had also made that precisely clear to
you. But come. The music begins."

"You have made a great many things clear to me, my lord,
and I do not appreciate any of them. However, in this instance

I can see that I cannot refuse you without making a scene. You seem to be very accomplished at putting me in that position, although I cannot think what compels you to do so.'' She took his arm and followed him onto the dance floor, suffering his hand on her back as he took her other hand in his.

"What compels me?" he asked, looking down into her eyes. "There are many reasons, Eliza. As I explained to you, you and I have much that is practical we can offer each other. You did not choose to hear me out, but I hope that you will give me the opportunity very soon to finish my proposition. I can be very persuasive, you know, when I am given a chance." He swept her around in the first of the circles, and she followed, unable to think of a suitable rejoinder.

His arm was firm and he guided her expertly and effortlessly around the room. Eliza did not know where to look, and so she concentrated on a spot over his shoulder. She had often dreamed of waltzing just like this and had secretly practiced many a time on her own, but she had never thought to be dancing with the Marquess of Seaton in the middle of his ballroom floor. She would have liked to sink right through it, and to bring him with her, for it would have afforded her great satisfaction to see him appear as foolish as she felt just then.

He took the wind out of her sails by quietly saying, "You dance very nicely."

"I thank you, my lord." Suddenly feeling utterly helpless, she blinked back unaccustomed and unwelcome tears. It was all too much. She felt Sackville being wrested from her inch by inch, and all done by sheer force of will. She brought her own will to bear, refusing to allow herself to be beaten down by the brute. "I know I am hopeless in most social areas, but not totally devoid of all graces. I can still perform the essential movements of the dances. Consider me remedial if you will, but I doubt I will disgrace you overmuch. I would, however, appreciate your lightening your grasp. It really isn't necessary to humiliate me any further."

Edward stared down at her, and it was testimony to his skill that he did not stumble. "Humiliate you? Is that what you think I've been doing? My God, woman, you are impossible to divine! Here I've been doing my very best to make you welcome in my circle, and all you can do is insult me. Are you such a numbskull that you cannot appreciate the honor I'm doing you?"

Eliza glared at him, her temper exceeding her fragile control. "Honor? Honor, you conceited ass? Have you for one minute thought about my honor, about what these people must be thinking? You are making me into a laughingstock."

Edward opened his mouth to give her a stinging rejoinder, but then thought better of it. He was, after all, supposed to be courting her, although at this particular moment he couldn't think what lunacy had overcome him. "Eliza," he finally said, "I cannot see why in trying to make you comfortable I am making you into a laughingstock. Perhaps you will explain yourself so that I might understand."

She looked up at him with accusing eyes. "I don't see why I should explain anything at all. You understand me perfectly well. There is nothing in me that would ordinarily recommend itself to such as you, and no reason why ordinarily you should have any cause to make me feel comfortable. I know perfectly well your opinion of me, and I am sure that your friends feel the same."

"I hope they have the good sense to follow where I lead."

"You, my lord, have an extremely high opinion of yourself if you think such a thing."

"And you, Miss Eliza Austerleigh, have a tongue in your head that is going to bring you to grief."

"I have told you, my lord, that I am not possessed of subtlety. If you did not insist on hovering about me, you would not have to suffer my shortcomings."

Edward laughed. "If I did not wish to suffer your shortcomings, then surely I wouldn't hover, would I?"

Eliza glared up at him. "You really are a very cruel man. Do you imagine I enjoy enduring your barbs? I cannot help being the way I am, but I do try to make the best of my situation. You were born with all the advantages, Lord Seaton. I would think you'd try to be more gracious to those less fortunate rather than making sport of them."

"But why do you persist in thinking I am making sport? I have offered you a way to improve your situation. I hope I will be able to bring you around, but I think it is very bad of you to accuse me of cruelty when it is you who has refused me. I do find your logic difficult to comprehend, Eliza."

"Do not call me Eliza. And nothing you do to attempt to persuade me to your will is going to work. Don't you see how unfeeling it is to try? You cannot come marching back to Seaton and decide that just because you are the marquess and have a great deal more money than I have, you have the right to do as you please.''

"But it is not as if I haven't consulted you, Eliza.''

"Consulted me? You made a bald statement, my lord. How did you expect me to respond? "Certainly, my lord, help yourself to my land, my animals, my house. It's my privilege to hand away all that I have worked so hard for.' Is that what you expected? You do not seem to understand that Sackville is my home. I love it.''

"Yes, you've made that very clear,'' he said with a frown. "I had not realized you were concerned about the disposition of Sackville. Actually, to be honest, I hadn't even thought about it. I suppose I thought I was offering you so much in return, that it would not matter to you. But it would be easy enough to create a trust property, although it seems a great deal more sensible to have the land fully joined to Seaton. I must say, this is the most curious thing to be discussing while waltzing, but if you agree to my terms, I could see to it that you would retain control over Sackville—''

"What are you talking about?'' she demanded. "I have just told you that you may not have Sackville. Therefore, there is no point in talking about trust properties or anything else you've been prattling on about, not that you've made any sense.''

"Eliza,'' Edward said, by now quite sure that she was slightly unbalanced in the head, "I don't think you've understood me correctly. I know it is complicated, but—''

"I have understood you exactly, and it's no good trying to confuse me further just because you think I'm simpleminded and you can take advantage of me, because you can't. I will not sell you Sackville! I begin to think that your pigheadedness makes you deaf, not that I would insult a pig by comparing it to you, for pigs are actually possessed of understanding and devotion. And furthermore, I think you are a deceitful, manipulative snake, although I shouldn't insult that good species either, and I wouldn't trust you not to sell your firstborn child if you saw a profit in it for yourself.''

Much to her surprise, Edward merely stared at her for a moment, then threw his head back and howled with laughter. Eliza stopped dead in the middle of a turn, and Edward, whose reflexes fortunately had always been good, grasped her firmly about the waist with both hands to keep them both from stumbling, although he was laughing too hard to be completely successful.

"My dear Lord Seaton," Eliza spluttered furiously, "I cannot think you have any feeling at all. And I wouldn't see you owner of Sackville if I were starving." And with that, she tore herself away and walked quickly across the room and through the door to the entrance hall, the crowd of people quickly enveloping her.

Edward watched her go, trying terribly hard to control himself, for it all had finally become clear to him. Here he had been doing his very best to offer for Eliza, and the whole time the idiotic woman had been thinking he'd been offering for Sackville.

And then, not oblivious to the looks of fascination they had drawn with their performance, he went to see to his other guests as if nothing at all were out of the ordinary.

Eliza fled up the stairs, feeling quite ill. It was just as she had thought: he had already worked out a complicated legal way to steal Sackville. She would have to hire a solicitor, and goodness only knew how much that would cost, not that she had any faith that she, an unmarried woman with no protection, could win her case over the wealthy Marquess of Seaton. He had already made it appear as if they were on the best of terms.

She hurried toward the retiring room, desperate for some privacy in which to collect herself. She was about to enter when she heard a conversation in progress and realized that the subject was herself, and she pressed herself against the wall so as not to be seen.

"Really, my dear, I cannot imagine what Lord Seaton can possibly be about," one voice said with a little titter. "She really is the most unattractive thing. And her clothes! The way he's behaving, one would think he's utterly enamored. It really is most baffling, not to mention nauseating."

"Well, I must say I find it rather disgusting the way the Austerleigh girl is flinging herself at his head. What is he to do? Although I cannot think why he invited her. Quite scandalous I find it. It's not as if she has any redeeming qualities at all, nor any respectability. Imagine living quite alone! One would think he had set up her house."

"I would not be surprised in the least. They say they are acquaintances from Jamaica, but still, why he would make any sort of effort when there are a hundred eligible beauties here to choose from, I cannot say."

"They've always said he was slightly different and without any scruples. I can well believe it. Imagine choosing to live in those disease-ridden islands when he has Seaton, not to mention his other estates. But then, one only has to look at the Austerleigh female, quite devoid of looks or social grace, and one cannot help but question his judgment."

"I suppose there's no accounting for taste," said a third voice. "Come, let us return downstairs. I have no inclination to miss any more of the evening, although I do wish Miss Austerleigh would develop a sudden migrim and have the good taste to take herself off."

Eliza, whose face had gone crimson with mortification, pushed herself away from the wall and, picking up her skirts, fled down the corridor, turning once and then again. But she heard footsteps and male voices coming from the other direction. Trapped, she pushed open the nearest door and slipped inside, trying to catch her breath. The voices passed, and she heard a burst of laughter drift past. She waited a few moments and then slowly turned the handle, intending to find Marguerite and ask her for the use of her carriage to take her home.

But the handle would not turn. She jiggled it and jiggled it again, and then, to her complete dismay, it came off in her hand.

She stared at it for a moment and then told herself not to panic. Panic never got one anywhere, no matter how much the dark terrified. And a bloodcurdling scream really wouldn't serve any purpose. What she needed was light. Light, she kept telling herself, slowly inching her way across the room, her hands out in front of her, for she could see nothing at all in the suffocating blackness. Searching for the far wall, she finally felt the fabric of heavy velvet draperies under her badly trembling fingers and thrust them aside. The faint glow of the half-moon came in a merciful shaft through the window, and she could see that she was facing the west side of the gardens. There was not a soul to be seen outside, but why should there be? It was early October and cold.

Eliza turned and looked about her, orienting her eyes to the thin light. She was in a bedroom. The four-poster bed sat against the wall, its hangings matching the deep velvet at the windows, but she could not be sure of the color—deep blue or claret, she guessed, trying to remain calm. A plush armchair sat to its right. There was a writing desk, delicate in design, and a dressing table with a mirror over it. Both surfaces were bare of implements. The room looked as if it hadn't been used in many years, although there were no Holland covers over the furniture to protect it from dust, which seemed to lie in a thick coat over everything. It appeared as if its occupant had simply moved out one day and no effort had been made toward the room since. It was not dissimilar to the feeling that pervaded the rest of the house.

Tapestries lined three of the walls, and she could make out one of them quite clearly where the thin shaft of moonlight struck it. It was a hunting scene, a hare being pursued by baying hounds. It described her feelings exactly.

Eliza crossed the room, handle still in hand, and tried to insert it into the massive door, but it would not cooperate. In a fit of frustration, she finally flung the knob to the floor and began to pound on the thick door, her pride no contest to her fear of being locked in. But no one came, and after a time her hands became raw and sore. She gave a hiccup of a sob, then bit her lip hard. She never cried. Crying was a sign of weakness.

Instead, she stretched out on the bed, hoping against hope that Marguerite would worry about her absence and come looking for her. She tried very hard not to think about what might happen if she was still there in the morning, for no matter how she looked at it, it could only mean disaster.

5

It does not appear to me that my hand is
unworthy your acceptance, or that the
establishment I can offer would be any
other than highly desirable.
                    Jane Austen *Pride and Prejudice*

Edward was on his way to the stables for his early-morning
ride, despite the fact that he had slept only three hours.
It was not his habit to stay late abed, and never had been,
no matter what the revelry of the night before.

The ball had been judged a grand success, but by Edward's
standards it had failed miserably, for Eliza had taken herself
home immediately after their waltz. He could hardly be
surprised, but her behavior had done nothing to further his plans.

He frowned as he considered his next step. Eliza was proving
to be a blasted nuisance, and he was damned if he was going
to expend much more energy bringing her around. Perhaps a
quick abduction would do the trick.

A noise from behind distracted him, and he looked around,
wondering where it had come from. But the garden was empty
and he could see no one on the path that led to the front of the
house. It came again, a knocking and what sounded suspiciously
like a muffled voice. He looked up. Eliza Austerleigh appeared
to be in a second-story window, in his mother's old bedroom,
if he wasn't mistaken. He blinked to be sure it wasn't last night's
brandy that was affecting his vision and then grinned, for it was
most indisputably Miss Austerleigh, and she looked quite
distressed. He signaled that he would be right up, for it became

immediately apparent that she did not wish to be in the second-story bedroom at all.

He could hardly believe his good luck. Edward had never had any trouble with slowness of the brain, and various ways of taking advantage of the situation flashed through his mind with alacrity as he reentered the house. It now appeared that there would be no need to abduct Eliza. She had abducted herself. By the time he reached the bedroom door, he had a plan well in place.

"Oh, my lord," Eliza said thankfully as the door swung open. For once she was delighted to see Edward. "I am so embarrassed. I cannot think how the handle came off, but I could not let myself out. I—I fell asleep." She tried to smooth down her badly wrinkled gown.

"Eliza," Edward demanded awfully, "what were you doing in this room in the first place?"

She blushed. "I—I was in need of solitude, my lord, and so I thought—I thought . . ."

Edward bent down and picked up the errant doorknob, turning it over and over again in his hand.

"My lord?" she said uncertainly. "You look disturbed."

"No, Eliza. I am not disturbed. Actually, I'm delighted. Surely you must realize the consequences of your need for solitude?"

"The consequences, my lord?" she said, her heart sinking, for she had a fair idea of what was coming.

"Yes. The consequences."

"I cannot think what you mean." Her eyes darted down to her feet and she bit her lip nervously.

"It is quite simple. You have irredeemably compromised yourself, my dear, and put us both in an interesting position."

"I most certainly have not," Eliza said indignantly. "Don't be utterly absurd. It was a perfectly genuine mistake—anyone could have made it."

"Anyone did not make it. You made it, Eliza. It doesn't seem worth mentioning that no one else of my acquaintance would think to invade a gentleman's living quarters."

"Living quarters? But no one has used this room for years. Look, you can see for yourself—"

"You're quite correct, Eliza, no one has used this room for years, most precisely not for twenty-nine years. These were my mother's rooms. They connect directly to what were my father's and are now mine.''

"Oh . . .''

"Oh.''

"Well, never mind, my lord,'' Eliza said brightly. "I shan't say a word about it, and I know that you won't, so we have nothing to worry about.''

Edward leaned back against the door, his arms folded across his chest. With a sense of removed horror Eliza saw the door swinging closed. "Oh, you idiot,'' she cried. "Look what you've gone and done! You will never be able to get the handle back in. I tried half the night! Now God only knows how long we'll be shut up in here.''

"We will be shut up in here for exactly as long as I wish, certainly as long as it takes to come to an agreement.''

Eliza eyed him warily. "What sort of an agreement? I have already told you that I will not sell you Sackville, so you may keep me here as long as you wish. I am not changing my mind. You think to blackmail me with all this talk of compromise, but it won't work.''

"You really are an impossible girl. I don't want Sackville. I thought I made that quite clear last night.''

"You don't want Sackville?''

"No, I don't. I never have.''

"If you don't want Sackville, then why have you been plaguing me?'' Eliza said, looking for a trap.

"I am in need of a wife, Miss Austerleigh. You will suit my purposes very well.''

"Oh, don't be ridiculous. This is no time to joke, and it is a joke that is not in the least appreciated.''

Edward's brow snapped down. "It is no joke, I assure you. I do not propose marriage lightly, nor have I ever proposed marriage before. I meant exactly what I said. I am in need of a wife. It is the reason that I journeyed back to England.''

"But . . .'' Eliza swallowed hard, completely taken aback, for it was clear that he really was serious.

"But?'' Edward asked with a raise of his eyebrow.

"But we hardly know each other, and you know that I dislike you, and I know precisely what you think of me, so I cannot think that we'd suit at all. And anyway, I do not wish to marry you.''

"That is neither here nor there, and I haven't the time or the patience to argue with you. You removed any choice you might have had in the matter when you shut yourself in my mother's bedroom last night, although you did save me a great deal of trouble."

"You are despicable. I would sooner marry a—madman than be wedded to you for five minutes."

"That is unfortunate. As I have just pointed out, you have little choice in the matter."

"I could not care if I am compromised and the entire world knows it," Eliza said stubbornly.

"But I could. I have a reputation to uphold, and I will not have it said that I did not do the honorable thing."

"That's the most arrogant statement I have ever heard."

"Come, Eliza," Edward said more coaxingly, seeing that he had better point out the advantages of the match, for he was getting nowhere. "Do you not want to be a marchioness?"

She stared at him, transfixed, thinking that she couldn't possibly have heard him right, for surely he could not think such a ludicrous thing. "I, a marchioness?"

"Yes, a marchioness. And wouldn't you like to see your beloved Sackville prospering as you so obviously desire?"

"Naturally, but that has nothing to do with you." Eliza had to suppress a strong desire to laugh, for the conversation was growing more ludicrous by the moment.

"But it does. I will make you a full gift of Sackville, and I will also bestow upon you a hundred acres of Seaton land that adjoins it. You may do with it as you please."

"I don't understand you. Why ever would you want to make an offer like that when you needn't give me anything at all?"

Edward sat down on the bed. "See here, Eliza, it is really very simple. There is really no other way out of your embarrassing situation but to marry me. I do need a wife rather badly, and I have had you in mind from the first, for a number of reasons that I will explain to you later. I do not pretend to love you, but I had thought to offer you a comfortable life."

"Have I understood you correctly? You are saying that you actually want to marry me?"

"Yes, I do," Edward said with exasperation.

"I really don't think I understand."

"I'll try to explain more clearly. I need a wife. You need

to extricate yourself from a difficult position. We each have something to offer the other. I happen to know how badly in need of funds you are, and that you are struggling to keep Sackville. This scrape of yours presents a fine solution for both of us. You cannot refuse my suit, for to do so would put you quite beyond the pale. There is no way you can leave this house with your reputation intact unless you do exactly as I say. So the advantages for you are manifold. With my title and position in society, you will be accepted without question. You will have the funds to make Sackville everything you wish, without my interference. It will be a marriage of convenience, save for the necessary consummation, but I promise you I will make that as brief as possible. You will have to live here at Seaton, but I shall shortly be returning to Jamaica, so you will have the advantage of being here on your own. I shall make a generous settlement on you, so you will have more than enough money to live very comfortably, even extravagantly if you wish."

Eliza glared at him. "How can you be so cold-blooded? You speak to me as if I were a prize heifer to be bought."

"Not at all. I would hardly wish for you to think that. I am merely trying to point out that for you there is much to be gained by marrying me."

"And for you, my lord? Where is the gain in this for you? Why is it you need a wife so badly, and why, of all the women in the world you might have chosen, did you decide on me?"

"That is slightly more complicated. I need you to agree to practice a deception."

Eliza was beginning to think this had to be a bad dream. Lord Seaton lounged on the bed as if they were having the most commonplace conversation in the world, as if it were perfectly normal for them to be locked in a bedroom together discussing marriage and deception in the same breath.

"Eliza, did you hear me?"

"I heard you. You want me to practice a deception."

"That's correct. I need you to be willing to pretend that we have been married for three years. Since your last visit to Jamaica, in fact."

Eliza sank into an armchair. After a few moments she looked up at him. "Assuming you are in your right mind, which I somehow doubt, what might your reason be?"

"I will tell you that only when I have your word on the

marriage. Agree to the deception and you will have everything I have just promised you. Without your agreement, you will be forced into marriage with me anyway, but I will not be prepared to be nearly so generous. It would be very foolish of you to choose the latter, for you would find your position uncomfortable indeed. Those are your only choices left, Eliza.''

It was slowly and painfully being brought to bear on Eliza that she really did not have a choice. If she refused, she knew he would not hesitate to ruin her. If she agreed to marry him but refused to agree to the deception, he would not hesitate to take Sackville from her, and she could imagine countless other miseries he might perpetrate upon her, for by law he could do nearly anything he chose.

Never in her life had she felt so trapped. She tore her gaze away from the window. Edward was about to snatch her freedom from her without any more thought to her feelings than he would give to crushing an ant underfoot. She met his eyes. ''You, sir, are a cad.''

''Maybe. Do you agree?''

Eliza bowed her head.

''Eliza? I suggest you choose wisely.''

She walked to the window and pressed her hand against the cold pane, thinking of a trapped bird, and the image made her throat constrict. As a child she had been punished for letting a finch out of its cage at the house of her mother's friend. She had never regretted her action.

''I grow impatient, Eliza. Surely it cannot take this long to see the advantages and disadvantages. All you need say is 'I agree.' Two small words—I am sure you can manage them. Where is the difficulty?''

She turned to face him. At that moment she truly hated him. For whatever perverse reason, he had had this in mind since he had first appeared, and no doubt he would have found some other way to force her to his will if she hadn't so conveniently locked herself in his mother's bedroom and delivered herself right into his hands.

''Please do get on with it, Eliza. I would rather we didn't have to spend the rest of the day in here.''

''Very well, then. I can see no way out. I agree,'' she said, her voice shaking.

''A wise choice. I knew you would make it eventually.'' He

stood and crossed over to the tapestry. To her surprise, he lifted it to one side and a door appeared, which he opened. She saw his room beyond. He held out his hand. "Come. Let us begin, Lady Seaton. We shall descend from my quarters together. But first I shall tell you just a bit more of the role you are to play. The rest can wait until later."

By three they were on their way to London, by five they were married, and by seven they had stopped for the night at a respectable posting house. Eliza felt like a sleepwalker as she descended from the carriage and entered the inn, the circle of gold heavy on her fourth finger.

She watched as Lord Seaton made arrangements for their rooms and then guided her upstairs. He had been cold but unfailingly courteous to her, carefully explaining the story he had devised and how he intended to go about it.

"You see, Eliza," he'd said on the way to the church where they were to be married, "it is of utmost importance that people do not question the fact that we were married three years ago, but naturally I want the marriage to be legal. The reverend was quite willing to accept a large sum of money in exchange for a special license and his silence."

Eliza had merely nodded and looked out the window at the bleak landscape. The day was windy and gray, and heavy black clouds threatened to open at any moment. The weather suited Eliza's mood perfectly. From the moment they had descended the staircase together and he had introduced her to the gaping housekeeper as his wife, a bleakness had crept into her very bones. His valet had bowed and said how very nice it was to see her again, and it had been all she could do to keep from choking, for she had never seen him before in her life.

It had become clearer by the minute that Lord Seaton had set the stage very well indeed, apparently very confident that he would have no trouble convincing her to go along with his little scheme. The more she had a chance to think about it, the more she realized that his public behavior had been in exact accordance with how one might treat an estranged wife one was trying to win back. But why? Why would he need to do such a thing? That he had not yet seen fit to tell her.

Edward ushered her into the church and she waited while he had a quick word with the minister, who appeared to be heavily in his cups. It was just as well, she thought, for the ceremony was a mockery as it was. They spoke their vows quickly, the words heavy on Eliza's tongue, and then he slipped the ring on her finger and brushed her cold lips with his.

They signed the marriage lines and they were off again. The sky had opened and the rain had come pelting down, and Eliza had huddled in her corner of the carriage, in no mood to converse. They had exchanged hardly a word since.

Eliza brushed out her hair and put it up on her head again, then changed from her traveling dress into a dinner dress. At least Lord Seaton had allowed her to stop at Sackville and pack a small case before he dragged her off to her wedding. Annie had been struck dumb when Eliza had tearfully told her the lie, saying that she had no time to explain, but would tell her everything when they returned from London. But she did give Annie very careful instructions about how things were to go on at Sackville while she was away.

Annie had hugged her. "I always did think there was more to your story than you'd let on, miss—I mean, my lady. Specially when the marquess showed up and threw you into such a fluster of unhappiness. Well, all's well that ends well, I always say, so off you go with your husband, miss, and this time around you make each other very happy."

She'd dug into her apron pocket for her handkerchief and given her nose a great blow, and it had occurred then to Eliza that Lord Seaton might be right: people will generally believe anything they're told.

She sighed and gave herself a last look in the mirror. Her skin was unnaturally pale, hardly surprising, given all the shocks she'd had in one day. Her eyes fell down onto her wedding ring. It was the most ironic thing: here she was, newly married, and she was more miserable than she'd ever been in her life.

There was a knock on the door and she stood, smoothing down the pink muslin over the silk underdress. "Yes?" she called.

Edward came into the bedroom. He, too, had changed his clothes, exchanging his buckskin breeches and top boots for fawn-colored pantaloons, slippers, and a blue swallowtail coat. "I have bespoken a private parlor. You must be famished." He looked her over with a frown. "We really must do something about your clothes. I'll have that taken care of as soon as we arrive in London. Pink is most unattractive on you."

Eliza colored angrily. "I am aware, my lord, that my clothes are not the finest in the land. I have had to make do with Miss Chandler's cast-offs, and unfortunately she favored pinks and yellows."

"It's no good flying up into the boughs with me, Eliza. If you are to be my wife, I would see you suitably dressed. Marguerite will be in town, or so she mentioned last night, so I shall send for her. She will know exactly what is to be done."

Eliza bit her lip. She hadn't thought as far as Marguerite. Now she would have to deceive her one and only friend. It was almost more than she could bear—lie upon lie upon lie. Where would it end?

Edward's face softened slightly at the desolate expression on hers and he reached out a finger and chucked her chin. "Come now, Eliza, it surely isn't as bad as all that. I know it has been a long day, but food will do you good. You will settle into your new life quickly enough, and before long you will have forgotten that it was ever any other way." He held out his elbow and Eliza took it, but as they went downstairs, she knew that she would never forget. Never.

The dinner tasted like sawdust to her, although she attempted to choke it down, for her new husband was watching her impatiently over the rim of his glass.

"Have some more claret, Eliza. It will help you to relax. We have one more matter of business before the evening is done, and I would not have you in this frame of mind."

Eliza, who had been pushed to the edge of self-control, looked at him with outrage. "Have you no delicacy of feeling, my lord?"

"Very little, I'm afraid. I am a practical man, Eliza. It seems best to me to be straightforward when it comes to matters such as this. You have said yourself that it is straightforward language you understand best."

"Directness is one thing, my lord. Insensitivity is another. In one day you have taken from me my pride, my independence, and my honesty. Now you plan on taking my virginity. And why shouldn't you? No doubt you think you have a right to that as well as to everything else. So be it. I can hardly fight you off."

Edward drained his claret and poured them both some more.

"You are being unreasonable, Eliza. And do try to call me Edward, won't you? Trust me, it is better to have it over and done with." He took another deep drink.

"You would know better than I, my lord."

"Edward."

"Edward," she snapped.

"That's better. In any case, you cannot arrive a virgin at Grosvenor Square. That is quite out of the question."

"Why, my lord—I mean, Edward?" Eliza asked wickedly, knowing perfectly well what his reasoning had to be.

"Because, you silly girl, there would be blood all over the sheets, and the word would be out among the servants in no time at all."

Eliza stared at him openmouthed, beginning to enjoy herself. It seemed that the one way to provoke Edward was to behave in as moronic a fashion as possible. "Blood, my lord?" she asked in a little whisper, delighted by his harassed countenance. "Why blood?"

"Did your mother tell you nothing?" he said distractedly, running a hand through his hair and thoroughly disarranging the dark locks.

"No, my lord. I imagine she thought there would be time enough when I was to marry, and then I didn't take, and she died."

Edward swore under his breath.

"I beg your pardon?" she asked sweetly. "I did not understand you. I was hoping, you see, that you would explain it all to me, for I have heard that losing one's virginity is a difficult thing for a woman, although I haven't the least understanding why. If we are to do this thing together, it would be best if I knew what was to happen." She took a sip of her wine, and now she watched him over the rim.

"Very well," Edward said with resignation. "It is very simple." He quickly and clinically ran over the basics with nary a blush, and Eliza was quite impressed with his skill with words, for he managed to make it sound quite matter-of-fact.

"Oh," she said ingenuously when he had finished. "It sounds very like when the bull covers the cow. Not much different at all. I had no idea they bled, though. How uncomfortable for the poor cow. And such an awkward position."

Edward closed his eyes for a moment and rubbed his forehead.

"You can only lose your virginity the first time, Eliza. After that there is no bleeding and no pain. And the position is not usually the . . . Never mind. As I have told you, I shan't trouble you after tonight, so you need not concern yourself."

Eliza had to bite her cheeks to keep from laughing. "Very well, but I can't think why people bother so much over something that sounds deadly dull. I suppose it's the only way they can get children. I had wondered about that, but you've explained very nicely. I think I shall go up and prepare myself. As you said, the sooner it's done with, the better, and I really am quite exhausted." She rose and swept out without another glance in his direction, but when she reached the safety of her room, she collapsed against the door in a fit of giggles. Really, it had been amusing, and he really must think her the biggest cork-brain ever. She was going to make very grand sport out of Edward March. She'd see that he would rue the day he forced her into marriage.

But then she sobered abruptly as she thought of what was to come. She squared her shoulders and began to undress, telling herself that after the day she had just been through, she could face anything.

Edward opened the connecting door and managed to walk over to the bed in a straight line. At least, he thought it was a straight line. He'd had much more to drink than was good for him, having finished a second bottle of claret and then consumed most of a decanter of bad port. But the prospect before him seemed no better for the wine. If anything, it seemed worse. He was about to bed a wife—his wife, he thought dismally, his virginal, bird-witted wife, whom he'd actually had to instruct in the basic points of sexual congress. Now he would have to follow through on that instruction.

Oh, dear God, he thought miserably.

Eliza sat beneath the covers, her hands folded in her lap, her legs straight out before her. She'd braided her hair and put on a white cotton night rail. She most certainly didn't look like a bride on her wedding night, but neither did she look as if she would succumb to hysterics, he considered as he sat down on the side of the bed. At least that was something.

"So, Eliza. I am glad not to find you cringing in the corner."

"I can see no purpose in cringing, my lord, for it seems it

would only make things more unpleasant. Unless, of course, by my cringing, you would take such a disgust of me that you would go away.''

"I fear not, Eliza." He reached out a hand and stroked her shoulder. "I am not an ogre. Come, you need not be frightened."

"I am not frightened. As I told you, I am tired. I almost fell asleep waiting for you, thinking you were never going to come. That would have suited very well, but since you have come, I would have you do this thing and then leave me." She was certainly not going to admit that she was utterly terrified and had been staring blindly at the wall for nearly two hours.

"Very well," Edward said with a sigh, and blew out the candle next to the bed. Pulling the covers back, he shrugged off his night robe and slipped in next to her, sliding his hand over her waist. Indeed, she did not cringe at his caress, but neither did she respond. Her arms remained at her sides. He felt as if he were holding a block of wood. He slipped his other arm under her back, pulling her toward him, and he kissed her hair, finding it to be surprisingly fine and smelling of rosemary. He closed his eyes and tried to pretend he was with someone else as he brought his lips to hers. But there was no mistake that he was kissing Eliza, for her mouth was as tightly screwed together as if he were trying to insert a bar of soap into it. No one had so steadfastly refused one of his kisses before, and he found her resistance extremely annoying. It was very difficult to make love to someone who could barely comprehend what he was doing, save in the context of a bull and cow.

Giving up the effort to slowly arouse her and wondering if he were going to be able to manage the act at all, he moved his hand down and cupped her breast, fuller and softer than he'd expected. He stroked it for a few moments, more for his benefit than for hers, pleased to feel the involuntary tightening of her nipple in his palm. He was delighted to feel a responding tightness in his groin. Amazing what a woman's breast could do, he hazily thought, but he'd better get the deed done quickly, before he lost his ability altogether.

Eliza had been doing her very best to be as passive as possible while loathing and resentment burned in her chest and she felt like thrashing him off her. But as his hand slowly caressed her breast, she found her teeth unclenching and the burn of loathing and resentment seemed to be replaced by a different kind of heat. The warmth of Edward's palm radiated through the cotton of her night rail, doing alarming things to her. A slow throbbing began deep in her belly and she had a terrible desire to press her breast up against his hand, as well pressing other parts of her body to him. Her arms loosened, and just as she was about to slip them around his back and succumb to this treacherous desire, she felt his hand suddenly move away and he pulled her nightdress up around her hips. In one swift movement he was over her, pressing between her legs.

"This is the part I said would hurt," he said over her head, with no more inflection in his voice than if he were removing a splinter from her finger, and he pushed hard.

Eliza stiffened and gasped, and then she could not help a sharp cry as he thrust into her. The pain was acute indeed, but bearable. What she felt was far worse than physical pain. She turned her head and buried her cheek in the pillow as she suffered his driving movements in her, praying for it to be over quickly. She could not think, felt suffocated not only by his body but also by her humililation. This was not lovemaking; this was nothing more than bestial coupling. She felt ugly and somehow sullied.

He made a slight noise in his throat and then he rolled off her, his breathing hardly disturbed. "Sorry, Eliza. It's over now, all finished. I shan't touch you again." He pulled her night rail back down over her thighs. "All right?"

Tears stung at her eyes, and she only nodded, not turning her head to look at him.

"I'll leave you, then." He reached down, and feeling along the floor with his fingers, he collected his dressing gown, wrapping it around himself, and then he crossed to the basin and poured some water into it. Dampening a cloth, he brought it over to her. "Here. You might want to clean up. I'm sorry, Eliza," he said again to the back now completely turned from him. He felt a pang of guilt and then irritation that he should feel such a thing at all. He had done nothing more to her than any husband did to his virginal wife. Why, then, did he feel as if he'd just committed an act of rape?

"Good night," he said as civilly as he could, putting the cloth on the nightstand. "We'll talk more tomorrow." With that, he turned and went back to his own room.

As soon as the door shut behind him, Eliza rolled onto her stomach and buried her face in the pillow, crying as if her heart would break. It wasn't so much the hurt in her body, the heavy throbbing between her legs, where she felt bruised and swollen, that caused her tears. Eliza had never been one to cry over physical pain, not even when she'd been very small and had fallen from a tree, breaking her arm.

Nor had she cried even when her mother had died, for her stepfather had made it very clear that he would not stand for tears. She had learned very early to put a good face on things, not ever to show her feelings. Feelings only caused trouble. Far better to be invisible.

Eliza rubbed her eyes on her sleeve and sat up. Much good she had done at being invisible. She couldn't even get that right. First there'd been her stepfather, and now Edward, but she hadn't managed to fend him off so successfully. The awful thing was that for a few moments, she really hadn't wanted to.

Three years ago she'd first laid eyes on Edward March from a distance. She'd been taken not so much by his fine figure and good looks, nor by his charm, as by something less definable. There had been something in his face as she had watched him, a quality beneath the surface that had hinted at a very different man than the one he chose to show the world. But that had merely piqued her curiosity. What had touched her heart had been the day she'd come upon him unawares as she had been out walking. He had not seen her. She doubted very much whether he'd ever noticed her anyway, although they had been introduced and several times she had been on the outer fringes of a group of which he had been a part.

But on this day he had been alone, crouched by the riverbank, watching something with great intensity, unmoving for a long time. Finally he'd left and she'd moved out from the position she'd taken in the shelter of a banana tree. Upon quietly approaching the spot he'd abandoned, she discovered a nest of baby mice, curled up against their mother, who had obviously only just finished giving birth to them. It was this process Edward had been watching so intently, a most surprising interest for a fashionable marquess, but an interest similar to her own.

It was then that she had well and truly lost her heart. She had sat and sketched the scene, thinking of Edward as she'd done so. It had been amazing to her to discover a man who could take the same enjoyment in nature that she did, that he could be fascinated by a small animal giving birth. She had been correct then about the sensitivity she'd sensed in him. She decided that the next time she saw him she would somehow summon up her nerve and contrive to enter the conversation.

But the next time she'd seen him had been at the Denighams' ball, the night she had overheard the mocking words that had wounded her so deeply.

She had seen only his back through the open window where she'd been standing hidden on the balcony. Still, his voice had floated out into the night air with crystal clarity. She had started when she'd heard him mention her name, for she had gone out onto the balcony for privacy, trying to think of a way to approach him without making a complete fool of herself. And then her heart, which had for the only time in her life felt the stirrings of romantic love, had been crushed under the brutal impact of his words.

"Eliza Austerleigh?" he'd said with a laugh. "A veritable pantry, do you not think, with her carrot top and bran face? Pamela Chandler lamentably may have no brain, but she's no fool when it comes to protecting her self-interest. She has chosen herself the perfect foil for her beauty. No risk that the Austerleigh girl will be noticed by even the hoariest old gent."

A murmured question with a smothered laugh, and then his answer. "A seduction? Now there would be a challenge. I wager it could be done if one exerted enough skill, but for me, no, thank you. Keep your money. I know some think my prowess is legendary, but I leave that challenge to some other unfortunate. I prefer to warm myself over something with a touch of appeal. In any case, aside from a negligible personality, the girl has no eyebrows."

He and his friends had wandered away, and Eliza had stayed hidden the rest of the evening, too ashamed to come back into the room and face Edward's mocking eyes.

And now he had wounded her again, and this time she could not run away and hide.

Eliza winced with the fresh memory. No matter how much she had tried to deny it to herself, she had fallen in love with Edward March. Fallen in love with him because she thought he was different, not like all the other men she'd known. She'd spent three years chastising herself for so foolish a sentiment, for he'd proven himself to be a callous, insensitive rake, after all. And now she was married to him, not for any finer reason than he'd needed a wife and she'd landed herself in a predicament from which she'd been unable to extricate herself.

Perhaps tonight, somewhere deep in herself, she had harbored a tiny seed of hope that he would find the person she was beneath, that he would take the time to be caring of her, to discover that she had the beginnings of passion in her. Perhaps she had even hoped that she'd been wrong about him, that there might be a chance that they could find affection, if not love, together.

Her heart had threatened to pound out of her chest with fright when she'd dimly seen his naked body, when his arms had gone around her, and she had secretly prayed that he would whisper some tender words to ease her fear, anything to help her to let go. But nothing. Nothing but a neutral word of warning as he poised over her, ready to rip into her body. If only he had waited a few more minutes, had given her some time to become adjusted, to experience fully the stirrings he had set off in her, maybe it could have been different.

The fact he had just taken her in an act of incredible intimacy, with no more thought to it than a rutting stallion, pointed out to her just how loveless her marriage would be. That he had been able to take her at all, given his admitted disgust of her, must have been a supreme act of will.

Well, too bad for him, she told herself belligerently. She had been wrong, badly wrong about him, and tonight had just proved it to her finally: she'd been a foolish, naïve woman of twenty-five, stricken by a handsome man with an interest in mice, convinced that beneath the arrogant facade there was a person of sensitivity. Now she was twenty-eight, far too old for illusions, and she knew that Edward March had not a sensitive bone in his body. She had every reason to hate him and none at all to love. The Denighams' ball had been the first time she'd cried over him. Tonight would be the last time she ever shed a tear on his behalf.

Eliza numbly reached for the cloth he had left for her. She scrubbed at herself and the sheets until no trace remained that he had ever been there. And then, changing her night rail, she climbed back into bed, swearing to herself that he would never know just how deeply he had hurt her. She would surely never let him touch her heart again.

6

I have heard that something very shocking indeed will soon come out in London.
                    Jane Austen *Northanger Abbey*

The next day began badly. Edward woke with a pounding headache and a foul taste in his mouth. He squinted against the light coming in from the window and it took him a moment to orient himself. And then memory returned—all of it, in one great fell blow—and he groaned and rolled onto his back, staring moodily at the ceiling.

He'd drunk a great quantity of bad port and then broken a cardinal rule he'd always adhered to: he had taken a woman to bed when he'd been far too drunk to give either of them any pleasure. What was worse was that the woman he had taken to bed had been his wife.

He wished that his drunken state had induced a complete loss of memory, but unfortunately it hadn't, and he was well aware that he had never in his life made such a poor showing.

It was Eliza's fault, he told himself, knowing perfectly well it wasn't Eliza's fault in the least.

It was the fact that she was a virgin that had put him off, he silently insisted, and once again a voice somewhere in the back of his throbbing head told him that because she had been a virgin he should have shown her even more consideration.

She was hopelessly dim-witted and felt like a broomstick with breasts. But he had slept with hopeless dimwits in his less discerning moments, and as for a broomstick . . .

"It's a blasted legal contract," he roared, sitting up abruptly and immediately regretting his impulsive action. "You don't make love to a legal contract," he finished on a whisper, his head in his hands. "Oh, damnation."

A half-hour later he made his way down to the private parlor, where he found Eliza already ensconced, halfway through a breakfast of bread, cold meat, and cheese.

She looked up as he entered and her expression was less than warm. Edward, who did not deal well with emotions, least of all his own, had worked himself into a temper. Guilt did not sit easily on him, and since it was Eliza who had caused him to feel guilty, she became the object of his wrath.

"Good morning, my lord," she said quite without expression. "Did you pass a pleasant night?"

"If by that remark you are referring to my taking you as my wife—"

"I am not, my lord. You have assured me that it will not happen again, and so I consider the matter closed. I'd thank you not to mention it again."

He scowled, then sat down at the table and poured himself a cup of coffee. "I've ordered the carriage to be ready in a quarter of an hour. I trust you will be finished with your meal?"

"Do you not care to eat, my lord?" Eliza asked, glancing over at him, quite pleased to see that he was very out of sorts.

"I do not. And I would prefer to drink my coffee in peace. I do not enjoy conversation early in the morning."

"Certainly, my lord. As you wish. I imagine you have a great many habits I shall soon discover for myself. They are probably mostly unpleasant, or so has been my experience."

Edward shot her a foul look and she returned her attention to her plate, finishing her meal as she had begun it—in silence.

Fifteen minutes later exactly they were on their way.

Eliza sighed and shifted slightly on the cushion. She was still very sore from Edward's assertion of his marital rights, although she viewed it as more of an assault. She could not help but wonder if a child would result from that union, and she did not know what she felt on the matter. Where she had always very much wanted children, she now had mixed feelings on the subject, given who the father would be. But a pregnancy was so improbable as to be discounted entirely, so she didn't know why she was even thinking about it. Yet, for some reason she felt sad.

"May I ask why you are frowning so, Eliza? It is a most unbecoming expression," Edward stated from his seat opposite her.

"I assume that now it is nearly eleven we may speak, my lord?"

"Insolence is also unbecoming."

"I beg your pardon. I must depend on you to tell me how to go on, my lord, for you know I have no sense of my own. It is just as well I have you here to instruct me, for I should not want to make a fool of myself or you." Eliza had spent the better part of her sleepless night thinking how she was to deal with the monstrous marquess, and she had decided that continued stupidity was probably the most effective way to aggravate him and therefore keep him far away. Add to that frivolity and she should soon be left very much on her own. She had decided to use Pamela Chandler as the perfect model for her behavior, and she had had much experience in observing Pamela.

"I shall tell you exactly how to go on, madam, do not doubt it. Whether you like it or no, you are my wife and shall behave accordingly."

"Indeed, my lord," Eliza said with lowered lashes. "I shall behave just as a marchioness should. I shall develop airs and graces and flirt with my fan. I shall also attend parties and routs and balls. In truth, my lord, I have decided that since our marriage is to be one of convenience, I shall take advantage of every convenience I can. Don't you think that is most sensible? You promised me wealth, my lord, and if my plan is to succeed, I cannot go about without it. When may I expect to see my settlement paid?"

"As soon as you fulfill the terms of our agreement," Edward said, wearily rubbing his aching forehead.

"But you have not explained those terms, my lord. All you told me was that we were quietly married three years before, on my return to Jamaica from British Honduras. We kept the marriage a secret and resided elsewhere—you have not specified where, my lord. After a number of months I left you, quite understandably, and returned to England, where you had arranged through my relative Lady Westerfield that I should have Sackville upon her death because it bordered Seaton and you wished to keep an eye on me even though from afar.'' She drew in a deep breath and continued, like a child reciting by rote. ''You decided that the estrangement had gone on long enough and returned to persuade me to this. You finally convinced me at your ball to return to you—''

''Enough! That's quite enough. I do not need chapter and verse of my own story, Miss Austerleigh.''

''Lady Seaton,'' she corrected demurely. ''I am now a marchioness.''

''I have not forgotten,'' he said, a storm cloud lowering on his brow. ''It is one thing I fear I shall never forget.''

''That is good, my lord, for short of divorce you are leg-shackled to me. I find the prospect less appalling today, now that the unpleasantness is over with—that is, of being leg-shackled, not divorced, I mean. I had never dreamed to be a marchioness, but I find the position gives me a newfound confidence. Why, the way the innkeeper and his wife simpered and bowed, I felt quite the most important thing.'' She lowered her eyes again. ''I know I am not a diamond of the first water, my lord, but I think that my elevated position might make up for that, don't you?''

Edward gave an inward groan. He could hardly believe that the painfully shy, confused girl he had wed the day before was already beginning to transform into this creature.

''My lord? Do you not think?''

''What I think, Eliza, is that you had better listen to me very carefully if you wish any of the things you have mentioned to come to fruition. I have yet to explain to you the circumstances behind our agreement, and it is vitally important that you attend carefully.''

''My concentration is not the best, but I shall try very hard.''

''Good. We are less than an hour away from London, and so I have not much time. As you know, when one is a peer, it is important to ensure the succession—''

''I had wondered about that, my lord. You said last night that the desire for children was the reason that married people endured that disgusting act. But if we are never to have to endure it again, does that mean that I shall have a child quite soon? I cannot think why else you married me, but I do think it most unfair of you not to tell me I would begin immediately increasing.''

"No, you silly woman. You are not increasing. Please, try to attend to what I am telling you.''

"Yes, my lord.''

"And please, do try to remember to call me Edward. We might as well put on some kind of a display as man and wife.''

"Yes, Edward. I will try to please you in all things. But if I am not increasing, how can you ensure the succession?'' Indeed, Eliza was very puzzled as to this point, which had only just occurred to her.

"Because I already have an heir, Eliza.''

"Well, of course you must have, somewhere or other. Doesn't everyone? But surely you would want a son of your own?''

"I have a son.''

Her eyes flew to his in shock. "You—you have?''

"Yes. His name is Matthew. He is two and a half years old.''

"But surely you have not been married before, my lord?'' Eliza said, all sorts of pieces falling far too quickly into place.

"No, I have not been married. Matthew's mother is dead, and I only recently discovered his existence when he was brought to me. Because he was born out of wedlock, he is not allowed by the rules of succession to inherit, which I wish him to do. Therefore, it became necessary for me to find a wife, someone willing to say that we had married two years and six months ago.''

Eliza was struck dumb. Even her fertile brain had not come up with an explanation this bizarre. She was to masquerade as this poor child's mother?

"Please, do close your mouth, Eliza, and wipe that pious expression from your face. You were only just now carrying on about the advantages of your new position.''

"Yes, but, but you said nothing about my having had a child two and a half years ago. I won't do it.''

"Yes, you will. It's already done. You have already perpetrated the lie to a number of servants that we have long been married. Is it asking so much to add a child to it? I cannot see the difficulty.''

"You—you want me to become an instant mother to a child I've never before laid eyes on?"

"You needn't do anything maternal. The boy has a nurse. Just behave as if he is yours by birth, that's all I ask."

"You expect me to allow people to think such a thing? What sort of unnatural mother would give up her cihld at birth?"

"My dear Eliza," Edward said, leaning back against the squabs with crossed arms and a bored expression, "nearly every mother in society today does just that. It will excite no comment, believe me. In fact, the only thing that will excite comment is the fact that I seduced you in the first place."

Eliza did not even wince. She was too busy counting months. "I see," she finally said. "You seduced me, no doubt on a dare from one of your friends, and then I discovered I was with child."

"Yes," Edward said, giving her a sharp look, and then decided she couldn't have known what she had said, as usual. "That you should return to Jamaica, pregnant and terrified of the consequences, and demand that I marry you, is quite ordinary a reaction for someone in your position. That I should have accepted and maintained the child because he was my legal heir is also a normal if somewhat embarrassing reaction for someone in my position. And that I should have decided after a period of reflection that the child needed his mother is not so unusual."

"My God, you are despicable."

"I am no more despicable than any other member of my class. It is unfortunate that, because of your own position, to which a series of circumstances brought you, you seem to have absorbed the values of a less-exalted class."

"My values are my own, sir, and not for you to tread on," Eliza said through clenched teeth. "And I would far rather answer to mine than to yours."

"Listen, my girl. You might not have the best understanding in the world, but if you value all you said you have, then do not cross me in this matter, for as God is my witness, I shall make your life a living hell."

"God is indeed your witness, and you have already made my life a living hell," Eliza shot back.

"Eliza, do try to curtail this proclivity you have for melodrama. It really isn't necessary. This is only a slight twist on common behavior. Do you have any idea how many women present their husbands with children that have been fathered by someone else? It is not unknown to have five children in a family, each with a different sire.''

''And that makes what you are doing right.''

''Morality bores me. But if we must speak of right and wrong, it seems to me that what I am doing is quite correct, if slightly illegal. Matthew is my firstborn son. I will have no other children, as we have agreed. I would not have Matthew go through his life with the stigma of illegitimacy when it was no fault of his own that he should be so. By the by, had I known his mother was pregnant, I should have married her, but she did not have the good sense to inform me of her condition. As she was already dead when I learned of Matthew, I could not correct the situation; therefore, the only solution left to me was to find a wife willing to pose as Matthew's birth mother. Am I making myself clear? Good. That is why I came to England. I discovered that you happened to have been in the right place at more or less the right time, and that the set of circumstances was virtually tailor-made for this situation. It also helped that you were now living just down the road and you were unmarried.

''I have given you my name, and providing you do as you're told, I will also give you your settlement and your freedom to do as you please, so long as you behave in a fitting manner to your new position. I cannot see how any of those things are so terrible. I have also given Matthew a mother and his birthright. So do not tell me that what I have done is wrong, or think to judge me.''

Eliza only shrugged, but she was thinking that Edward made a very persuasive argument. The only thing he had left out was the feelings of the people involved. Edward seemed to see life as a series of circumstances he could manipulate to suit himself.

Perhaps she might be able to make some good come out of the disaster he had tossed them all into. She really didn't see how she could turn back at this juncture, in any case. She had already married Edward, after all. And he did have a point: it wasn't Matthew's fault that he had been born out of wedlock. Why should he have to carry that through his life, when at a word from her he would be Edward's legal heir?

But if Matthew was ever going to become the next marquess,

then she'd have to play her assigned part very well, for if the
truth ever came out, there would be an unthinkable scandal.

It would be a complicated role indeed: the cork-brain for
Edward, the marchioness for the staff, and for the rest of the
world the shy, awkward girl who had run away from her child
and husband and was only now prepared to take her place in
society. She bit her lip, wondering if she was up to it. Well,
why not? Perhaps it would be easier playing a role than having
to be her rather unsatisfactory self for as long as Edward chose
to keep her in London. It would certainly keep her busy, and
as soon as she had done her job, she could return to the country
and live out her life in peace, as Edward had promised. In the
meantime, she would continue to annoy him every chance she
had.

"Eliza? Do you agree to my terms? As I pointed out to you
yesterday, you have a great deal to gain if you do, and a great
deal to lose if you cross me."

She took a deep breath, her decision made. "Jewels?" she
asked, turning from the window. "Will you give me jewels?
If I'm to be forced to play this silly charade, then I think you
should make it up to me. And as a marchioness, I should like
to look the rank."

"I'll give you far more than jewels," Edward said with
exasperation, thinking once again of Swiss cheese. He had
clearly wasted his breath with his persuasive moral argument.
The girl couldn't hold a thought together for more than an
instant. "I shall bestow upon you money and clothes and all
the jewels you might desire if you behave yourself. If not, you
shall go back to poverty and rags."

"I cannot in all conscience do that. Very well, my lord. I
shall be Matthew's mother." But only for the child's sake, Eliza
swore. The marquess, his jewels, and his money could burn
in hell for all she cared. "But you had best do all the
explaining," she finished.

"Don't worry about that. I shall. The less you say, the better.
Now be a good girl and be quiet. I want to sleep."

Edward rested his head against the squabs and dozed for the
rest of the journey.

Hamlish, who had been well-versed, had gone ahead to
Grosvenor Square to alert the staff that Lord Seaton would be

arriving with his wife. Naturally this created a tremendous stir and great excitement, but all was in readiness by the time the carriage pulled up in front of the house, one of the larger residences gracing the square.

Edward had taken a great gamble that Eliza would capitulate, and his gamble paid off, for when they alighted from the carriage, she played her part to perfection, sweeping into the house as if to the manner born.

He watched her, actually amazed at the transformation in her in so short a time. Just over twenty-eight hours before, he had been persuading a reluctant and very upset Eliza that she had to marry him. Last night . . . Well, he wouldn't think about last night. She had obviously decided that there were advantages to her new position and also intended to forget about it. Now he could only hope that her scrambled wits would not bring about disaster, but perhaps people would find her so confusing that they'd take anything she said as a hum.

Eliza greeted the housekeeper and the butler and nodded to the rest of the startled staff who had lined up for her inspection.

"And now," she said anxiously, turning to Edward, who stood at her side, "where is dear Matthew? I cannot wait another moment, Edward, for I have been all in fidgets. I am convinced he will look exactly like you. When I last saw him, he was so tiny one could not tell anything at all, and as you know, I wasn't quite myself. But I do remember that at least he did not have red hair."

"And he still has not," Edward replied, well-pleased with the thunderstruck looks on both Grigson's and Mrs. Chubb's faces, for he knew the word would go out instantly to other households and filter upstairs. "He should be in the nursery. Come upstairs, my dear, and let me reacquaint you with your son." He took her by the elbow and led her up the grand staircase.

"You did well, Eliza," he murmured in her ear.

"Oh," she said lightly, "I always did enjoy acting. I grew up without brothers and sisters and so was very much on my own. I am convinced this is one thing I can do very well. I did so long to go on the stage, but of course it wouldn't have been the thing."

"Well, you needn't act in front of Mavis, for she knows the entire story. She was nurse to Matthew's mother and has looked after Matthew from the day he was born. It was she who brought the boy to me." He opened the door to the nursery as he spoke and Eliza stopped quite still in the doorway as a sweet little face looked up at her from his position on the floor, where he'd been playing with a pile of blocks.

Matthew was every bit as dark as his father, but his eyes were a lighter blue, a cornflower to Edward's indigo. He wore a white linen shift, and a little woolen shawl had been wrapped about him. His face was very solemn as he took them in.

Eliza's heart began to melt. She could not help but feel sorry for this little boy who had had the misfortune to lose his mother so young. Almost worse, he had the misfortune to have Edward for a father. Well, she decided briskly, at least she'd see to it that he had a decent future.

"Hello," she said, and Matthew looked quickly over to the corner where Mavis sat scowling at them, her knitting held in midair.

"Eliza, this is Matthew, and this is Mrs. Mavis Bugle," Edward said, leading her farther into the room, shutting the door firmly behind him. "Mavis, I have brought Lady Seaton, Matthew's new mama."

"Humph," Mavis said, having pulled herself to her feet. She looked Eliza up and down, her hands on her hips.

"Mavis is rather outspoken," Edward said, scowling right back at her.

"Edward," Eliza said, lightly touching his arm, "will you leave me alone with Mavis and Matthew? I think it would be the best way to get acquainted."

Edward was about to protest, but then it occurred to him that perhaps Eliza had a point. She was, after all, supposed to be a mother, so he supposed she might want some time alone with her child. "Very well. When you are done in here, pull the bell cord and someone will show you to your quarters. I have business to attend to."

Eliza nodded, and as soon as he'd left, she dropped to her knees and sat back on her heels. "Hello, Matthew," she said softly. "I'm very happy to meet you. I hope we're going to be great friends."

"He ain't said much since his mammy passed away," said Mavis. "So don't think you's going to go fooling him with these tricks."

"I don't intend to fool him, Mavis, but the child does need a mother, don't you think?"

"What I think and what I's told to think are two different things."

Eliza sighed, seeing that she was going to have to do some very plain speaking. Mavis had every right to her resentments. "See here, Mavis, I think you and I should have a talk, but perhaps it would be better if we did it privately. I don't think Matthew needs to hear what we have to say, and he does look like a bright little boy whether he chooses to speak or not."

Mavis nodded approvingly. "I can see you's got some sense. It's time for his sleep, so's I'll just put him to bed, and then you and I can see what's what."

She scooped him up and was back five minutes later, and in those five minutes Eliza had had a chance to think the situation out carefully and had outlined her strategy.

"I can quite understand what you must be thinking about his lordship's behavior. Quite honestly, Mavis, I don't think very much of it myself. He was not completely honest with me when he discussed the terms of this marriage, and so I only learned about Matthew an hour ago."

Mavis' eyes widened. "He's downright dishonest, that man, as well as wily."

"Perhaps, but his lordship did have good reason for the deception, whatever we might think of his tactics. The way I have decided to look at the situation is to think of Matthew's good, for he cannot be held responsible for his father's actions. I should like very much to be his mother, Mavis, although I know I could never take your mistress's place. But if Matthew is to inherit as his father would like him to, then I'm afraid that he must believe me to be his natural mother, and he cannot ever be told the truth. It's a terrible shame, but I cannot see any other way around it, can you?"

Mavis shook her head. "It ain't right, God knows, and what Miss Martha would have said, I can't think."

"I think Miss Martha would have wanted Matthew to have had as much love as possible, as well as a good life. I am sure she would have rather seen her child go through life being regarded as legitimate, for you must know how difficult it can be for bastard children. Why don't you tell me about her, Mavis?

For you to so obviously love her as you do, she must have been a wonderful person.''

And so Mavis did. She talked for over an hour, wiping her eyes on her apron as she went, for her tears were profuse. By the time she had finished, Eliza had a very clear picture of a woman of a sweet and undemanding nature—certainly a romantic, with her head in the clouds and not an iota of common sense to guide her. Eliza could only feel impatience with Martha's idiotic refusal to summon Edward to her, and so land all of them in this pickle, but then, she, too, had once been foolish enough to fall in love with Edward. Who knew what might have happened if he had taken notice of her? She could very well have been in exactly the situation she was now pretending to be in. It was really all too ridiculous.

"I am terribly sorry for all the pain you have suffered," Eliza said gently when Mavis finally fell silent. "And I am very glad that you have been caring for Matthew and had the good sense to bring him to his father. You must have been very worried that his lordship might not accept him.''

"I wasn't all that worried. And he accepted him straightaway, not that I like him any better for it. He's a cold one, he sure is. Like to freeze your bones with that look of his, but I never bowed before no man and I's not about to start now. I's a free woman, ma'am, given my freedom by Miss Martha, and I's got papers to prove it. Nobody tells Mavis Bugle what to do, no, sir.''

"I am sure his lordship is appreciative of the fact, Mavis. But I would be thankful indeed if you and I could be friends, and you might give me the benefit of your advice. I know absolutely nothing about mothering, although I do like children, and I should like to learn how to go about it.''

"Humph," Mavis said, but this time there was approval in the sound. "I reckon we can turn you into a mother if we try hard enough. Maybe you could come in before his bedtime and read him a story. His mammy used to do that every night, but I don't read, so it's just one more thing he's been missing.''

"I'll be happy to. Is six o'clock a good time?''

"It'll do.''

Eliza smiled, and as she left, she wondered who had really won the skirmish.

* * *

Eliza's room was most attractive, looking over the garden and flooded with pale sunlight. It had been decorated in sea-green silks, which suited Eliza very well, for she didn't think she could bear the sight of any more pinks or yellows. The bed was high off the ground, but the mattress was comfortable and had been freshly turned. Her clothes had already been unpacked, and Eliza smiled to think what the reaction of the housemaid must have been to see what little she had. And she was now very glad she had disposed of the soiled and stained night rail she'd worn last night, having fed it into the morning fire, for she hadn't ever wanted to see it again. It hadn't occurred to her that someone might unpack her valise, but she could imagine the reaction that the bloodied material might have aroused.

Edward came through the door just as she was sitting down at the small writing desk to compose a letter to Annie, who did read, thank God.

"Writing for rescue already?" he asked dryly.

"Why should I desire rescue when I see how comfortable life is to be, Edward?" she asked, and fluttered her eyelashes.

Edward looked away, determining to spend as little time with his wife as humanly possible. "How did your interview with Mavis go?"

"Well enough. She is very fond of Matthew."

"Yes. It is the only reason I have kept her on. But enough about that. Your room suits?"

"It is very nice, thank you."

"If you like, you may certainly have it refurbished. The fabrics are old, and you might want—"

"I like it well enough, Edward. I imagine your mother lived in this room? She liked garden views."

"I have no idea. I have come to tell you that Marguerite has arrived. I summoned her, and I have just explained our situation. She is very anxious to speak with you."

"Oh . . ." Eliza went quite pale. "She is downstairs?"

"In the front drawing room. I'll escort you down. I am on my way out."

He left Eliza at a pair of closed double doors, took his hat, cloak, and cane from Grigson, and vanished, leaving her to face Marguerite quite alone.

"My dear Eliza," Marguerite exclaimed as Eliza walked toward her. "The news—it is such a surprise, I hardly know what to say.'' She held out her hands and took Eliza's between them, squeezing her fingers.

"I feel so ashamed, Marguerite,'' Eliza said, her voice trembling slightly.

"Don't be absurd. I wish you had felt you could confide in me, but naturally I understand why you did not. You did worry us most dreadfully when you disappeared the other night, but Edward said he had upset you and that you had gone home. At the time I could not understand, but I see much better now why you have behaved as you have. But a child, Eliza! It is the most wonderful thing. A little boy of your own. Now I know why your eyes seemed so distant when you watched my children at play.'' Her own eyes twinkled. "It all has the most delicious touch of scandal, my dear. I am thrilled to the core.''

Eliza smiled. "You would be, Marguerite, but I find it is all very awkward.''

"Nonsense! Tell me. Do you love him?''

"Edward?'' Eliza sank down onto the sofa. "I thought I did once, but now? No. Nor does he love me, no matter what story he has been telling you. He wanted me back for Matthew's sake, and he was right, of course. I was very wrong to leave my child, but I—'' Eliza searched in her brain for how to go on. She was feeling such acute guilt that it was hard to think clearly.

"No, no, my friend. I understand. Do not torture yourself with the memories. He was not a child you wanted. Edward explained how it happened, that you could not bear the sight of either of them after the birth, for you felt it was all a terrible mistake. Now that I know you are a married woman, we may speak plainly. Feelings of passion overcome us all at one time or another, and sometimes they are impossible to resist. It was like this with George and myself. We could not wait for the wedding,'' she said in a mock whisper. "Darling Elaine was born a month early. It is a miracle we haven't six children by now instead of only three, for my George is insatiable, despite how correct he always appears. And naturally I can never resist him, for he is a wonderful lover.''

"Oh . . . No, of course you cannot,'' Eliza said in confusion, for she was completely confounded by the revelation that Marguerite seemed to think the sexual act a thing of joy.

"Ah, my dear Eliza, I can see that I have embarrassed you

yet again. It is perhaps not like this now with you and Edward?''
she asked with her usual perspicacity.

"No, it is not. We have agreed not—that we won't . . . Oh,
dear. It is to be a marriage of convenience. I am to go my own
way and he his. I'm afraid I only disgust him, Marguerite. He
has made it very clear, and I cannot say it bothers me any
longer.''

Marguerite tapped her finger thoughtfully against her mouth,
her quick brain working even faster than usual. "Hmm, she
said. "This is most interesting. I cannot say I am surprised about
this arrangement, given the circumstances, but this is most
certainly not how it should be. Edward appears to be a cold
fish on the surface, but beneath, no, I think not. And you, you
are the same. Quiet, not cold, and you are shy, perhaps, but
shyness can be overcome, and underneath—that is what we must
bring out. So, we begin at once.''

"Begin what?" Eliza said, puzzled.

"Why, your metamorphosis, my dear. You can be such a
goose. If you are to go about as a marchioness, then you must
do it with *élan*. Edward has told me that you have resigned
yourself to your position and have agreed to let me take charge
of your wardrobe. Very well, and your wardrobe shall far
exceed Edward's expectations, but your wardrobe is not enough.
We have things to do, and I have decided to hire my maid's
sister to be your personal maid. She has just left Lady Greystone's employment, which is just as well, for no matter
Jeanette's skill, Lady Greystone has absolutely no material to
work with. I shall speak to her in the morning. Ah, this shall
be such fun, Eliza. I have always wondered what I could make
of you if given half the chance.''

"Have I understood you correctly, Marguerite? You think
to make me into some kind of beauty so that Edward might find
me attractive?''

"But of course! You have never learned feminine wiles, have
you, my dear? It is a shame, but then you were not born a
Frenchwoman. I shall teach you, however. We shall make
Edward a jealous man, and then you may do with him as you
please.''

Eliza looked at her with sheer disbelief, then she began to
laugh. Once she had started, she could not stop, and Marguerite,

delighted, joined her. Soon the drawing room was ringing with
their peals, and the footman and the underparlormaid stopped
in their work and exchanged meaningful glances. Life was
certainly going to improve at forty-three Grosvenor Square,
which by all accounts hadn't rung with laughter in more years
than anyone could remember.

7

Oh! Worse than cold-hearted!
    Jane Austen, *Sense and Sensibility*

The next few days went extremely swiftly. Eliza did not
once see Edward. Clearly this was exactly the way he
intended their lives to be, and Eliza could hardly mind.
She was kept too busy to think much about Edward at all. The
first morning Eliza spent in the nursery playing with Matthew,
and that afternoon Marguerite collected her and took her off
to a dressmaker's, where she was measured and pinned and re-
measured for the remainder of the day by a perfectly charming
Frenchwoman who was responsible for most of Marguerite's
elegant wardrobe. Fabrics, ribbons, bows, fashion plates, all
flew around her in a constant and rapid discussion in French,
of which Eliza understood one word in five.

The second day they visited various milliners and bought all
sorts of furbelows that Marguerite seemed to think were indis-
pensable to a well-dressed woman. On the third day Marguerite
appeared with Jeanette.

Jeanette was as French as could be. Her nose was long and
sharp, her eyes bright blue and intelligent, and she looked Eliza
over as appraisingly as Madame Girondaise had. Eliza was
becoming quite accustomed to being examined in this manner
by the French, who seemed to view her as an object upon which

to exercise their considerable talents. Jeanette finally nodded at Marguerite, and Eliza realized she'd been taken on.

Jeanette wasted no time. She marched straight out to the shops and returned with a number of jars, vials, and powders, and Marguerite sat and amused Eliza while Jeanette smeared various of these concoctions on her face and body. It was a good thing that Marguerite stayed close by, for Eliza would not have suffered such treatment for long. No explanation was given, and after a while, she gave up her protests, for she could see they were doing her no good. Jeanette had an iron will and would not be distracted.

Eliza knew that at various and sundry times she smelled cucumber, certainly lemon juice, and even a wash of something that had smelled suspiciously like hydrochloric acid. She'd asked Jeanette and had her suspicions confirmed. After that, she had kept her questions to herself, not wanting to know what her poor skin was being subjected to. At night she suffered having Roman balsam spread all over her face in a nasty thick paste, and she was expected to sleep with this mess on. It hardly mattered; after a supper taken by herself in the dining room, she went early to bed. There was no one but Jeanette to see the sticky mask. At least it smelled pleasantly enough of almonds, but the honey did nothing for the pillowcase.

So her nights and days went, but she set aside the mornings to spend with Matthew. It was an interesting education, and she had to admit that she was beginning to enjoy herself. She read to him and drew him pictures and played silly games that made him laugh, and his laughter was a delight to her, although she did wish that he would begin to speak.

At the end of the week, Eliza received her first reward. She had Matthew on her lap and had just finished sketching a picture of Sackville as he'd quietly watched.

"Horse," he said, squirming with pleasure and pointing at the picture she had drawn, and Eliza gave him a great squeeze.

"That's right, Matthew. Horse. It is my horse, and his name is Parsley, for he likes it above all things. One day I shall take you to Sackville, which is my home, and you shall meet Parsley and feed him a sugar cube. Would you like that?"

Matthew smiled his sweet smile, looking up into her face, and Eliza spontaneously dropped a kiss on his hair. "Look,

Matthew," she said, quickly adding two cows. "What are those called?"

"Cows," he said. "They are cows." He pointed with a lovely plump finger.

"You are a very, very clever boy, and they are indeed cows. My two favorite cows in the whole world, Buttercup and Clementine. You see, this is Clementine with the black mark on her forehead. She will have a baby cow in February. Isn't that wonderful?"

Matthew nodded.

"And this is my cat, Leopold. He is very large and very silly. You shall meet him too." She sighed, suddenly missing her home acutely. "You will like the country, Matthew, for there are many animals and lots of trees and grass, just like the park."

Matthew adored going to the park, and Mavis never missed an afternoon, although she didn't hold with taking children out of doors unless they were buried under blankets, no matter what the weather. Eliza had learned this when on a fine afternoon two days before, she had seen Mavis on her way out, and Matthew was all but invisible under his layers of blankets. She'd tried to persuade Mavis to allow the child some air, but as far as Mavis was concerned, the air outside was the enemy, to be avoided at all costs. Eliza had conceded, determined to win the smaller battles one at a time.

Matthew reached for the pencil, and Eliza gave him a fresh piece of paper, on which he produced a broad scribbling.

"That's a cow," he announced when he was finished, and Eliza agreed with him that it was a very fine cow indeed, and she fervently wished she could take him by the hand and show him a proper cow, for she was quite sure he'd have the good sense to be suitably impressed. And then she remembered that she sadly had an appointment with Marguerite for her final fitting at the dressmaker's and called for Mavis to take Matthew, giving him a hug before she left. Mothering, she was finding, came even more naturally than she'd expected.

After three hours of being pinned and turned and pinned yet again, Madame Girondaise allowed her to change back into her old dress. The new wardrobe was promised to be delivered the next day, a record for Madame Girondaise, but well worth her trouble for the price she was paid.

Marguerite had no trouble playing fast and loose with Edward's purse, and she directed the enormous bill to be sent to Grosvenor Square, thanked Madame Girondaise, and directed Eliza out again, but not before Eliza caught a conspiratorial glance exchanged between the two Frenchwomen.

"What was that about, may I ask?" Eliza said suspiciously.

Marguerite smiled. "I told her that your husband wished only the finest materials to touch your tender skin. But seriously, Eliza, the Marchioness of Seaton is a customer to court. Do not forget that you will have influence now. Madame Girondaise certainly did not forget this fact. She will have done a particularly fine job, you shall see tomorrow. And, of course, I have explained to her Jeanette's plan for you, so she knows what I expect the result to be. Madame's clothes will be displayed to their best effect. Now back to the house. It is time for your next treatment. The ball is only three days' time."

"What ball?" Eliza said, giving her friend a horrified look.

"Why, the ball Edward has planned for you. Really, my dear," she added, "you cannot think he would one day simply decide to casually take you to a rout and announce you as his wife? He will introduce you properly. Edward may be an unusual man, but he does know how things should be done. Now, remove that grimace from your face and think of Edward's reaction when he sees what we have produced. The invitation list is very fine, for I have seen it myself, and the acceptances have been pouring in. Town is not as full as it might be, but I do believe that those who are here will be in attendance. Do not look so, Eliza. It will not be so large as to be overwhelming. Just think how it might have been had this been a truly fashionable time of year. Edward planned his timing rather well, I think. The announcement of your marriage was in yesterday's papers, did you not know?"

"No, I certainly did not," she said, trying to calm the panicked pounding of her heart. "I had wondered how Edward was going to handle the matter," she managed to say calmly enough.

"It was all the talk last night at the Chandler supper. And Matthew, my dear. His birth announcement, almost two years delayed, was also there. In the *Gazette and* the *Post*. Edward never does anything halfway." She laughed her lovely musical laughter, and Eliza was forced to smile. "The announcements will be sure to set all of society on its ear. Does he not speak to you of anything?"

Eliza shook her head. "No, he does not. I have not seen him at all this last week. We keep separate hours."

"Hmm. This is good. I would rather he did not see you until the time is right."

"A fine dress is not going to turn his head, nor do I want it turned. Irritating Edward is the only thing I wish, for then he will tire of this charade and let me return to the country, where I belong."

Marguerite nodded. "And Matthew?" she asked gently enough.

"Matthew?" Eliza said slowly, for the first time thinking of what would happen when she left. "I don't know. I hadn't considered."

"But you cannot leave him again, Eliza. I cannot believe you would want to. You are his mother."

"Yes . . . yes, I am," she said, turning to look at Marguerite with something akin to amazement, as if the idea had never before occurred to her. "Do you know, you are quite right: there is no reason that I should not bring him with me. I was thinking of Edward, for he has had responsibility for him all this time, but London air is not good for a child, and now that we have had a few days to learn about each other, I think that we shall manage famously together. No, perhaps Edward will not object to my taking him with me. He needs to be with his mother."

Marguerite patted her shoulder. "It is the years ahead that are the most important, and I think that now you have made your mind up to it, you will be a very fine mother."

"Yes. That is what I hope."

"Seaton House will be much the better for having a child there. It has been empty for far too long."

"Seaton?" Eliza said with surprise. "But I was thinking of Sackville!"

Marguerite gave a delicious gurgle of laughter. "Eliza, my dear, sometimes you do not think carefully enough. Now that you are publicly known to be Edward's wife, you cannot go back to living at Sackville. It wouldn't do at all. And you certainly cannot take Matthew there. He is heir to Seaton, after all. Do you not think he should grow up in his future home?"

"Oh! Yes—yes, I suppose he should. Oh, dear. I haven't been thinking very clearly at all, have I?"

"Never mind, dearest. You have had many other things on your mind." She squeezed Eliza's hand and launched into the next phase of her campaign. "I know how much you love your Sackville and how important it has been to you to see it prosper. But now you can do the same with Seaton. Just think, all that lovely, lovely land, so neglected. Did you know that Edward dismissed that awful steward—and a good thing, too, George said, for he was running it very badly."

"Yes, I'd heard," Eliza said slowly. She lapsed into a thoughtful silence.

She had just surprised herself very much, suddenly realizing that she did indeed want to be the finest of mothers. Somehow, at some point in the last week, a genuine affection for Matthew had crept in under what she had seen as her duty. For the first time she found it hard to imagine going back to her old life without him. And really, there was no reason why she should, for Marguerite was quite right: Matthew should by all rights grow up at Seaton. Seaton . . . A little stirring of excitement started in her. She imagined that she could turn even that hollow place into a home if she tried hard enough. Indeed, it would be a challenge. And with a child running about, it would be so much happier. Matthew was bound to flourish there. She could always visit Sackville, although it would be wiser to hire it out and receive a rental income from it. It would be difficult indeed to see someone else living in her house, but she couldn't very well live two places at once. And she could move the cattle to Seaton, and of course Parsley and Leopold and Annie. They ought not mind too much. Sackville would only be down the road, and if she could bear it, they could.

That was what she'd do: as soon as possible, she'd retire to Seaton with Matthew and Mavis. Really, the place did need lots of work, and Edward did not seem to have any intention of seeing to it himself. She certainly didn't think he'd have any objections to her taking Matthew; according to Mavis, he had not once been to see his son.

She wondered just how soon she could leave. As much as she loved Marguerite, there was a limit to how much of this foolishness she could take, although she knew Marguerite had only her good in mind. She only hoped she would not let Marguerite down when it came to the point, for her friend had made such an effort over her.

The day of the ball finally arrived, and Eliza, who had been kept a virtual prisoner in the house for the last three days and had done nothing but work herself into a state of nerves, was now captive in a chair at her dressing table while Jeanette applied the finishings touches.

Marguerite regarded Eliza critically. The various washes and masks and baths given her skin had not exactly removed her freckles, but they had gone a long way toward lightening them.

The daily chamomile rinse that her hair had received had subtly highlighted the gold among the red, so that her hair looked like an autumnal forest streaked with sunlight. Today Jeanette had carefully dyed her brows and her lashes, causing them to stand out in her face. Finally, Jeanette had cut her hair, allowing the natural wave to assert itself, and with the heavy weight of its length no longer pulling it down, it danced gently about her head in a loose cloud of curl. It had then been washed, rinsed yet again with chamomile, and then half-dried as Jeanette pulled it into the exactly style of her choosing, using only her clever fingers. She threaded a gold ribbon through it and pronounced herself content.

Marguerite now watched with great concentration the final process of Eliza being dressed. The gown Jeanette slipped on her had been the subject of much discussion between herself and Madame Girondaise. It was made of deep-blue silk with an overdress of gold netting embroidered with butterflies, and was cut in a low, straight line over Eliza's bosom. The swell of her breasts, milky-white in appearance, peeped enticingly over the bodice, which finished directly under her bust. The widened skirt fell with just the hint of a train in the back and emphasized Eliza's tall, trim figure and long, well-shaped limbs beneath, for the silk was fine and moved softly about her as she moved.

Jeanette lightly powdered Eliza's face, then applied the very slightest touch of rouge to her cheeks.

"*Et voilà*," she said with satisfaction, moving away as Eliza stood.

Marguerite jumped to her feet and clapped her hands with delight. Before her was perhaps not a beauty, but certainly a great improvement on the old Eliza. One could even call her handsome, for she was tall and had a fine figure, now that it could be seen to advantage. "*Magnifique*," she exclaimed triumphantly, clapping her hands. "Really, it is very good. Now, Eliza, you must see yourself. Jeanette, fetch the mirror."

Jeanette obligingly rolled the standing glass in from the dressing room next door, and Eliza came to stand in front of it, terribly nervous of what she was going to find reflected in it. She did not hold with paints and would have insisted that Jeanette stop when she felt what she was doing, but Marguerite had firmly hushed her, reminding her to keep their mutual goal in mind, and that had silenced her. She would enjoy for once not appearing to be a complete dowd, and she thought it might put Edward in his place to see her dressed and groomed as one of his own kind, although she could not be comfortable with the low cut of the bodice.

Eliza certainly did not expect what she saw, and Marguerite gave a great peal of laughter as she caught the bewildered expression on Eliza's face.

"Oh," Eliza cried. Her nose still turned up and she still had a dent in her chin, but her despised freckles seemed to have completely disappeared, the rice powder having removed the last traces. Her hair shone with unaccustomed color, not the carrot red she had so loathed, but softer. It reminded her slightly of the color it had gone the long winter she had spent in Jamaica, too often hatless under the strong sun. But it no longer looked like a great bird's nest atop her head. Now it curled softly about her face, a face she just only recognized as her own.

"You see, my dear, your lovely full mouth is your finest attribute, next to your eyes," Marguerite said, coming to stand behind her. "Now one's attention is drawn to both, don't you agree?"

"It is an interesting effect," Eliza said hesitantly. "I do not feel quite like myself."

"But you are not quite like your old self. You are the new Eliza, who has been waiting for years to come to the fore. And do you not feel quite like fluttering your fan and bowing your head at the various gentlemen who will do their best to engage your attention this evening?"

"No," Eliza said bluntly.

"And what about making my lord jealous?"

"Jealous?" said Eliza uncertainly, picturing the sight in her mind's eye but not quite able to believe that Edward would ever feel anything resembling jealousy over her.

"But naturally, jealous, just as we discussed. Perhaps not instantly, but you are a talented pupil and shall make me proud," Marguerite said, whose strategy ran far beyond what she had revealed to Eliza. "Now I shall leave you. Your husband has requested a brief audience with you."

"Oh, please, don't leave me, Marguerite. I am quite terrified enough as it is, and I do not think I can bear to deal with Edward just now."

"Do not be silly, Eliza. It is Edward who shall have to deal with you. You must trust me in this: I believe that I have a much better understanding of men than you have."

"Yes, of course you have, and it was amusing when it was just a game, but now, this is real!"

Marguerite laughed. "Yes, it is real, my darling Eliza, and you are about to make a new beginning with your husband. It was all very well when he thought of you as shy Eliza, not quite up to snuff, although it is beyond me how such an eminently sensible man could be missing what is so obvious. But that is in the past, and it is time to get on with the future. At least he had the good sense to make a child with you. Now we must see what else can be made. Eliza, you must try not to blush. With your fair complexion it is not so appealing as with someone of a darker skin."

"Marguerite," Eliza said with the hint of a smile, "there are things that even you cannot change. My appalling tendency to blush is one of them."

"Perhaps, although a good Frenchwoman never admits defeat. Now, see to your husband. I am sure he grows impatient. And, Eliza, remember that the game between men and women has been going on since the beginning of time. You have the advantage." She kissed Eliza's cheek and said she would see her downstairs shortly, then slipped out the door.

Eliza paced nervously, wondering how she was ever going to make it through the evening, then wondering what it was Edward wanted to say to her. She did not have long to wait to find out. A knock came only minutes later and she took a deep breath to steady herself, for her knees were shaking.

"Please come in," she said, standing in the middle of the room, her hands folded in front of her.

Edward looked horribly handsome, she thought as he came through the door. His eyes were the blue of a deep lagoon, his hair thick and darkly glossy, his facial bones sharply defined, never mind his imposing figure. It was too unfair that he should have been born with such perfect looks, looks that he took completely for granted. He never blushed, and had no doubt never had had a freckle in his life, nor any other sort of physical flaw. He also had never known what it was like to feel as she did at that moment, terribly insecure and vulnerable. And it was also really quite rude for him to be standing in her bedroom looking her up and down in that analytical way as if she were some kind of a potted specimen.

"Good evening, Edward," she said tightly, amazed she could speak at all.

His eyes went to hers, and she could not read the expression in them. There was no approval, no disapproval. There was nothing at all. "Good evening, Eliza," he said coolly. "I trust you have been enjoying yourself?"

"Oh, very much, thank you. Marguerite is so amusing."

"Yes. I am happy she has been able to keep you entertained. You understand, naturally, that without a proper introduction as my wife, it would not have been appropriate for you to go about. After tonight, should everything go well, you may go where you please."

"Thank you. I am looking forward to my freedom."

"Your dress is most satisfactory."

"Marguerite is very clever."

"Your hair is much improved. The style suits."

"Thank you. It is less heavy."

"I have brought you the Seaton sapphires. They will match your dress well. I have had them cleaned and reset this week. The previous setting was not inspired." He put the large square box he'd been holding on the writing desk and opened it.

Eliza's eyes widened as she saw what it held. A sparkling necklace of diamonds in the shape of delicate petals, each petal surrounding a large sapphire, was flanked by a pair of similar earrings. A ring lay beside them, a solitary sapphire cut in the shape of a rectangle.

"Edward," she said haltingly, looking up at him, "I cannot think you mean for me to have these."

"You are my wife. I cannot think whom else you think I should bestow them upon. You surprise me, Eliza. It was you who asked for jewels."

"Yes—yes, I did, didn't I?" she said, belatedly remembering her absurd demand. "I am so absentminded sometimes. How thoughtful of you to have remembered. They are very nice."

"Very nice? Yes, I suppose that is one way of describing them. I will see you downstairs, Eliza. The guests will be arriving shortly and we shall receive them together. No doubt Marguerite has instructed you as to how to behave. I would only ask you to smile as much as possible and limit your conversation to the simplest of subjects. Tonight our story will either be accepted or exposed for the lie that it is. I caution you to be very careful."

Eliza inclined her head. "I will speak of nothing more than love under the bougainvilleas, my lord."

"Eliza! You will speak of nothing more than how happy you are to be reunited with your husband and son. Any other questions that might arise you will properly ignore. Do you understand?"

She curtsied. "As you wish. As I have told you, I endeavor to be the finest of peeresses, and so will do my best to see that I do justice to my rank. I have observed you often enough, my lord, to have noticed that you ignore those whom you consider beneath you and give your attention only to those who amuse you, or flatter you, or who might be in a position to pay you a service. I intend to follow your example, for I have no other to fall back upon. That is how it is done, is it not?"

Edward opened his mouth to object and then, as with so many times when attempting to deal with Eliza, closed it. "Simply follow my example this evening, Eliza, and I shall be satisfied. Five minutes."

He banged out the door and Eliza collapsed into a chair in a fit of genuine amusement. It seemed Marguerite might be correct, and there was a way of besting Edward, after all, even in this sort of situation.

But then her eyes fell on the case of jewels, extraordinarily beautiful, and she felt a terrible stab of guilt. Many generations of Seaton women had no doubt worn these priceless stones. She would be the next, and was the least deserving of all, for her marriage was a complete sham. How different she might have felt if Edward had placed them on her himself, truly happy to do so.

It was with a genuine sadness that she called Jeanette in and felt her fasten the clasp around her neck, with genuine sadness that she slipped the ring on her finger and secured the earrings to her lobes.

And it was with a genuine terror that she went down the stairs to greet their guests.

"Eliza, my very dearest friend!"

Eliza turned from the last person whose hand she had clasped in the interminable receiving line to look upon the face of Pamela Chandler beaming prettily up at her. She had always stood nearly a head above Pamela and so the comparison between them had been even more exaggerated than just Pamela's pretty blond looks next to Eliza's. And then there had been the matter of trying to alter the hemlines of Pamela's cast-offs.

"Welcome, Pamela," she said unenthusiastically, bending down to accept the kiss on her cheek. "I had not realized you were in town."

"You were the sly puss, weren't you?" Pamela whispered. "You might have at least told me. Scandalous, Eliza! And to think you were meant to be chaperoning me! I have had more questions asked. I must be the most popular person in London at the moment."

"I am most sorry, Pamela," Eliza said quietly. "We will have to speak at some other time, for I fear there is a line accumulating behind you."

"Well," said Pamela, extremely put out. "It seems to me you have gained quite a mighty opinion of yourself since your marriage. I think you were a deceitful wretch, but far it has been from me to let that fact be known to those who had asked, as well I might have. I have been everything loyal, defending you to the hilt, proclaiming your match one of star-crossed lovers. And now you think to snub me?"

"I do not think to snub you in the least, Pamela. We can speak later. Surely you must see this is a difficult time?"

"I would have made a much better marchioness, you know, for you are not the least suited to the position in any way. It is not as if I'm unaware of what you did to gain your place. I am quite sure I would have had a good chance with Lord Seaton had you not interfered.''

Edward turned to her, just as she was trying to think of an answer to this preposterous statement. ''Eliza, perhaps you can speak with Miss Chandler later. I am sure it has been an age since you have seen each other, but we do have guests to greet.''

''Indeed we have, Edward.'' She turned away, thankful to be saved the necessity of a reply and determined to prove Pamela and her vindictive judgment wrong.

The rest of the evening went by in a blur. Eliza did not know quite how she managed it, but she both conversed and danced, and managed each without stumbling, thinking only of the role she was expected to play. As Marguerite had said, there were not so many people as to make it impossible, but there were still a great deal too many for Eliza's comfort.

Edward stayed mostly at her side, playing his role to perfection, the attentive husband performing introductions, parrying questions with facile grace about the marriage, deflecting what might have been construed as rudeness with good humor and, when necessary, with *sangfroid*. Overt curiosity was rarely expressed, however. There was something in Edward's bearing, his natural hauteur, that discouraged it.

Eliza was so fascinated with his performance that she found she hardly had time to worry over her own. Edward made it very easy for her to play to his cues, and she needed to say little beyond the commonplace. Oddly enough, this seemed to free her to speak more easily, and on the occasions when she was on her own, conversation came more readily than it had in the past, although it didn't exactly flow with ease.

But at one point she nearly lost her carefully kept composure when an elderly matron, Lady Horsley, apparently a paragon of society, examined her through her lorgnette, up and down, until Eliza felt every hidden freckle had surely been discovered. She suffered the inspection without flinching, but she could not help but give Edward a look of entreaty. He merely raised his eyebrow in the characteristic way she was coming to know.

''An interesting choice, Seaton,'' Lady Horsley finally pronounced, and three other people standing around them exchanged long, deliciously shocked looks.

''I am delighted you approve of my taste,'' replied Edward

dryly. "If memory serves correctly, you have not always done so. I find Eliza to be unique among women."

"I was referring to the new setting you have chosen for the Seaton sapphires. Much an improvement on the old, although I don't usually hold much for diamonds myself. Garnets are more the thing, don't you know?"

Eliza choked back a laugh, but Edward didn't miss a beat. He inclined his head. "Garnets suit you, Lady Horsley. However, I would have nothing compete with the color of my wife's hair, and I fear in this instance garnets would most definitely not be the thing."

"My husband is most considerate to have given me the sapphires, ma'am," Eliza said, wishing to soak his head and forgetting her shyness in her indignation. "His taste is so exquisite that I'm sure if he had wished to give me garnets, I would have had to color my hair green so as not to offend."

Lady Horsley gave a great crack of laughter. "I think the color of your hair is an indication of your character, child. Perhaps Seaton has not done so badly, after all." She patted Eliza's cheek. "Don't you let the silly gossips bother you. You've brought Seaton to the point and given him an heir, and that's more than the rest have been able to do." She walked off, leaving Eliza blushing furiously and Edward with a funny little smile in his eyes, which only made Eliza even more discomposed.

He danced with her three times, the first time leading her out in the opening dance, the second time in the second set, and the third after the lavish supper. Edward had spared no expense, Eliza noted as she viewed the heavily laden tables overflowing with delicacies of every sort. She had little appetite herself, but accepted a plate from Edward, for she could think of no way to refuse. But they talked between themselves not at all, and Eliza could not help but wonder what had happened to cause this constraint. He had behaved like this since the marriage, and she could only imagine that now he had achieved all he had wanted, he no longer had any reason to be the least bit pleasant.

That suited her perfectly, she thought, watching him as he conversed among his friends. In the morning she would ask him for her promised freedom. He could have Pamela Chandler, who had hovered about them like the dearest of friends, ignoring

Eliza and batting her lashes at Edward until they were all but falling off. Now she was leaning toward him and whispering something in his ear. Eliza picked up her skirts and went to find Marguerite, unwilling to observe such foolishness for a moment longer.

Edward had had quite enough of Pamela Chandler's fawning attentions, but she was a valuable tool and he could ill afford to let her go to waste. For the last ten days he had spent most of his time convincing various segments of the polite world that his marriage was all that he said. He needed Pamela to back his story, and so he was now busy carefully and confidentially planting the information he wanted her to spread.

"Really, Miss Chandler, I do know how close you and Eliza were, but surely you cannot have expected her to speak of something quite so intimate as our brief relationship, can you? Forgive me for being so blunt, but you seem to feel that we deceived you. And indeed we did, but neither of us expected anything to come of it. I would like to set the matter straight. It was a diversion, nothing more. Eliza did not know that she was with child. Surely you can understand."

"Oh, indeed, Lord Seaton, I understand all too well. Eliza always was overly concerned with things of the earth." She giggled at her cleverness. "I am merely saddened that she did not come to me in her time of trouble and instead turned to Hermoine Ludlupe."

"But Mrs. Ludlupe was a widow, Miss Chandler, and as such, she was better suited to dealing with such a situation. As she was planning to return to Jamaica on her way home, Eliza's decision to go with her was most sensible. I am quite sure that my wife meant to bring no embarrassment to you or to your family. It was one reason she left immediately after Matthew's birth, for, being very distraught and not thinking clearly, she wanted to put the episode behind her. Can you not understand that and forgive Eliza? I have."

"You are very good, my lord. I think you are overly generous toward her, for I of all people do know how difficult she can be. But you are an honorable man and you did the honorable thing, although Eliza never should have led you on the way she did. Indeed, I feel extremely sorry for the position she put you in."

Edward was reaching the limit of his patience. "Miss

Chandler, you forget you speak of my wife. Whatever happened three years ago, it is in the past. We have a young son together, and it is Matthew's life we must consider. Eliza has seen that and so agreed that the marriage should be made known. I would thank you also to keep that in mind and not bandy Eliza's name about.''

"Certainly not, my lord," Pamela said indignantly. "I would not think of such a thing. I would see your marriage accepted and I will do what I can to still the gossip, for I am in a position to make the circumstances sound quite acceptable. I only wish you happiness, my lord," she said, meaning it quite sincerely.

Edward bowed. "Thank you, Miss Chandler. Excuse me, for I must return to my guests." He left, well-pleased that he had set in motion everything he had wished for the continuance of the fiction, but extremely sorry that the vehicle had to be Pamela Chandler, for he was finding he truly could not abide her.

8

A woman especially, should she have the
misfortune of knowing any thing, should
conceal it as well as she can.
                    Jane Austen, *Northanger Abbey*

E liza presented herself in her husband's study at ten o'clock the next morning. She was wearing a morning dress of bottle-green merino wool with long sleeves, its white lawn bodice finishing in a high ruffled collar. She felt she looked exactly as a wife should: dignified but demure.

She cleared her throat. "Good morning, Edward."

Edward looked up from his paper with surprise. "Good morning. What are you doing awake at this hour?"

"I am always awake at this hour, and for a good many hours before it."

"I would have thought you'd be exhausted from the exertions of last night."

"Not at all. I am sorry to interrupt you, as I know you dislike conversation in the morning, but I would like to speak with you on a matter of some importance."

"And what would that be?"

"May I sit?"

"I beg your pardon. Please do," he said, indicating the chair opposite his desk.

"Thank you. I hope you felt the evening went well."

"Did I not say I did?"

"No, actually, you did not. You said nothing at all, but then, I don't know why I should have expected you to. I have become quite accustomed to a lack of conversation with you."

"Are you chastising me?" Edward asked, wondering why his head always ached when he was around Eliza.

"Not at all. As you know, I have no conversation. It is not this I wish to discuss with you. Now that I have performed my duty and been introduced as your wife and Matthew's mother, I should like to return to the country. I would like to leave as soon as possible, if you would be so kind as to arrange transportation."

Edward uncrossed his ankles and sat up straight, putting the paper down on the blotter and leaning across it to stare at her. "Have you lost your mind?"

"I don't think so. You said I might have my freedom, my lord, if I fulfilled the terms of our agreement. I believe I have done so."

"Eliza, you chuck-head, can you imagine how it would look if you picked up and left now? I have not spent the last ten days convincing the polite world that we have reconciled, only to have you flee from London the day after your introduction."

Eliza sighed, her eyes wandering over his head to the bookcases, and she tried to make her eyes vacant, despite the fact that her hands were clenched with anger in her lap. "You *said*, my lord—"

"I know what I said," Edward roared, his temper in shreds. "You don't seem to have grasped the point. You may have your blasted freedom, but not until I have decided the time is right. You will stay in London throughout the Little Season, and you will have me at your side while you do it. Do not think I will enjoy the process any more than you. Now that you have been introduced and have the appropriate clothes, we will attend whatever routs and suppers and musical evenings that I deem fit, and then we will return to Seaton. There you may molder for the rest of your days if you wish. By the time April comes around and the Season begins in earnest, the world will have quite forgotten the shocking revelation of our marriage in favor of some other delectable scandal, and that will be that. I will be back in Jamaica, the marriage will be said to have been just another one of those mistakes, for it was never a love match, and you can do as you damned well please. Do I make myself clear?''

''Very clear, my lord,'' Eliza said, her eyes flashing with outrage, but she managed to keep a civil tongue, for she could not see the gain in provoking him further. ''Please let me know when you decide the time is right. In the meantime, I shall do my very best not to disgrace you.''

Edward tapped his forefingers together. ''You confuse me, Miss Eliza. Two weeks ago all you could speak of were cows and chickens. Last week you gave me the impression that all you wanted in the world was to be a fashionable marchioness and to prance about London bedecked in jewels. Last night you had those jewels and behaved to all the world as if you had been born to them and the position. Now, this morning, you want to go running back to your chickens. Would you please explain yourself?''

Eliza thought quickly, for she could see that she'd made a serious tactical error. ''I did not think that I had done a very good job last night, my lord.'' She lowered her eyes and tried to make her mouth tremble. ''You did not say anything to me. Marguerite tried so hard to make me presentable, and I did so want to behave properly, but all those people . . .''

Edward ran his fingers through his hair, trying to remind himself that Eliza's brain did not work precisely as other people's and that she seemed to respond best when treated as a child. ''See here, Eliza. I am sorry if I did not praise you. You behaved yourself very well, and I suppose I forgot that you are not accustomed to such things. With your new clothes and your hair nicely dressed, you looked exactly like every one else.''

Eliza could not help the sudden bubble of laughter that slipped out unbidden. Raising her eyes, she said, "I think not precisely like everyone else, my lord."

Edward smiled, absently thinking that Eliza looked quite pretty when she laughed. "Well, perhaps not precisely. But you looked very nice. If you continue to behave just as you did last night, I am sure you will do very well. You will find that people do not expect clever conversation, only that you observe the properieties."

"I see. Mostly everyone was quite polite to me. It's what comes of being a marchioness, I suppose."

"I suppose." He looked up as Grigson appeared in the door. "Yes?"

"I beg your pardon for interrupting, my lord, but you have a visitor, and he felt you would want to see him immediately." Grigson stepped aside as the visitor came up behind him and Eliza turned in her chair to see a lean, blond gentleman.

"Hello, Edward. And this must be your wife."

"Peter, what on earth! How marvelous to see you." He stood and went around the desk, clasping his friend's hand. "When did you arrive?"

Grigson melted away and Eliza observed the two of them with curiosity. Edward was obviously very pleased to see this visitor, but what was far more interesting was that Edward looked a completely different person. The tight, guarded expression had fallen away and there appeared to be a much younger, light-hearted man beneath. His eyes were alight with pleasure as he directed a rapid-fire series of questions at his friend.

"Oh, I beg your pardon," he said, suddenly remembering Eliza when Peter gave him a meaningful look. "Eliza, may I present Mr. Peter Frazier? He is a close business associate from Jamaica. Peter, my wife."

"How do you do?" Eliza rose and offered her hand.

"I remember you, Lady Seaton," he said, bowing over it. "You were at one or two of the same engagements as I in Kingston a few years ago, although I don't think we were formally introduced. May I offer my felicitations on your marriage?"

"Thank you," Eliza said, scanning her brain to see if she remembered him, but coming up blank. "I will leave you gentlemen in peace to discuss your business. You must have a great deal of catching up to do. Good day." She went out, softly closing the door behind her, then went up the stairs, wondering why such a look of concern had come over Edward's face when Peter Frazier had claimed to have met her.

But she shrugged the thought away, for she had other, more important things on her mind, such as how to annoy Edward so much that he'd wish her away to the country immediately. With that to occupy her mind, she made her way up to the nursery.

"Suppose you tell me just exactly what game you are playing at, my friend?" Peter said, taking the chair Eliza had vacated and leaning back in it.

"What game?" Edward said calmly. "Pray tell. What game do you think I'm playing at?"

"I arrived in London yesterday. Had I known you were also here, I would have come directly to see you. Imagine my surprise when, last night at White's I was regaled with the latest *on-dit*. Lord Seaton was hosting a ball to present his wife to society. That did not particularly surprise me. It is high time you were married. What did surprise me, however, was the knowledge that this marriage was one of long standing and had produced an heir well over two years ago. What was even more surprising was your choice of bride. Miss Eliza Austerleigh? Really, Edward."

"No doubt you heard the reason for the marriage."

"Oh, yes. The aftermath of seduction. 'Poor Edward,' everyone is saying, 'but how honorable.' " Peter shook his head. "You, my dear man, are a fraud."

Edward smiled lazily. "Are you doubting my word?"

"Call me out if you wish, but yes. I think you are putting out a whisker, and for the life of me I cannot think why, for it is a very dangerous one. Why would you seduce a woman for whom you expressed physical disdain? I remember thinking at the time that you were being most unkind, so do not attempt to deny it, for I recall the conversation quite well. Lowdry actually challenged you to a seduction and you refused. Fortunately for you, Lowdry is no longer with us, and so I am the only witness to the conversation."

"I changed my mind. Upon consideration, the challenge was too great."

"Indeed. Then I asked myself how it was possible for you

to have married Miss Austerleigh and for her to have had your child without my having any knowledge of it.''

"You may be a friend and partner, but you are not privy to all my affairs, Peter.''

"Nor would I expect to be. This, however, seems a rather large step for a man like yourself to take. And where, may I ask, did all of these events supposedly take place?''

"Right under your nose.''

"I see. And the boy? I understand you have been raising him.''

"Not I. A nurse. I sent them both to the Carolinas after Eliza returned to England, not wanting a reminder of my mistake. I changed my mind recently and summoned them home, then decided to return to England for Eliza. I was tired of living a lie.''

Peter laughed with genuine amusement. "An interesting choice of words, given what you have just set yourself up for. Well, you have an excellent imagination, and I must say I admire your nerve.''

"I see. You don't believe me.''

"See here, Edward, I would never think to expose your story for what it is, but I think you should tell me the truth of the matter. You might need someone to back you up, and I'm probably the best person for it. And I do have a stake in your future, so you really do owe me an explanation.''

Edward walked over to the window, his brow creased, and he looked out over the square. It was a bright day, but there was a hard frost on the ground. A carriage stood outside one of the houses down the street, the horses' breath thick in the cold air as they stamped their feet. It was the first real autumn he'd experienced in years. He turned and looked back at Peter, drawing a deep breath. "I didn't think I'd be able to pull the wool over your eyes.''

Peter nodded. "I'm glad you've decided to give up the effort. Why don't you tell me what this is all about? You are married to Miss Austerleigh?''

Edward leaned his hip against the low windowsill. "Yes. For nearly a fortnight.''

"So. That's something, at least. And the child?''

"Is mine. But not by Eliza. By Martha Medford of Charleston, now deceased.''

"Good Lord." Peter pulled a cheroot from the pocket in his coattail and lit it. "I think you had better start at the beginning." He settled back in his chair quite calmly and prepared to listen.

Edward told him the whole convoluted story and Peter attended carefully without interruption until Edward was finished. Then he stubbed out his cheroot and stood, his head bent in thought. "I see why you chose Miss Austerleigh. In fact, I see everything quite clearly with the exception of one glaring omission." He looked up and regarded Edward's back. "Why have you gone to such extraordinary lengths to make Matthew your heir? I know your feelings about Justin Brixtose, but he's on his last legs. Surely you could have married and produced an heir in the usual fashion?"

Edward shook his head without turning around. "No, I could not. I have had an illness. Matthew will be my only child."

Peter, who was no fool, was silent. He knew what it must have cost Edward to make this admission. "I see," he eventually said, having turned the implications of this over in his head and now seeing everything in a new light. "Does Eliza know?"

"No. And I don't plan on telling her. She has agreed to a marriage of convenience. There is no reason she ever need know."

"This was what had you so blue-deviled all of the last two years, or thereabouts?"

"Yes." He was not willing to go any further and admit that he had been rendered sterile by a childhood ailment. His pride had already suffered enough. "But none of it signifies any longer. Matthew is indisputably my son. He will inherit the marquessate. That is all that matters."

"And Eliza?"

He turned and looked at Peter. "What about her?"

"Edward," Peter said with admirable calm, "she is your wife. I hardly think that is insignificant. She must have some thoughts about this peculiar deception you've dragged her into."

"Eliza hasn't a thought in her head, Peter. She is delighted to be a marchioness. Tomorrow she will be delighted to be a hen-keeper again. I don't know, and I doubt she knows herself. She has about as much wit as one of her chickens and even less of an ability to attend to anything for more than two minutes. She has agreed to the lie, and no doubt by now is believing it for herself."

"Maybe. Tell me, what happens if someone begins to poke into your story?"

"I cannot think who would bother, quite honestly. No one would stand to gain, and the story is so bizarre that who would think to doubt it? But before I left Jamaica I made quite sure that I had a parson who would swear to the marriage, and I have since sent him the details of the bride along with a large sum of money. I seem to have been bribing rather a lot of parsons lately; it's astonishing how easy it is to corrupt them. The marriage is legal in England, and before you bother to ask, it has been consummated. No question will be raised about that."

"I see. And how will you feel if Eliza produces a child, or two or three?"

He shrugged. "I cannot imagine who will want to bed her, but she can do as she pleases. I know none of them will be mine."

"So you have said. Well, it seems you have thought of everything."

"I sincerely hope so. You will not turn me over to the magistrate, then?" he said with a wry smile.

"Certainly not. I would say that you have justifiable cause for your rather unorthodox actions. If asked, I shall say that I knew of the marriage all along and that I was present at the ceremony. I cannot think why, but I would hate to see you caught in this particular lie. So. In my haste to speak with you, I left my papers at my club. I shall get them and we can discuss business this afternoon if it is convenient."

"I will make it convenient. You have yet to tell me what brought you."

"Actually," Peter said with a grin, "I came exactly on schedule. You seem to have forgotten that we have a large and very valuable cargo to prepare for shipment the beginning of February. We also have a large cargo to sell here, with which I have just arrived, and another due in November. Then the *Kestrel* is to be reoutfitted."

"Oh, yes," said Edward, smiling with a trace of embarrassment, "I had quite forgotten about this month's delivery. I have been very distracted of late. Let me make it up to you. Why don't you collect your things and stay here? There is more than enough room, and I would enjoy the company."

"Thank you. I should like that, and I was hoping you might ask." He walked over to Edward and clapped his back. "Thank you for trusting me."

Edward smiled ruefully. "If not you, Peter, then, who?"

Peter returned his smile. "Who, indeed?" He left.

Eliza was most surprised to hear that they were to have a guest. But she smiled brightly at Edward, who even more surprisingly had deigned to tell her at all.

"I do not know myself how long Peter will be staying. He will no doubt be coming about with us on occasion, but I don't want him in any way to feel responsible for your entertainment, so you are not to plague him."

"How nice," she said vaguely. "I must change my dress. Marguerite said I would surely be receiving callers this afternoon, and I must be ready just in case. Will you join me, my lord?"

"I have business this afternoon."

She looked so crushed that he relented. "If you are very good and do not make a fuss, I will take you driving in the park afterward."

Eliza immediately brightened. "Then I shall be very brave and deal with my callers on my own. I must learn to be an independent marchioness if we are to live separate lives. But I would so like to see the park. It has been rather tedious being stuck away for nearly a fortnight, and I do like the fresh air. Perhaps my new cloak will do. It's exactly the color of Spanish fly. Good day, Edward."

She could feel Edward's irritation vibrating down the hallway after her, and it was all she could do not to laugh.

She did indeed have callers, but the experience was not as painful as she had anticipated. Eliza had learned the night before that if she he held her head high and behaved as if she had every right to her new position, people generally responded quite well. No one had yet tried to have her removed from the house, at any rate.

Eliza, Marchioness of Seaton, was a far cry from Eliza, slightly questionable spinster with no prospects. She now discovered that whatever subject she chose to bring up seemed to be met with no objection. As she had never in her life attempted to bring up any subject at all, having been told early in life that she had nothing to say, she discovered that the practice had some pleasant results, for she could converse about things that interested her.

This particular subject interested her very much, for Mrs. Chatterly had arrived with her pug, Loulou, and Loulou was causing some serious distress among the other guests. Mrs. Chatterly apologized volubly with every new whiff that billowed out into the room. "It is so distressing, you know, but I cannot seem to find a cure. Poor Loulou, I know she must be so ashamed."

This Eliza doubted very much, eyeing the self-satisfied dog who lay like a fat bread roll at her mistress's feet.

"Please, Mrs. Chatterly, allow me to pour you some more tea," she said, lifting the teapot. "You must tell me more about your pug. Loulou's problem sounds most interesting and I believe that I might have an idea. When did indigestion first begin?"

"Well, my dear, I believe it was shortly after the new house-maid arrived last month. I cannot think she has been feeding Loulou properly."

It did not take Eliza long to divine that the problem was not the new housemaid but Mrs. Chatterly, who had recently developed a passion for bonbons and felt that her beloved dog was as entitled to the treat as she was. Since then, the dog had been parading about emitting great clouds of noxious gas. Mrs. Chatterly described Loulou's condition most delicately, "an unpleasant disturbance of air, my dear," which had had the other visitors privy to this extraordinary conversation trying terribly hard to maintain their composure.

Eliza suggested a very simple diet, no rich foods of any sort, and daily vigorous exercise, and she also suggested that the stout Mrs. Chatterly be the person to take darling Loulou on her expeditions. "She will walk more vigorously if she knows you are leading her, ma'am, than if she is being taken by a person with no real attachment to her. And where authority walks, affection will follow."

Eliza had absolutely no idea where she'd pulled that from, but it seemed to have been a great success, for Mrs. Chatterly repeated it at least five times before she left, determined to put Eliza's advice immediately to work.

"Just as I thought! You are an original, Lady Seaton," pronounced Lady Horsley, who had condescended to visit. "I can think of no other person who could manage the subject of Lavinia Chatterly's dreadful Loulou and her digestive weakness so well. Perhaps you will have cured Lavinia as well as her monstrous dog.''

Eliza burst into laughter. ''I had no idea that Mrs. Chatterly was suffering from Loulou's problem, ma'am.''

Lady Horsley chuckled. ''Not that I am aware, but since she brings the dratted dog everywhere, who's to know which is which? No, I meant that you might have given Lavinia an interest in something other than paying interminable calls. I do believe you are a tonic, my dear. It certainly seems that you have cured your husband, for he has been remarkably well-behaved since his arrival here. The last time he set foot on these shores, he had every mama in a panic—and a well-deserved panic, I might say. I believe that the way you handled the situation finally brought him to heel.''

''Oh, but I have no need to handle him, I assure you, Lady Horsley. My husband is a man very much of his own mind, and he would not suit well at my heel. In any case, I go on much better with animals than people. He merely decided that our situation was not acceptable, and so he came to correct it. I was quite happy as I was. Well,'' she amended, blushing at the lie she was about to tell, ''in all truth I was not happy. I missed my child. But he was Seaton's heir, you see, and I felt I had no right to interfere.''

''Oh, you poor dear,'' said Penelope Leavington, who had come hoping to find fault, but instead found herself utterly in sympathy. ''It is so difficult when one has no rights.''

''Please, do not fault my husband in any way. Indeed, he did his duty where many would not. And he came back to set things to right. I would have no one think ill of him.''

''I think you must love him very much to be able to forgive him,'' said Mrs. Leavington.

''No. It is he who has forgiven me, and I am grateful, for Matthew's sake and my own. I never thought to see my child again. Please, let us not discuss it any further. It is too painful.''

It was indeed painful, Eliza thought, more painful than she had realized it would be to perpetuate the lie. It came to her mind to deny the entire fiction and have done with it, rather than live with the guilt. But then the image of little Matthew rose before her eyes and she strengthened herself. Edward and his machinations be damned. Matthew would not suffer because of his father. He certainly would not suffer because of her.

"I am sorry," she said into the silence, blinking hard. "I did not mean to sound harsh. All of this is new to me, and I am not quite sure how to go on. It was kind of each of you to come here today, for I am sure I am not at all the thing and I know you came for my husband's sake."

"Nonsense," said Lady Horsley. "We came because we were curious, and why not? But I find you perfectly acceptable, even enjoyable. I haven't had such an amusing visit in weeks. Your story is touching, child, as is your bravery. Do not be discouraged. To be very candid, I do not believe your husband would have made such an effort if he did not intend a real reconciliation. And it is heartening to see how much you care for your son. It must have been difficult to leave him. I can only be happy he has been returned to you." Unaccustomed to making such an emotional display, Lady Horsley took her leave, warmly pressing Eliza's hand. "I shall see that you are received everywhere, my dear," she whispered. "Do not concern yourself about that. It is your husband who should be horsewhipped."

Eliza laughed. "Thank you, my lady," she whispered in return. "I do indeed think he probably should be. But marriage to me is horsewhipping enough, I think. Any more punishment would be a cruelty."

She heard Lady Horsley's laughter all the way out.

Edward appeared two hours later, after the last of the callers had left. "Are you quite ready for our drive, Eliza?"

"Indeed, Edward. I should like it very much after spending the day indoors."

"Let us be on our way, then. Peter shall come with us. Do fetch your bonnet and pelisse."

Eliza obligingly hurried up the stairs, feeling inordinately pleased with herself, for she judged the afternoon to have been a success and was proud that she had not once fallen into a fit of the jitters. Well, once, perhaps, when Pamela and Mrs. Chandler had arrived and quizzed her excessively, but that didn't signify, for that would have thrown her into the jitters under any circumstance.

She was glad to have it over with and felt she quite deserved to be taken out to the park, for she had missed being surrounded by a large expanse of grass and trees. It was a pity that she had to tolerate Edward's company in order to go, but it was an opportunity she felt she really couldn't refuse. She would simply ignore him.

Edward's carriage was exactly like Edward, Eliza thought as she climbed in: sleek and sophisticated. It was black and very shiny, of the finest lines, and the Seaton crest was painted in gold on the side. The four horses, perfectly matched grays, were magnificent and equally shiny.

It was chilly and Eliza gladly accepted the blanket that was placed over her lap and the hot bricks to warm her feet, and they set off, Eliza very quiet as she took in the sights and sounds and smells.

As it was now into October, the park was relatively empty, but they did see a few of the people who had graced their house the night before. Eliza was quite happy that the weather did not permit overly lengthy pausing, and so only brief conversation could be exchanged. Much of that was directed toward Peter Frazier, who seemed to be a popular gentleman, for everyone expressed himself most delighted to see him.

Peter, in his turn, was a gregarious sort, with an open, friendly manner and an easy laugh, and she found herself relaxing in his company, for he seemed to expect nothing at all of her. He was a complete contrast to Edward, of whom one would never think in terms of relaxation.

Eliza bundled further into her cloak and watched him as he spoke with a Mr. Gripshaw, wondering at this man who was now her husband. She had seen a number of different sides of him, but however she tried, she could not make all the pieces fit. He smiled and chatted amiably enough, but at the same time he seemed to be holding a part of himself back. He was always elegantly but simply turned out, just as he was now; he was usually polite, if a trifle frosty; and she knew he had a sense of humor, for on the rare occasions that he did laugh, he did so with genuine amusement and usually over something subtle she could appreciate. She also knew he possessed a fine intelligence, for he had certainly shown that, despite how inadvertent.

She frowned. He was a brute, possessed of a vile temper and incapable of the simplest sensibility or understanding, unless it was his own. Edward had apparently never learned that there was any point of view in the world except for his. And yet that didn't really explain to her the inconsistencies she had noted in his character. She shivered, thinking that whatever had gone into making the man before her could not have been very pleasant material.

"Lady Seaton?"

She looked away from her contemplation of Edward with a start, to see Peter Frazier watching her. "Yes?"

"You were shivering. Your husband told me you enjoy fresh air, but it is perhaps a trifle cold now that the sun has dropped."

"Oh, yes, now that you mention it, there does seem to be a nip in the air."

"Yes." He gave her a rueful smile. "Truth to tell, it is a nip I am not yet accustomed to. My blood is still thin from the tropics."

"Indeed," she said with a smile, "I remember how I had to adjust when I returned to England. I have never much minded extremes of temperature, but I must admit that I found an English summer unexpectedly cool. You must find October positively arctic."

"Perhaps not arctic, but a touch daunting. It is most selfish of me, but my heart lifted immensely when I saw that you, too, were cold. I confess, a blazing fire would not go amiss."

"Then we must return home immediately," she said sympathetically. Peter was truly frozen, she realized, seeing his blue lips. She distracted Edward from his discussion with Mr. Gripshaw about his horses' bloodlines. "I beg your pardon, Edward, but do let's turn back. The air grows chill and the horses cold."

"Certainly, my dear." Edward made his farewell and gathered up the ribbons, and the carriage started off again. Peter gave Eliza a smile that hinted of conspiracy. "Thank you," he said in an undertone. "I could not have admitted my weakness to Edward. It was kind of you to put it off on the horses."

Eliza laughed. "But it is true, is it not, that one should always think of one's animals before oneself? They are helpless, after all, and depend on us for their comfort."

Edward overheard this and threw Peter a speaking look, which only made Peter smile more broadly. He was beginning to wonder if Edward had not been mistaken about Eliza, and he determined to set out to find out more about this odd woman Edward had taken to wife.

"We dine at home tonight," Edward said to Eliza when they had returned to Grosvenor Square. "I think a quiet evening after last night would be in order; I do not want you becoming exhausted. I have invited Marguerite and George, and Peter will dine with us as well. Are you prepared to be hostess at your own table?"

This comment had the effect of inciting Eliza to mutiny, but she lowered her eyes and whispered, "I think I can manage, my lord. As long as you are there to give instruction should I go wrong."

"I am sure you will try to be and do all that is correct. We dine at eight."

"Yes, my lord." She raised her eyes. "I don't suppose I can wear the sapphires this evening," she said wistfully.

"Certainly not, Eliza. Those are only for formal occasions. I am sure I can find something more appropriate. Perhaps a string of pearls."

Eliza sighed happily. "I have always wanted pearls. I hope they are very large." She turned and went up the stairs. She had not missed the black look that had come over Edward's face, and she hoped he was regretting with all of his being having married her.

Eliza spent an hour dressing for dinner, determined to enjoy the evening. She would be among friends and had no need for shyness, she told herself. Besides, she'd had a very successful afternoon on her own, and disaster had not struck. Furthermore, since Peter Frazier was unexpectedly pleasant and congenial, there was no reason she should feel uncomfortable in his presence, either. Then why did she still feel terrified? Would she never learn to relax and enjoy herself? Edward was right, she thought despondently: she was completely without personality or appeal.

Jeanette placed the beautiful string of pearls about her neck. They had just arrived by the good graces of Hamlish, Edward's valet, who had presented a box to Jeanette with a bow.

"Oh la la, madame. These are very fine indeed," she'd said

as Eliza had opened the box. "They shall be perfect with the green velvet. His lordship will be very pleased with the effect. You are in particularly fine looks tonight. The air did you good, and the wind has given your cheeks some color. See how milky the pearls look against your skin? The color is exactly right for you."

"Thank you, Jeanette." But she couldn't help the pang of remorse that gnawed at her; these were Edward's family treasures and by her foolish behavior she was practically blackmailing him into giving them to her. "His lordship is very generous," she said colorlessly.

"Forgive me, madame, but his lordship is a practical man. He wishes for his wife to play the part. He cannot see that beneath, he has chosen a wife who is exactly what he wants."

Eliza stared at Jeanette.

Jeanette did not blink an eye at her unthinkable forwardness, taking out the hare's-foot brush and sweeping it across Eliza's face, evenly distributing the rice powder on her skin. "It is very often so with gentlemen, you must understand. They see only what they think they want to see. Soon he will realize that what he wants to see is not what is, and that what you truly are is of real value to him. It is only a matter of perception. Your guests will soon be arriving. You look very well, madame. Have an enjoyable evening."

Eliza, feeling she had just been dismissed, went downstairs, considering what Jeanette had said. Perhaps she wasn't completely without personality or appeal, even if Edward couldn't see it. And she would have an enjoyable evening, despite Edward.

Her spirits lifted and she felt for the first time since the monstrous marquess had shown up on her doorstep that life might not be quite so bad, after all.

9

One cannot always be laughing at a man
without now and then stumbling on
something witty.

Jane Austen, *Pride and Prejudice*

Eliza was more than aware of Edward's foul mood immediately she entered the drawing room. It came as no surprise, for he seemed constantly to be in a foul mood, but she had had quite enough of it and assiduously set herself to ignore him.

She spoke with Marguerite and George, both who complimented her on her appearance; she had a pleasant-enough exchange with Peter; and with each conversation she felt her confidence growing. She was also cognizant of the fact that to whomever she spoke, Edward remained outside of the conversation. This was not always easy to achieve, but he managed it quite well, and also managed to direct his icy gaze her way on a regular basis.

Eliza was amused that the tables seemed to have turned, for it was usually she who chose the outskirts and Edward who was always in the center of things. Just as this thought was making its way through her head, she noticed an extraordinary thing: Peter, in his haste to warm himself, had stepped a touch too close to the fire. A small ember had leapt out and landed with a shower of sparks on the back of his pantaloons, just where the tails of his coat separated. Eliza, who had been standing off to one side, saw it immediately and hesitated for a moment, waiting only to see if Peter noticed he was about to catch fire before she embarrassed him. Then, seeing that he had not and the coal was not about to extinguish itself, she moved quickly. Her hand came down hard on his backside and stayed for a moment, smothering the ember.

Peter, to his infinite credit, did nothing more than stiffen momentarily, although she was quite sure that he must have been completely taken aback. But he missed not a beat of his conversation. Eliza stepped forward and Peter, after a few protracted moments, turned to her, giving her a long, extremely eloquent look. She had never before seen such expression in the raise of an eyebrow, not even in Edward's, and she smiled, discreetly holding out the coal in the cupped palm of her hand and dropping her eyes to it.

His eyes, following the movement, fell down to her side. Then, seeing what she held, they shot back to hers with unspoken amusement. Eliza looked meaningfully at his tails, and his hand crept behind, his fingers finding the small singed area. This caused an even wider smile on his part, and now his eyes held gratitude as well as amusement. "You are an exemplary hostess, Lady Seaton," he said easily. "I quite envy Edward."

"Oh, you mustn't do that. Edward wouldn't like it at all."

Peter smiled. "But then perhaps he's never been quite so close to the fire."

This remark caused Marguerite to turn from the comment she'd been making to her husband. She looked at the two of them very sharply, but Eliza missed the glance, having caught Grigson's discreet entrance, announcing that dinner was served.

Edward watched Eliza from his position opposite her at the head of the table. He was a mass of conflicting emotions, all of them unpleasant. He wanted to strangle Eliza, certainly, although he wasn't sure whether he first wanted to immerse her in boiling oil. No, strangulation would do. She wouldn't be able to speak that way. It wasn't that he could fault her behavior. That was the problem. There she was, wearing a most attractive dress of deep green velvet, unmistakably cut with French genius and Marguerite's direction. His grandmother's perfectly matched string of pearls was draped around her neck, a neck that was surprisingly long and slender. Oh, yes, he thought gleefully, taking a long drink of his claret, his fingers would fit about her neck nicely.

Eliza Austerleigh March, Marchioness of Seaton, was a fraud, a puppet he had created, shining in the finery he had bought, wearing his family's jewels. She was a blasted fabrication, a result of the fiction he had so successfully flummoxed the world with. And she, damn her, had become the fiction and was enjoying herself to the hilt. It was hypocrisy of the worst sort. What had happened to Eliza, the shy girl who blushed and stammered whenever he came anywhere near her? At least she had been genuine. But that Eliza had disappeared somewhere on the road to London to be replaced by this travesty!

Eliza laughed with Marguerite, spoke with George as if she actually had some wit, although George was diplomatic enough to make anyone appear to be clever and amusing. But Peter, he thought stormily . . . With Peter she was actually being flirtatious, if he could credit such a thing. He had seen her near the fireplace, standing far too close to him, looking into his eyes and smiling as if they shared some great secret. Worse, Peter had responded in kind.

How his closest friend could behave in such a way with his bird-witted wife was beyond him. Indeed, Edward took it as a personal slight. Had he not explained the situation, told him the truth about everything, including Eliza and her unsteady brain? Why, then, was Peter behaving as if Eliza was the most fascinating of creatures? Really it was beyond anything. Let Peter discover for himself the sapscull behind the act, he thought irritably. Better yet, let him discover that behind the act Eliza was as frigid as a . . . He quickly dismissed that thought. Still, if Peter knew the real Eliza, he wouldn't be smiling at her quite so charmingly.

Dinner was going very well, Eliza thought with relief, for although the staff was efficient, it wasn't particularly well-trained, and she had had to speak with Grigson, who actually seemed to be appreciative of the direction rather than resentful. She had had some meals recently that had been quite inedible, with curdled sauces and mangled vegetables and a variety of other problems resulting from a cook trying to please the new mistress with a less-than-perfect grasp of French technique. She'd instructed him to serve the simplest of English fare. Although she had not been given the opportunity to approve the menu on this occasion, it was appropriate and not overly ambitious, and the service was unremarkable. She relaxed on those accounts and gave her attention over to the conversation.

"I am so happy you have taken enjoyment from the book, George," Edward was saying. "I found it noteworthy not only because of the assiduous attention paid to detail, but also because Mr. Babcock's observations ring with a sentiment that suggests he has the true understanding of a natural historian, although he makes no claim to be so. It is the first chronicle I have read of the natural history of Jamaica that is not purely scientific, but indeed speaks with genuine feeling. I have too often read books that discuss such things without any real comprehension of the place itself. Did you not find it so?"

"I did. Marguerite also expressed her pleasure. It has instilled in us a strong desire to visit your island." He exchanged a quick look with his wife, who smiled.

"I must read this book you all think so illuminating," Peter said.

"You must indeed, now that you are here and not there, for you'll miss Jamaica sooner than you think. I do, I know, but then I haven't been back to England as often as you have, so I am not accustomed to such long periods of time away. It's a good book for relieving a certain homesickness, and I've often found myself late at night going through the pages. Even Eliza has read it, Peter, or at least looked at the pictures. Our tastes differ when it comes to pen and ink. She prefers color plates, don't you, Eliza?"

Eliza, who had been listening to him with a certain degree of incredulity, found her voice. "That depends entirely on the subject matter. I thought in this instance the colors were properly vivid and did justice to the foliage. A banana tree simply doesn't look the same in black and white."

Edward looked weary. "No, it wouldn't."

"I also have found Mr. Babcock's book pleasant bedtime reading," she continued. "Despite what transpired there, I have retained a fondness for Jamaica."

"But I can understand perfectly," Peter said quickly, seeing the annoyance in Eliza's eyes and not wanting to stray onto treacherous territory. "If one is receptive to such things, the island does indeed exert a magic pull. The disadvantages are far outweighed by the advantages."

"I assume you mean the climate?" Eliza asked wickedly. "I

have observed that some of those who live in that kind of heat for a period of time become completely impervious to it, sometimes to their detriment.''

"Their detriment?" Edward asked, wondering what sort of outlandish observation Eliza was going to hand down now, and wondering at the same time why Peter was looking as if he was about to be overtaken by a fit of sneezing.

"Yes," Eliza replied evenly. "One can become overconfident and find that even the thickest of skins cannot sustain long exposure to high temperatures. Really, extreme heat can cause the most volatile of situations without warning."

Peter dissolved. "Pepper," he said, the tears rolling down his cheek as he choked into his napkin. "Sorry. Pepper up my nose."

"I'm terribly sorry," Eliza said. "Perhaps some water would help? I've found that it has a dampening effect."

This only resulted in Peter going off again, snorting even more volubly into his napkin, while the tears streamed and his shoulders shook.

Edward gave them both a long look. He knew Peter well enough to know he was not suffering from pepper up the nose at all. He had seen him in the position of unrestrained mirth often enough to conclude he was now suffering from exactly that, and he could only assume that Peter was beginning to see what a lunatic Eliza was and was transported into hysterics thinking of the fate of his poor friend.

"Oh, dear," Eliza said fretfully. "Don't you think you should do something, Edward? I simply cannot think how Mr. Frazier came to have pepper up his nose when we were eating a blancmange, but then I've known the strangest things to happen at dinner tables."

"I think Peter will recover shortly, Eliza," Edward said quickly, before Eliza could launch into one of her monologues. She had gone all the way since morning without doing so, and the strain was clearly showing, given her last remarks. "You might want to retire next door so that he might do it without embarrassment?"

His words were nearly drowned out by a fresh hoot from Peter, and he looked at his friend with annoyance, while George wore his typically quiet expression of amusement.

Eliza simply gave him that infuriatingly vacant smile of

hers and excused Marguerite and herself from the table.

"So, my dear," Marguerite said, settling on the sofa. "What is this game you are playing with your husband?"

"Game?" Eliza said innocently. "Whatever makes you think such a peculiar thing?"

"Because your eyes have had the most devilish expression in them all evening. I have never seen you so animated. You look marvelous, Eliza, and you should be animated, for it gives me great pleasure to see this side of you. But I cannot understand why you turn that extraordinary look on Edward."

"What look is that?" Eliza asked with trembling lips.

"Why, that bovine stare as if you were one of your cows."

"Marguerite, please, do not insult my cows so!" The laughter spilled over and Eliza held her sides, gasping for air. "It is too awful, isn't it? It quite maddens him, you know," she managed to say.

Marguerite tapped her fan on Eliza's knee. "I see. I know you wanted to annoy him, but now you would have Edward think you stupid?"

"Yes, I would. It takes very little effort, for he has thought me quite hopelessly stupid from the beginning."

"Eliza, darling, you most certainly will annoy Edward, for he does not suffer fools gladly. He prizes intelligence above almost all things."

"As he prizes beauty?" she said with a touch of bitterness.

"I think you do not know your husband very well," Marguerite said gently. "He prizes beauty, indeed, but there are things he holds in higher regard. Certainly intelligence is one of them. There are other things as well. Tell me, Eliza, for I do not think I understand. Do you truly wish to give Edward a disgust of you?"

"Yes. I do. I told you, Marguerite. All I wish is to be returned to the country. It is not a pleasant thing to be in the presence of a man who finds it nauseating to look at me, especially when that man is my husband."

Marguerite considered. "I do not think this is true, although when people have had a difficult time together, that colors the way they see each other. When Edward looks at you, perhaps he still sees his failure."

Eliza squeezed her hands together hard. "No. That is not what he sees."

"But, Eliza, darling, you have changed much since your marriage. You have changed much just since being here in London. Look at you, glowing with a new confidence. Why will you not let that work for you? You are highly intelligent, very sensitive and caring, wonderful with Matthew, who is clearly beginning to adore you. Do you really think it is impossible to build something between you and Edward, so impossible that you are bending over in the other direction to send him away?"

"Yes. I have done what he has asked, Marguerite. I have done my best to make myself presentable as Edward's wife and not to disgrace him in public. I owe him that much. But I have not done it to make him happy with me, or in any hope that he will wake up one morning and discover that he is in love with his wife. Believe me, there is absolutely no hope for that."

Marguerite sighed. "I cannot help but feel that you are both too proud and too stubborn for your own good. I don't seem to be able to talk any sense into you at all, but perhaps Peter can talk some sense into Edward. He's the only person who's ever had any real influence on him."

"Really? But they seem quite different."

"They are. Perhaps that is why they are such good friends, like the closest of brothers. Of course, George knew them long before I did. It was he who introduced Edward and Peter at Cambridge, for Edward and George played together as children, growing up so close to each other."

"Marguerite . . ." Eliza said suddenly.

"What is it, dearest? You look troubled."

"No, not troubled. But I am curious. What was Edward's childhood like?"

"He has not talked of it to you? I suppose I cannot be surprised about that, either."

"I told you, we do not speak of anything beyond the mundane."

"Yes, of course. It is a pity, for I am sure you would find each other quite interesting. Ah, well, I shall not beat a dead horse. As for Edward's childhood, I'll tell you what I can, although George has not given me very much detail. I know that it was not at all a happy time for him; Edward's father was not a very nice man. I gather he made life very hard for Edward, who was the only child and quite ungovernable. I have been told he was very rebellious and naughty.''

''I can imagine. And his mother?''

''Ah, this was another matter. I do not know the exact truth, but there was a scandal. She ran off with another man when Edward was quite small. I believe she went to Italy and died there some twenty years ago. I really can't remember any more. I'm so vague.''

''You're not in the least bit vague, Marguerite,'' Eliza said fondly, storing away these facts to mull over at another time. ''Actually, I think you're one of the brightest people I know.''

''Really?'' Marguerite said with interest. ''If I were so bright, then perhaps I would better understand why A.E. Babcock, author of *An Observer's Jamaica*, which Edward so admires, has not let her identity be known.''

Eliza flushed deep red.

''It will do you no good to deny it, my dear. I know you too well, you see, and many of the thoughts you have expressed to me are in that fine volume. I also recognize the style of your pen and inks, for your sketches hang on my drawing-room wall for all the world to see. If anyone asks, I shall be hard-pressed to explain how it is I know the mysterious Mr. Babcock well enough to have some of his original works.''

''Oh,'' Eliza said uncertainly, feeling extremely foolish.

''I did not see any reason to mention it before, as you clearly had your reasons for wanting to keep it a secret, and indubitably you thought I would never see the book. But I think it is very foolish of you to keep it a secret from your husband, when it would give him much regard for you.''

''No! No, please, Marguerite, don't say anything,'' Eliza said, panic-stricken. ''I don't want him to know,'' she said more softly, swallowing hard.

''Naturally, I will keep your secret to myself. You should be very proud, Eliza. It is a fine piece of work.'' She smiled. ''It is very amusing, you see. Edward brought us a copy when he came to tea his first day back at Seaton. He said it was the only thing he'd ever read that accurately described his feelings about his adopted home. This is why George was not so surprised to learn of the marriage between you. He, too, guessed that you were the illustrious Mr. Babcock after reading the book, and he could quite see how you and Edward might go on. He's been longing to discuss certain passages with you, but has been tactful enough to hold his tongue.''

''I—I see. I do feel quite an idiot, Marguerite. I would have told you, but . . . Well, it just seemed a very private thing, a part of my life I wanted to keep to myself.''

''Of course, my dear. George and I would never think to censor you for that. We are all entitled to our privacy.''

''Thank you,'' Eliza said, her fiery head bowed.

''And you are entitled to your privacy when it comes to your relationship with your husband. I do not think to censure you there, either, my dear. I would only see you happy.''

Eliza looked up, her eyes slightly blurred. ''I know you would, and I do thank you, Marguerite. You have been the best of friends to me. But my future happiness does not lie with Edward. It lies at Seaton with Matthew, and that is where I shall build a new life.''

''We shall be happy to see you both there. We return to Keble Park tomorrow. Perhaps you will not be far behind.''

They heard the gentlemen coming in, and Eliza rang for the tea tray.

The next three weeks Eliza found pure torture. True to Edward's word, he took her to every amusement that was available during the last month of the Little Season. He also expected her to return calls, and thanks to Mrs. Horsley as much as anything else, she was accepted everywhere without question. Penelope Leavington, who was a dramatic sort in any case, had spread the touching tale of Eliza's courage and devotion, and it was now generally agreed that poor Eliza had been very ill-used by Lord Seaton, rather than the other way around. Within a week, Eliza was no longer seen as an upstart but a heroine. Within three, she was hailed as a true original.

She was also hailed as a lifesaver. The story of her conversation with Mrs. Chatterly had become the latest *on-dit*, along with Mrs. Chatterly's new passion for dieting and exercising Loulou at all hours of the day and night. This all had had a happy result on Loulou's digestive process, saving many a hostess from near expiration.

* * *

"Eliza," Edward said in the carriage on the way to the Buckingham rout, "I heard a most interesting tale concerning you and Mrs. Chatterly and a certain conversation you had some three weeks ago. I'm surprised it only just reached my ears, but I imagine no one wanted to offend me. Would you please attempt to limit your conversation to standard human topics? In this instance the *ton* has decided to be amused, but one day you will go too far and you might find the consequences unpleasant."

"Oh, but, Edward," Eliza said earnestly, "I think you are being rather high in the instep. You did not have to smell the result of Mrs. Chatterly's indiscretions with Loulou. When she appeared in the drawing room, every lady there immediately drew out a lavender-scented handkerchief. I feel it is my duty as a marchioness to do good deeds, and so I did."

"Please refrain your good deeds to the rescue of orphans."

"Oh, may I, Edward?"

"Certainly not. You have Matthew to look after. See here, Eliza, I only request that you abstain from discussing those things better left to the veterinarian."

Peter, who was also in the carriage while this conversation was taking place, had gone into a fit of laughter. "May I ask what you find so amusing?" Edward said, turning to him.

"No, you may not," Peter said, wiping his eyes. "If you have to ask, then you have completely lost your sense of humor and I cannot restore it to you with an explanation."

"You seem to be having rather a lot of these fits, my friend. Perhaps it is you who needs to reexamine your sense of humor."

"Sorry. It must be the London air that is giddying. Lack of oxygen, you know." Peter grinned and took a steadying breath, unable to meet Eliza's eyes lest he go off again. She really was a terrible tease, and there were times he almost felt sorry for Edward, for his friend had been completely taken in and was now being slowly tortured. He couldn't blame Eliza, for Edward really was dreadful to her, but he did wish the two of them would see how much they suited, rather than being at each other's throats every time their paths crossed. He had become terribly fond of Eliza, and to see Edward, lucky dog that he was, married to her and treat her as if she were poison made him furious.

Still he hadn't laughed so much in years. Eliza had a mind like a razor, he had discovered, and that she managed to use it so successfully to torment her husband, couching it in this garb of idiocy, amazed him. He grinned again. "I think the lack of oxygen has been affecting you as well, Edward. You haven't been at all yourself."

"I shall soon regret having you as a guest if you carry on in this fashion," Edward said to him irritably.

"Then it is a good thing I am disappearing in the direction of Southampton in only two hours' time. I would hate to wear out my welcome. Perhaps you will feel more charitable toward me after a few weeks' absence."

"I believe you are enjoying yourself at my expense, but you are not in my shoes."

"No, no, I am not. Although sometimes I wish I were, I must confess. I have often wondered what it must be like to be titled, handsome, and rich all at the same time." He looked out the window innocently, but he could not help hearing Eliza's hiccup of laughter, and it nearly sent him back into whoops.

"There are times, Peter, when I really have to question your reason. I think you have been spending too much time with Eliza, for I believe you are beginning to think like her."

"Do you question my reason, Edward?" Eliza said with a worried frown. "I have often wondered about it myself, but I didn't think it was a serious problem. I don't believe insanity runs in the family, but I would have to think carefully. Oh, dear, it's just as well we will not have children—other than Matthew," she amended. "But he seems perfectly normal. Maybe insanity only runs in females. I had so wanted a daughter, but now I don't at all, so really it is just as well we won't have one."

Peter leaned his forehead against his hand, doing his very best to keep a straight face.

"Eliza, please," Edward said curtly.

Eliza clapped her hand over her mouth. "I beg your pardon. I suppose I shouldn't have said that. But not a soul has asked me if I'm in an interesting condition, as they often do married women my age, so I assumed that everyone must know what our arrangement is. You said it was not uncommon, Edward."

Edward groaned. "Eliza, if we must discuss such things, let us please do it in private. It is a most improper topic of conversation."

"Oh! Well, at least it was human in nature. At least I think it was. I don't think you would discuss it with a veterinarian, although I'm sure he would understand the mechanics perfectly well. They always seem to know just the right time to get a cow with calf. It always surprises me how well cows take. Far better than people, I think, or you should no doubt have a hundred children by now.''

Peter quickly sobered, thinking that Eliza was about to go too far. He knew Edward well enough to know that he was at the very limit of his control. Eliza had definitely touched a nerve from the look on Edward's face. "Enough, Eliza," he murmured by way of warning in an undertone that Edward could not hear from his seat opposite.

Eliza's eyes flew to his in silent question and then she slowly looked back at Edward. "Oh, dear, I seem to have done it once more. I truly do beg your pardon, Edward. I shan't mention the subject again.''

"Thank you," Edward said tightly.

They were silent for the rest of the drive.

Eliza gave an inward sigh as they entered the Buckinghams' house. There, like a predator lying in wait for its prey, was Pamela Chandler, and her behavior was as despicable as ever. Pamela had never had a bone of tact in her body, nor had she ever had the simplest of consideration for others, but she was really going very much overboard when it came to hanging on Edward.

"Do not let her disturb you," Peter said quietly as Pamela came scurrying toward them. "She is only hungry for attention. She thinks she will find it in this quarter, but she will not.''

"It is merely awkward, Peter." Eliza had had quite enough of Pamela, more than enough of London, and she had completely had her fill of her autocratic husband, who deserved Pamela Chandler for all she cared. Too bad he hadn't married her, she thought spitefully.

"Edward is looking for escape, poor man.''

"Let him try," she said shortly. "It has been my experience that once you are in Pamela's clutches, it is rarely possible to escape.''

"So I have observed on many an occasion. It's an interesting situation, for she has a rare ability to repel people. Good evening, Miss Chandler.''

"Good evening, Mr. Frazier, Eliza. And how very fine you

look this evening, Lord Seaton," Pamela gushed, dropping a curtsy and a blush.

"Miss Chandler," Edward replied tightly.

"It has been such a dull evening, and I am so pleased you are here to enliven it. I find it difficult being in London when it thins so dreadfully. Now November is here, almost everyone has left. If my papa's work were not so important, we would be in the country, but alas, it cannot be. Mr. Buckingham is also a diplomat and a colleague of my father's, and of course a cousin of the duke's, but I am sure you know that."

"Would you care for some punch, Miss Chandler?" Peter asked. "I have not before been to this house and its design appears most interesting. Perhaps you will direct me to Mr. Buckingham so that I may ask him . . ."

Peter should have been a diplomat, Eliza thought as she watched him stroll off with Pamela on his arm.

"You seem to have become quite taken with my friend," Edward said, following the direction of her eyes. "You have been spending a good amount of time together. And I had thought you had agreed not to plague him. I imagine you shall be sorry to see him leave tonight, but I begin to think it a good thing. I wouldn't want there to be talk."

Eliza, who had wearied of Edward's surveillance of her behavior and of the need to put on any behavior at all, forced her shoulders to slump. "I hope you are not displeased with me, my lord. I am sorry I annoyed you in the carriage, but I have promised I shan't again."

"I was speaking of Peter. I noted that you address each other most familiarly."

"Oh! I hope that is not improper. Peter is most amusing and makes me feel quite comfortable in every way."

Edward, who had in the deepest recesses of his mind begun to wonder about exactly that, frowned. "I would hope not in every way, Eliza. You have been doing a fairly good job of behaving with propriety, at least in public. I trust you would not sully that in private."

Eliza's face went white at the implication. "Do you so little trust your friend, my lord?" she murmured. "You apparently have no trust of me beyond that I shall not give away your secret. But then, you did tell me it was to be a marriage of convenience, did you not, my lord? Or perhaps I misunderstood. I so often do, you know. It was to be a marriage of convenience for you and not for me, was that it?''

Edward's face went as white as Eliza's. "You impertinent chit," he hissed. "If I did not think you were incapable of understanding half the things you say, I would throttle you here and now.''

"Please do, my lord. I am quite sure that it would create the most marvelous *on-dit*, and we do want to keep our names in the forefront, as you have often told me in the last month. I am not quite sure if it is the sort of talk you would wish, however, but I would be happy to oblige. Here is my neck. Do help yourself. Oh, but then, you promised not to touch me again. Does throttling count?''

Edward gave a muttered oath and spun on his heel, rapidly walking away.

Eliza turned and walked in the opposite direction, for once caring nothing about who might notice. She had as much right, if not more than most, to a marital spat, and she could not give a fig as to who had witnessed it, including Pamela Chandler, who was gloating from across the room like a cat in the cream pot. She could have the cream pot and the spoiled cream, and Eliza hoped it would make her sick.

Eliza determined to enjoy the rest of the evening and Edward be damned.

"I will see you in the library," Edward said, slamming through the front door and handing Grigson his hat and cane.

"Certainly, my lord," Eliza replied, also slamming through the door, leaving Grigson looking after them, truly startled.

Edward closed the library door with a bang. "I have had enough, Eliza," he said, turning to her and towering over her menacingly. "Your behavior this evening was disgraceful.''

"In what way, my lord? Because I behaved as any married woman of the *ton* does and ignored my husband in favor of all the other attractive gentlemen dancing attendance on me? I noticed that you had no objections to the various women fluttering around you. Pamela has been most enthusiastic in her attentions.''

"Pamela . . ." He stopped for a moment to get a grip on himself. "Pamela Chandler is a complete nuisance, and if God had given you any sense, you would see that I cannot abide the woman. However, as she is willing to repeat anything I tell her regarding our supposed prior relationship, I cannot slight her either. Nor can I slight the other ladies of the *ton* whose business is hovering about men who have absolutely no interest in them, hoping against hope that some illicit pleasure might come from their efforts. Which brings me back to you, Eliza. You cannot be so foolish as to think that the gentlemen you were flirting with this evening thought it was in all innocence.''

"Of course I do. There was nothing wrong with my behavior.''

"You behaved like a light-skirt!''

The last thread of Eliza's temper, which had been fraying all night, finally snapped. "Surely you can say it more eloquently than that, my lord. Why don't you just out and call me a slut? You implied the same earlier this evening when you coupled me with your closest friend. I wonder what that makes him? I know it makes you a cuckold, but you could hardly care, could you? I can scarce think of how many husbands you've cuckolded in your time.''

"That's enough, Eliza.'' A muscle in Edward's cheek twitched rhytmically.

"Enough? It is acceptable for you to level such a charge, but not acceptable for me to reply to it? I have noticed that there is one code of behavior for you and another for me. Do you know, Edward, I cannot help but wonder one thing: how is it that you think anyone in his right mind would want to bed me? You had a difficult-enough time yourself, and your reputation leads me to believe that you would throw your leg over just about anything. Or do you still think that where Lord Seaton goes, all others are compelled to follow?''

All the color drained from Edward's face as he struggled to retain his temper, for if he lost it now, he knew he would do her bodily injury. "Tomorrow you will leave for Seaton,'' he said, his voice shaking. "Your London reign is finished, my lady. There you will stay until such a time as you regain your senses. Is that understood?''

"You forget I have no senses, nor feelings, my lord. But as you have no feelings yourself, I cannot see why you would see that as an issue. And you also forget that I have been asking to go back to Oxfordshire since you first removed me from it.

I would be happy to be released from my obligations here. I would ask to be released from this sham marriage if it were not for Matthew. And speaking of that, I intend to take him to Seaton with me. I cannot think you will miss him here. You needn't worry, my lord. I shall raise your son to be a proper marquess. Having observed you closely, I think I have the general idea, although I shall leave out arrogance, callousness, and lack of consideration for others from his training. Your father taught you those qualities overly well.''

Edward stiffened for a moment, and then he turned slightly away from her, rubbing his forehead. His hand fell to his side and after a long moment he looked up. Eliza was surprised to see that the anger was gone, to be replaced by a look of utter weariness.

"I may take Matthew?" she said uncertainly.

"Take whatever you want, Eliza. Take Matthew, take your damned jewels and your French maid and your expensive wardrobe. I don't care what you do. Just leave.'' He sat down at his desk and opened a drawer. "I have settled three hundred thousand pounds on you. Most of it is in investments that will generate a generous income, but I have cleared fifty thousand pounds that you may spend as you wish. You have clear title to Sackville and the hundred acres on Seaton that border it. Here are the particulars. They were settled shortly after our marriage.'' He removed a large envelope and pushed it across the polished surface.

Eliza drew in a sharp breath, stunned by the amount he had named, unable to comprehend such a sum, but even more shocked at the expression on his face. Edward looked utterly bleak, and she could take no enjoyment from the sight. Her hand slipped to her cheek as a dreadful realization crept over her.

"It is everything you asked for, I believe. If you have any questions, the name of my solicitor is in there, as well as the bank you may draw on. I hope you find everything in order.'' He looked up at her. "What are you waiting for? Take your thirty pieces of silver. I doubt we'll find you hanging from a Judas tree tomorrow. After all, the only person you sold was yourself, and it was a damned good trade, wasn't it, Eliza? Your virginity for a title and a fortune?''

Eliza blanched. He might just as well have slapped her, although he had hurt her far more with his words than he ever could have with a physical blow. "You really have no feelings at all, have you?" she said, fighting tears. "I wish you to hell, Edward March, although I'm sure you'll arrive there all on your own without my help. And I will take my thirty pieces, but not because you bought my virginity. I would have given you that willingly enough if you'd only thought to ask. I take it because it represents my freedom from you and a chance to bring Matthew up as he deserves. You have a wonderful little boy. It's a pity he isn't as lucky in his father." She stepped forward and picked up the envelope. "Good night, Edward. Thank you for keeping your word." She walked out, her back straight and her head held high.

Edward stared after the closed door for a moment, then put his head in his hands. He sat like that for a long time.

10

If anyone had told me a year ago that this place would be my home, that I should be spending month after month here, as I have done, I certainly should not have believed them.

Jane Austen, *Mansfield Park*

Eliza left early the next morning. She, Matthew, Mavis, and Jeanette traveled in one carriage, their baggage in another. It was bitterly cold. The journey took seven hours, two hours longer than usual, despite the improved roads. But the hail that pelted down made their passage hard going. Matthew became querulous, hardly surprising in a child that age, but it nevertheless caused Eliza to think that he had more of his father in him than his looks.

The carriage rattled passed Reading and then, some time later, Henley, and Eliza's heavy heart began to lighten as she saw the familiar landmarks quickly approaching. There was the spinney of ash trees, the church with the slatted lych-gate, the churchyard full of evergreen and yew. Her heart began to beat with excitement now as the outermost of the tenant farms came into view, and she could almost feel her blood quicken as the roof and chimneys of Seaton House appeared. They were approaching from the wrong direction to see Sackville, but it was good enough just to be this close. It was land, her lovely familiar land, and she could almost hear Clementine and Buttercup lowing in welcome. She could feel the dust of London blow away as she lowered the window and stuck her head out, breathing in the crisp, clean air.

"You'll be getting the child with croup, Miss Eliza," said Mavis in horror, clutching the sleeping child to her bosom in an effort to protect him from the deathly breeze.

Eliza laughed. "He'll be getting plenty of good country air in his lungs now, Mavis, and it will do him all the good in the world. I have trusted you in London, now you must trust me out here in the country. I promise you, no harm will come to Matthew from the outdoors."

"It is so," Jeanette agreed. "As I said last night, I grew up on a farm, and my sisters and brothers and I were all very healthy. I shall enjoy being back in the country."

"It was good of you to agree to come, Jeanette. You know I will not hold you to your word should you decide you miss the city. Look! Here is Seaton now." The enormous building rose up in front of them as they came through the wooded park and rounded the corner. It was set in front of a fold of hills, the situation very beautiful, and looked out over the Thames. Eliza took a deep breath as the carriage pulled up in front of the entrance and two liveried footmen appeared, looking extremely surprised.

"Wake up, Matthew," she said softly. "Look, we are finally arrived at your new home."

He struggled upright from Mavis' lap and rubbed his eyes, blinking hard, then popped his thumb into his mouth and looked as directed.

"Here you are, my little lord. Come, let's go in and meet everyone. I am sure they will all be very happy to see you."

She stepped out of the carriage and took Matthew into her arms, setting him down on the ground and firmly gripping his hand. Then indicating for Mavis and Jeanette to follow, she walked up the three steps and through the front door.

It did not take Eliza long to get started on making Seaton a home. The first thing she did after visiting Sackville was to have a long talk first with Mr. Wyatt, who seemed an elderly but loyal sort, and then with Mrs. Pringle, who expressed her fervent desire to retire. Eliza was happy to oblige her, having a perfect replacement in mind in Annie.

She discovered two things: first, Edward had put almost no appreciable money into the upkeep of Seaton House; second, as far as anyone could tell her, he had no plans to do so. That was a start. Eliza now had money of her own, and use it she did. It only seemed appropriate to spend the money Edward had given her to improve the property. The first two stories of the house were immediately turned out, new linens ordered, as well as fabrics to replace upholstery and draperies that had become old and faded.

As for livestock and land, Eliza had a joyous reunion with her beloved cows and then had them brought to Seaton, where she could supervise them more readily, along with her horse, Parsley, and naturally her cat. She then brought in her cowman from Sackville to ask his advice on the agricultural side of Seaton, for Edward had not hired another steward and the last had done a very poor job. For two weeks she walked the land, taking Matthew with her as often as possible, and then she sat down and began drawing up plans, which she worked over until late at night.

Eliza was astonished at the amount of energy she had. She had never felt better in her life and realized that city life had affected her more than she had realized. Matthew was a joy, a happy, wiggling, shouting bundle of little boy. He had been thrilled with the cows, overjoyed to finally meet the famous Clementine and Buttercup, who had peopled many bedtime stories.

There was one surprise that had greeted Eliza; it had been almost the first complaint off Mr. Wyatt's tongue. It concerned Archie, a large green bird who had been residing in an isolated downstairs room since his master's departure and who would let no one come near him. Feeding the bird had become the bane of Mr. Wyatt's existence, for it did nothing but fling food and epithets at his head, and worse, bit him whenever possible.

"It is quite simple, Wyatt," Eliza announced upon hearing this. "Archie is missing his master. Therefore we must find a way to distract him from his misery. I had a brief acquaintance with an Amazon parrot when I was in Jamaica. Let us move Archie to the morning room and see if we cannot coax him into a better temper."

Archie was indeed a challenge, Eliza thought constantly over the next few weeks as each day she patiently taught him to come to her hand, to take food from her fingers, and to cease his screaming and growling whenever she came near. Matthew found the parrot fascinating and longed to put his hands around him, and it took all that she had to convince Matthew that neither he nor Archie would be happier for the encounter.

But soon Archie came around, as indeed the staff had, relatively quickly, and soon he was putting his head down and demanding a scratch on his bright yellow nape, purring and prancing and spreading out his wings to be admired. Eliza adored him, and Archie knew it.

"Yes," Eliza said absently, looking up from her figures one morning shortly before Christmas. "You are indeed a very pretty bird, but really, Archie, you do have an insatiable need for attention. Hush now, let me get back to my work or we won't know what fields will be planted with what next spring. They will all be called Pretty Bird, or Hello Archie, and then everyone will be confused. Do you know, Archie, perhaps what you need is a mate, for I am sure it is not suitable for you to make these sort of overtures to me." She looked down at her figures again.

Archie trilled and bobbed his head, his pupils contracting and dilating with pleasure at the sound of her voice. He then walked pigeon-toed along his perch, and seeing he had lost her attention, he swung down and latched his beak onto her shawl. The next thing Eliza knew, she had a bird preening her curls and a cat leaping off her lap in horror. Archie looked after the cat with a gleam of satisfaction in his small orange eye. "Bad bird," he said, bobbing at Leopold's swiftly retreating figure. "Bad, bad bird."

Eliza dissolved into laughter, then firmly removed Archie and put him back on his perch and went to soothe Leopold's feelings.

Archie had gone so far as to learn to call Leopold in Eliza's voice and then scold the cat, and Leopold's dignity was sorely tried at the moment.

She suddenly stopped and straightened in the middle of stroking Leopold back into a semblance of self-respect. She felt almost happy, she realized with amazement. She had a wonderful sense of fulfillment: she felt a true mother to Matthew, who for some reason of his own had begun to call her 'Mama.' She was delighted—she couldn't have loved him more if he had been her own. She very much enjoyed running a large household and being the acting steward until she could somehow convince Edward to hire someone worthy of the job. She truly enjoyed being brought the manifold problems of the estate, inner and outer, every day and solving them.

Seaton had become an extension of Sackville, and it began to shine with the same reflection of loving care. It would take a great deal more work to make it truly come about, but she could already see the difference. The staff were happy and went about their work with pride, knowing that their efforts were appreciated and that Eliza was there to stay. Annie's practicality and penchant for hard work went a long way toward turning things around, and Mr. Wyatt, who had long ago given up doing anything but the minimal, now sprang into action as if he'd been reborn.

The pantries were restocked, the footmen retrained, a new cook was hired, and it was all done with a generosity of spirit on all parts. The atmosphere belowstairs was convivial for the first time in years, and although Eliza didn't know it, her praises were constantly sung by everyone, from Wyatt down to the footboys.

Eliza only knew that she was well pleased. She thought that, really, there might be hope for a good life. It would also be a truly happy life if only she could rid herself of the wrenching emptiness at the core of her being, which was all tied up with Edward. It had been a terrible night, the night he had banished her from him, and oddly, despite how much she had wished it, had worked for it, when it had happened, it had hurt her deeply. Perhaps it was the premise he had based it on, she thought as she put away her papers and called to have Matthew brought down for their daily inspection of the barns and henhouse. Perhaps it was that he had so badly misjudged her despite the fact that she had tried to mislead him. Or perhaps it was the fact that she still loved him.

That shocking moment of truth had hit her in the library that night as he had pushed the papers representing her freedom across his desk with that terrible look of desolation in his eyes. She had realized that it wasn't Sackville she wanted any longer. She certainly didn't want his land or his money. She only wanted his love.

When had that changed? When had she ceased to hate him for what he had done to her? How could she possibly love a man who treated her like a necessary but despised object, who had taken her virginity as if he'd been performing the most odious of tasks? And yet she did, although for the life of her she couldn't work out why. Edward had done only one thing that showed any kind of sensitivity, and that was to watch a mouse give birth. Oh, and he had had the good taste to admire her book. For that she was prepared to love him, when everything else he had done was either cruel, or thoughtless, or cold?

But there had been that look in his eyes, a look that she had put there, and she felt terrible for having done so. When it came down to it, she had been cruel and insensitive herself, taking every opportunity to torment him. And on that last night, even Peter had warned her off . . . She had been over and over what it was she had said in the carriage that had touched so raw a place, but she had only been talking foolishness. Perhaps she had embarrassed him in front of his friend by letting it out that they did not share a bed. To someone like Edward, she supposed, that would be humiliating, for he had a reputation to uphold. In any case, whatever it was had set the stage for the rest of the evening and their final, appalling argument.

Eliza squeezed her eyes shut for a painful moment, wishing she could take back what she had said, wishing that it was possible to change things between them, and knowing that it wasn't. Edward would never feel anything toward her but acute distaste, or perhaps, eventually, indifference. She was condemned to love.

And then she heard little footsteps coming fast and she pushed Edward from her mind. Matthew came barreling into the room and flung himself on her with a shriek, Mavis waddling in behind him, out of breath with trying to keep up.

"Let's go see how Clementine is coming along with her baby, shall we?" Eliza said, scooping him up in her arms. "She's getting very round, I think."

"Very round," Matthew said with a giggle. "I drawed a picture."

"Did you, sweeting? We'll look at it later. I'm sure it's very, very good. Let's go and bring her a carrot, for I know she's looking forward to her treat. You have to eat very well when you're going to have a baby." She smiled at Mavis and went out to fetch their coats and boots.

Peter handed Grigson his greatcoat, shaking the snow from it. "Good evening, Grigson. It's a cold night out there. Is his lordship in?"

"In the library," Grigson muttered. The last five weeks had been terrible, his lordship in an appalling temper and making everyone's life miserable, and right before Christmas, to boot. "He said he didn't want any interruptions."

"Very good," Peter replied, unperturbed, but wondering why Grigson looked so put out. "Have the footmen bring in my bags, will you?" He crossed the hall and knocked at the library door.

"What is it, damn you?" came the answer, and Peter considered that as much of an invitation as he was going to get. He entered.

"What the blazes do you want?" Edward snapped, looking up from his papers. He stiffened when he saw who it was.

"In a bit of a temper, are we?" Peter replied equitably, picking up a decanter of brandy and two glasses from the side table. He sat down and poured two glasses. "You don't seem to be in any better a mood than when I left you," he said, handing Edward a snifter.

"Considering that you are the last person in the world I want to see aside from Eliza, no. My temper has not improved."

"Hmm. I gather you and Eliza have not resolved your difficulties."

"Peter, you are treading on very hazardous territory. I would advise you to be extremely careful. If you were not an old friend, your life would be very much at risk."

Edward's voice was as cold as ice, which Peter knew meant he was in a far more dangerous frame of mind than a simple rage. "I see. It appears I have done something to give you offense."

"You could say that, yes." The quill Edward was holding bent and then snapped.

"Back to breaking pens? That is a bad indication. All right, Edward. Let's have it out. My conscience is clear, so I must have been an oaf about something I am unaware of. Is it Eliza?"

"You have the gall to ask me that?" Edward said incredulously.

"What else am I to do? You seem reluctant to help me discover what my offense is. As you are also apparently extremely annoyed with Eliza and want to have nothing to do with either of us, then I imagine we committed this imagined transgression together."

Edward came half out of his chair. "By God, Frazier, I should bring you to your knees."

"I wish you wouldn't. But I do wish you would enlighten me. Or maybe it would be easier to ask Eliza, as no doubt you've set her ears ringing a long time since."

"I did better than that. I sent her packing," Edward said with silky smoothness. "And if you wish to console your doxy, you'll find her at Seaton. Please, be my guest."

"My—my doxy," Peter said disbelievingly, choking on the fiery liquid that had gone down the wrong way. "Surely you can't be referring to Eliza?" He wiped his mouth and stared at Edward as if he'd lost his mind.

"I am perfectly serious," Edward said coolly.

"That's what this is all about?"

"That's exactly what this is all about. I have sent Eliza back to the country, where with luck she might remember who she really is. If you would like to go chasing after her, you may, although cuckolding a man under his own roof is a bit much. Not that you've let that stop you."

Peter calmly absorbed this, then shook his head. "You're a damned fool. You might possibly at this moment be one of the biggest fools in God's creation."

Edward slammed his hand down on his desk, and the glasses jumped with the impact. "Are you denying that you made my wife your mistress?"

"Naturally. Why would I want to go and do an idiotic thing like that? Wait! Oh, for the love of God, calm down, Edward.

What put this absurd notion in your head to begin with? Surely not Eliza? Even she wouldn't go that far . . . I don't think.''

"Eliza denied it, naturally. But my natural powers of observation have not completely failed me. You and Eliza have been like peas in a pod. For three weeks every time I turned around, the two of you were together, laughing and carrying on. I witnessed your fond farewell at the Buckinghams' rout. Such a touching moment.''

"I kissed her hand, Edward," Peter said evenly.

"What else could you have kissed in a semipublic place?''

"This is ridiculous," Peter said, trying to suppress his treacherous sense of humor, which had often enough before this landed him in trouble in equally volatile situations. "How does the fact that Eliza and I have become friends and enjoyed some harmless activities together suddenly transform into a clandestine arrangement?''

"It's very simple," said Edward, who had had five long weeks to think about it. "Why would you want to spend time with a hopeless idiot like Eliza unless you were bedding her?''

Peter couldn't help himself. He threw his head back and roared with laughter. "You're disguised, that's what it is," he finally managed to say. "That must be it. You've been in your cups since your marriage, for that was the last sensible thing you did.''

"You are going to find yourself without a head on your shoulders," Edward said curtly.

"Then I'll be in very good company," Peter replied, going off into fits again.

"What?" Edward said, completely confused by Peter's unexpected reaction.

"You fool, I haven't been cavorting with Eliza. She's your wife, for God's sake, even if you cannot see it. I wouldn't do a thing like that no matter how much I might want to, and if you weren't so turned about with jealousy, you'd know it.''

"Jealousy? Don't be absurd. I'm not jealous in the least. I do not like, however, being betrayed.''

"No one has betrayed you, dear boy. I like Eliza, as hard as you might find that to believe. At first I kept her company because I felt sorry for her, given the way you forced her to marry you and then ignored her and, when you weren't ignoring her, insulted her. Then I quickly began to discover the person she was underneath and looked forward to spending time with her.''

"No one," Edward said smoothly, hardly able to believe his ears, "likes spending time with an imbecile."

"Eliza's not an imbecile—that honor goes to you. You can't see what's under your very nose."

Edward frowned. "I do believe you have lost your wits altogether."

"Edward, you are my very good friend, although you have a gift for being trying. Now is one of those times. Let me give you a piece of advice. Why don't you see how you might put right the hash you've made of your marriage? Go to Seaton to see Eliza, and go with an open mind. I know you don't like the place and you think you don't like her, but you might be surprised. Perhaps I'll join you in a month or so, before I sail for home. I'll take care of everything that needs to be done until then. Agreed?"

"I've just rid myself of Eliza. It's ridiculous to expose myself to her again."

"Edward, you have accused me of all sorts of unsavory things tonight, and I have taken it on the shoulder like a good sport. Don't push me further. I would find it very uncomfortable to have to call you out. Go to Seaton. Stop being such a pompous ass and look at the good fortune you've been given, God only knows why. You've called Eliza a cork-brain often enough. It is you who is a cork-brain, my friend, for you have had the wool well and truly pulled over your eyes. You have a treasure, and you can't see it. You don't ignore a treasure and hide it from the light of day, simply because you think it doesn't suit you. You cherish it, you accept its imperfections as part of what makes it what it is, and you thank God that it is yours. Would that I will be so lucky one day. Please, do not throw away something of such value."

Edward regarded Peter with astonishment, for he was not one to wax eloquent, and he seemed genuinely sincere.

"Go to Seaton," Peter repeated.

"I'll think it over, although I certainly don't know why."

"You're a very tall, strong man. I'm sure you can take on a moderately tall, slim girl like Eliza." Peter smiled and drained his glass, then stood. "I won't find any snakes in my bed, will I?"

"Go to hell," Edward said, picking up a new quill and proceeding to sharpen it.

"Straightaway," said Peter, and bowed out.

Edward looked after him with puzzlement. He found himself believing that Peter had not taken Eliza to bed, nor anywhere near one. He'd always found the idea hard to fathom, although he'd done a good job of convincing himself that was the case. He did feel slightly ashamed that he had thought such a thing of Peter. If he was really honest, he had probably convinced himself so that he would have an excuse to send Eliza away.

But in his own defense, she was the most provoking creature—no man could be expected to keep his sanity around her. Given that, he couldn't understand the extraordinary way Peter had come to Eliza's defense. He trusted Peter as he trusted no one else. Why, then, did Peter think his wife was such a treasure? And what had Peter meant by saying that he'd had the wool pulled over his eyes? No one had ever succeeded in pulling the wool over his eyes. The entire situation was a mystery to him.

He resolved to leave for Seaton in the morning. Mysteries were for solving, even if they did include Eliza.

Edward arrived the next afternoon. He was rather surprised at the way the footmen snapped to, and there was an indefinable difference about the house when he entered it, although he couldn't quite place what it was.

"My wife, Wyatt?" he barked. "Where would I find her?"

"I believe, my lord," Mr. Wyatt said with great dignity and not without surprise, "you will find Lady Seaton and Lord Glouston collecting eggs in the henhouse. They are very regular about doing so, and it is two o'clock. Lady Seaton believes the hens are well-rested at this hour."

Edward muttered under his breath, wondering why he had allowed Peter to talk him into this fool-headed mission. He began to stride out the door and then stopped abruptly. "Where, may I ask, is the henhouse?"

"Where it has always been, my lord. It is adjacent to the barns, perhaps a two-minute walk to the west of them."

Edward gave him a vile glance, promising himself he'd deal with the man later, and went out. He picked his way over the snow, which had crusted underfoot. The surface broke occasionally, causing Edward to stumble and swear loudly, more from

simple aggravation with himself for being there at all than for
any other motive. But he reached the henhouse without catas-
trophe and paused as he heard voices within.

"You're quite right, Matthew, Ginger has not laid her usual
amount today. She has given us only three eggs."

"Is she ill?" came a worried little voice.

"No, I should think just off her feed or annoyed about something. I'll tell you what we might do. We might let her alone
for a day or two and see if she isn't feeling more the thing.
Perhaps tomorrow or the day after she might lay her usual
number. How many is that?"

"Five!"

"That's right, and two more than we had today. Maybe
someone needs to teach Ginger to count, do you think?"

Matthew laughed. "Hens can't count."

"No, perhaps not. But you can, and it's a fortunate thing,
for you can keep Ginger on the mark when she falls off. What
would she do without you, sweeting, to keep count for her? Just
think, you are two years old and can count prodigiously well,
and Ginger has seen at least three years by the look of her and
can't seem to count at all. Now, you'll have to help me with
the basket as Mavis was busy today and I need both hands for
the milk jugs. Look, darling, take the handle like this. That's
it. You are a strong fellow to manage all those eggs."

Edward stepped back around the corner as he heard them
approach the door. He had no idea what to make of the conversation he had just overheard, but he knew that it had made him
feel uneasily like an eavesdropper and, worse, a complete
stranger in his own home, where his wife and child seemed
perfectly comfortable. He watched them as they left, Matthew
carrying his basket as if it contained the crown jewels, Eliza
swinging a milk pail from each hand, looking as if she hadn't
a care in the world. He looked again, hard. Gone was the studied
elegance, the practiced manners of a marchioness. Also gone
was that vacant look he so abhorred. It was Eliza, only it was
yet a different Eliza, one he had certainly never seen before.
Was this what Peter had meant? He'd wanted him to see Eliza,
the milkmaid? No, surely not. And yet there she was, having
dropped her buckets, and was now tumbling Matthew in the
snow, rubbing the stuff into his hair and crowing with laughter

as he tried to do the same to her, his little hands not quite managing it.

Eliza? Was this some farce Peter had orchestrated? That seemed unlikely, given his sincerity.

"*Go with an open mind.*" Peter's words echoed back to Edward and he decided to do just that. How he was going to manage an open mind with Eliza was slightly beyond him, but stranger things had been known to happen, he supposed. He would simply have to make his best effort. He turned away and took a roundabout path back to the house, not sure why he felt quite so hollow inside.

Eliza saw Matthew safely in through the kitchen door, where Mavis was waiting with a very large towel that had been warmed by the fire.

"Thank you, Mavis. We have had a satisfactory visit to the cow barn and all appears to be well. As for the chickens, Matthew is most displeased with Ginger, who is off her laying, but I expect she will settle down. I think Matthew could use his nap after all that exercise." She ruffled Matthew's hair and smiled at Mavis, who grunted.

"Master Matthew's gonna outgrow his father if he keeps up like this. Never did see a child eat and run and sleep so much, but it seems to be doing him good," Mavis said grudgingly.

"I think it is doing him a great deal of good. Now I really must get back to my books. Do bring Matthew down at six. I'll be in this evening."

Eliza had spent many a contented night with George and Marguerite, but she equally enjoyed the peace of Seaton, which was gradually becoming as much home as Sackville had been. And she had to admit, it was pleasant not to worry about making every penny stretch, or to be constantly concerned about conserving fuel. She gave Archie a rub on his beak, then sighed and massaged her back as she bent over the accounts she had not managed to finish that morning. She was soon lost in concentration. Oats, barley, rye—that took care of the three hundred acres of the home fields. Feeding the sheep on turnips, clover, and sainfoin would cause them to produce more manure, so those fields whose soil had been exhausted . . .

"Good day, Eliza."

Eliza's head shot up and her heart seemed to stop. Edward was standing halfway into the room, a quizzical expression on his face.

"Edward!" She somehow managed to get to her feet, closing the book as she did so, wondering what could have brought him and trying very hard to compose herself. She was actually happy to see him, realizing how long it had been since she had laid eyes on his familiar face, his tall, muscular figure. "I—I didn't expect you."

"No. I hadn't planned on coming. You're looking well."

"Thank you," she said hesitantly. "Country air agrees with me."

"Apparently. Are you happy here at Seaton?"

"Yes, I am. I hadn't thought to find it so convivial, although naturally I miss Sackville. Would you like some tea, some coffee, perhaps?"

"What were you working so hard over? I was standing here for some time."

"Oh! I was—I ordered some things for the house. I hope you don't mind. I paid for them from the money you gave me." Eliza felt her cheeks flame.

"Why should I mind? But that is not how I intended you to use your money."

"It seemed a worthwhile expenditure."

"As you please. I have come to put Seaton in order. I hope that will not be an inconvenience."

"It is your home, Edward. I hope you will make yourself comfortable. If you wish me to retire to Sackville while you are here, I will do that, although I have arranged for tenants to move in after Christmas when the renovations are complete."

"Eliza, enough! You are my wife. You live here now. I am delighted to hear about your arrangements for Sackville, which indicates to me that you've come to terms with your situation. The fact that I have arrived for a temporary stay should not in any way make you feel displaced. Ignore me if you so desire."

"Edward . . ." Eliza could not think what to say. Their last argument had been so bitter that she had often wondered if she would ever see him again. And now there was something ineffably different about him, although she couldn't think what it was. "I do not wish to ignore you," she said falteringly. "I only wish that you should feel at home."

"Thank you. However, as I have never felt particularly at home here, I cannot think why I should start feeling that way now." His gaze wandered around the room and landed on Archie, who was stiffly glaring at him from a corner in the shaded sunlight. "Hello, bird," he said, crossing over to him. "I imagine you've been making life hellish." He put out his hand. Archie ducked his head and began to bob and hiss in an unmistakable display of wrath.

"What's this?" Edward said, his surprise evident. "A tantrum? It's not the first time I've been away."

"Bad bird," Archie said in reply, spreading his wings out and flapping them. "Bad, bad bird."

Edward looked over his shoulder at Eliza. "Where did he learn that? The bird swears like a pirate on a bad day, but that's a new one."

"I imagine he learned it from Wyatt, for it sounds exactly like him. You left him in a rather difficult position. I don't think he was too pleased with the arrangement."

"Ah. Archie is rather particular in his tastes."

Eliza couldn't help smiling. "I meant Wyatt."

"Did you? I suppose I should have brought him with me."

"Wyatt is very comfortable here."

"I meant Archie," Edward said with an amused twitch of his mouth. "I suppose I had better be off about my business. I'm planning on hiring a new steward, and I should catch up on things before he arrives."

"A steward?" Eliza repeated, knowing she should be delighted. She had been enjoying herself greatly, but she knew she couldn't continue to run Seaton single-handedly. Yet she couldn't help but feel a tinge of disappointment. She was also feeling the strain of Edward's presence. She ran a hand over her forehead.

"You needn't look quite so put out. He'll have a house of his own and won't bother you overmuch."

"I won't mind at all if he does. Seaton needs someone experienced. It's gone too long without."

Edward gave her a long look. "Yes, it has. You suddenly look pale, Eliza. Are you feeling unwell?"

"No, I'm a trifle tired. I think I'll lie down for a while." She picked up her book and hurried past him. "Will you be here for dinner?" she thought to ask, turning at the door, her hand resting on the knob.

"Yes. If it's not an inconvenience."

"No inconvenience, my lord. We eat at seven."

Eliza went directly up to her room, feeling more upset than she had in five weeks. She buried her face in her pillow, refusing to cry, refusing to think at all.

11

When so many hours been spent convincing myself that I am right, is there not some reason to fear I may be wrong?
                    Jane Austen, *Sense and Sensibility*

Eliza was about to enter the library when she heard the sound of voices from within. She paused outside the half-open door where she could just see Edward sitting in an armchair close to the fire. At his feet sat Matthew, cross-legged and dressed for bed, listening intently, his little hands on the floor beside him. "And then?" Matthew said insistently. "Then, what?"

"Then?" Edward's deep voice sounded perplexed. "Well, then the cow—ah, Clemmy—decided she'd had quite enough of the farmer taking her milk without so much as a by-your-leave or a thank-you for all her hard work. So she waited until the time was right, just when the farmer had filled the bucket with her warm, frothy milk. First she flicked her tail in his eye, and then she picked up her hoof and kicked the bucket over, and when the angry farmer jumped up, knocking over the milking stool in his haste, she kicked him, too, right in the—right in the stomach."

Matthew burst into a fit of giggles. "Clever Clemmy."

"Yes, she was a very clever cow, and she was also a happy cow, for she finally had her revenge after years of mistreatment. And ever after the farmer learned to say please and thank you when he wanted something."

Matthew clapped his hands in delight. "Tell another!"

"Certainly not. Surely it must be your bedtime by now?"

"I want Mama."

"Mama? Yes, well I'm sure she'll be down shortly. Now off you go to Mavis."

Matthew's face crumpled. "No. I want my mama!" A fat tear squeezed out of his eye.

"Oh, for God's sake, don't do that. Big boys don't cry." Edward looked so uncomfortable that Eliza took pity on him and moved briskly into the room.

"Here I am, Matthew. Has your father been telling you your bedtime story?"

Matthew immediately brightened and scurried to his feet, dashing over to her and wrapping his arms around her knees. Eliza scooped him up into her arms and dropped a kiss on his hair. "Your papa's right, sweeting, it is your bedtime. What a very fine story you had told you tonight! Look, here's Mavis to tuck you up. Good night, Matthew. I'll see you in the morning." She gave him another kiss and handed him to Mavis, who had come up behind her, giving Edward a long, highly suspicious look.

"I don't think either has come to any harm," Eliza said with a choked laugh at Mavis' mutinous expression. "Good night." She turned toward Edward. "Good evening, my lord. I didn't know your taste ran to cows."

"The child seems to have picked up your obsession. He insisted," Edward replied, coming to his feet.

"He is a very determined child. You were brave."

"I was terrified," Edward said with a reluctant smile. "I am not accustomed to children. Nor am I accustomed to telling stories—at least not that kind."

"I am sure Matthew took you well in hand." She wished he would not smile so, for it made her heart quite feel like turning over, and she did not wish to to do so. It had been much easier when she'd convinced herself that she disliked him thoroughly. How much more difficult it was to face him with the knowledge that she did not dislike him at all. She had spent the last half-hour thinking hard about the situation and had decided that she would not provoke him, nor play the imbecile any longer, no matter how vulnerable she felt. One did not intentionally torment the people one loved, no matter how foolishly.

"Seaton seems to have done Matthew some good," Edward said. "He has grown quite a bit."

Eliza took the chair opposite the one Edward had been sitting in. He leaned against the mantelpiece in his characteristic pose, looking down at her as if expecting a reply.

"Matthew loves Seaton," she said. "He has a great affinity for animals and things of the earth."

Edward nodded. "Then you will suit each other."

"Yes, we will. I am very fond of Matthew." She felt suddenly tongue-tied and looked down at her hands. Being simply herself with him did nothing for her poise.

"Eliza, I want to apologize for what I said to you in London. I have spoken with Peter and I know that I accused you unjustly."

Eliza flushed deep red. Edward looked terribly uncomfortable, and she knew that the apology had been very difficult for him to make. In fact, she wondered why he'd bothered to make it at all. "Thank you," she said simply. "I, too, said some things I shouldn't have, and I am sorry."

"You left your jewels behind."

Eliza smiled. "I hardly thought I'd need them here. We are used to being very informal, and there is no one to see."

Wyatt appeared to announce dinner, and so whatever comment Edward had been about to make went unspoken.

Eliza had asked to have the table set so that she sat next to Edward instead of across from him, given that the table was so long they would hardly have been able to hear each other. There was enough of a gap between them as it was, and she really didn't see the point in adding to it.

Edward brought Archie in to dinner and sat the parrot on the chair to the left, which made Eliza smile into her napkin when she saw the look on Wyatt's face. Archie had no table manners and so had not been allowed into the dining room, a fact that had pleased Wyatt enormously.

"Perhaps you will bring a cloth, Wyatt, and place it under Archie's chair," she murmured, and Wyatt bowed with a poker face and went off to fetch a towel. "Wyatt is fond of the carpet," she said to Edward when he gave her a sharp look, as if expecting a criticism. "He believes the naturally occurring pattern of flowers should be left as the weaver had originally intended."

"Parrots are not noted for neatness," Edward replied.

"No. But what they lack in neatness they make up for in other areas. I hope you enjoy mulligatawny soup, my lord. The new cook was most pleased to hear that you had arrived and so has made a special effort over this evening's dinner."

Edward only inclined his head. It had never occurred to him that the servants would care one way or the other if he was in residence. If anything, he would have thought they'd resent the extra work. He ate his soup in silence, which Eliza did not interrupt, a fact he was grateful for. He was not accustomed to Eliza and silence together, but it was not an unwelcome combination. He felt slightly off-balance, as if he'd entered a familiar world where nothing was quite as he remembered. He had worked out what was different about the house: it had a warmth it had previously lacked. He supposed it had something to do with women and domesticity, although he would hardly know. Until Eliza, he had lived most of his life in houses confined to men.

As for Eliza, he could not for the life of him work out what was different about her. She was quiet, yes. She was dressed very simply, but in a dress that flattered her figure and emphasized the swell of her breasts. He remembered the feel of her firm, round breast under his hand, and he shifted uncomfortably. He could not quite credit he was thinking about Eliza's breasts at the dinner table—indeed, thinking about them at all. It was what came of celibacy. He really did need to find himself a woman.

This thought was interrupted by the sight of Archie climbing off his chair and marching across the middle of the table. Edward watched with fascination as Archie happily plunged his beak into Eliza's soup bowl, and he waited for the shriek. Archie's ability to outrage had provided him with hours of entertainment, and he especially enjoyed the effect of Archie's table behavior on females, for it never failed to alarm.

Eliza, instead of shrieking, called Wyatt. "Wyatt, could you please fill an egg cup with soup and bring it? I am sure Archie will be very happy to drink it at his own place. Archie, don't do that. Off you go, back to your chair, please."

Edward could scarcely believe it when Archie fixed Eliza with his little orange eye, then turned around and marched back across the table, muttering, "Don't. Don't do that." He climbed back on his chair and sat there, looking broodily at Eliza.

"Good God," Edward said. "How did you do that?"

"Do what?" Eliza replied. "He's not stupid. He understands English as well as the next person."

Edward closed his eyes for a fraction of a second. This was the familiar Eliza. He knew the illusion of sanity could not have lasted for long. And when Wyatt brought the egg cup and placed it on a mat in front of Archie's chair, and when Archie climbed down and began neatly drinking from it as if such a thing was an everyday occurrence, Edward knew that he was back in Bedlam and nothing had changed. Eliza had simply rearranged everyone's brain to suit her own, his child and bird included.

The next few days brought more of the same. Everywhere Edward went, things seemed to have taken on a subtle air of Eliza. He was thrust into Matthew's company on a regular basis, for neither Eliza nor Matthew seemed to hold to the credence that children should rarely be seen and never heard. Matthew seemed to be able to talk about nothing but his mama and his animals, although Edward did find himself adjusting somewhat to the presence of a small child. What else could he do when the boy dogged his every step? Still, it was amusing in its own way, he supposed. At least Matthew appeared to have a lively and inquisitive mind, and for that he could only be thankful. Martha Medford had not been the brighest of creatures.

He was also thrust into Eliza's company, for they often sat in the library together, where a large fire blazed, the warmest place in the house. It seemed a natural spot toward which to gravitate, and he found that her company no longer rankled so much. In fact, there seemed to be an atmosphere of tranquillity that he found not altogether unpleasant. It somehow suited the short days and long winter evenings.

It snowed all of Christmas Eve and by evening a few inches had accumulated on the ground. Edward sat near the library fire reading the paper, with Matthew sitting on the hearth rug drawing pictures and keeping up a steady stream of chatter.

"Matthew, do leave your father in peace," Eliza said, entering the room, having changed for dinner. Annie came in behind her with a silver tray. "Here, it is time to tidy up your pencils and paper. Mavis is waiting to give you your supper."

"Look, Mama, I drawed a barn. Here is you, and here is Papa, and here is me with Clemmy. And this is Buttercup."

Eliza smiled and examined the paper. "It's a lovely picture, sweeting. Don't you think so, Edward?"

Edward took it from her and looked at it, trying to decipher it. "Very nice," he said, handing it back to her.

"Ask Mavis to put it on your wall. I'll come and kiss you good night later. Edward, would you care for some mulled wine? Cook has made some especially, given the day."

"Thank you. Will you join me?"

"Yes, I will. Put the tray just there, thank you, Annie." She handed Edward a glass, then settled down in front of the fire and picked up her needlepoint. "I imagine it's been some time since you last celebrated Christmas with a snowfall."

"Yes. Since I was eighteen, if I remember correctly, although we never really did celebrate Christmas at Seaton."

"Didn't you? Why was that?"

"My father was not interested in such things."

"You never speak of him."

"No, I don't."

"Why, Edward? Did you not get along? What was he like?"

Edward sighed and put the paper down. "I suppose you are going to plague me until I tell you."

"Yes, I am," Eliza said with a little smile. "I want to know about your childhood. I'm afraid you're not going to be able to beg the question."

"Very well, then, if you insist. We'll do it quickly. My father was a large man, quite imposing, and brutal when he chose to be. He and I were much alone here, although I did not see him often. I had a tutor. He was responsible for my day-to-day activities. My father appeared only when he wanted a progress report."

"And was he pleased with your progress?"

"No," Edward said shortly, then smiled. "I did not wish him to be. It gave me a certain amount of satisfaction to annoy him, although I found myself constantly paying the consequences. It was a painful process and I often had cause to regret my actions.''

Eliza swallowed hard, recognizing the similarity in her own recent behavior. ''And your mother?'' she asked.

Edward gave her a long, penetrating look. ''Surely you have heard the stories, Eliza. It was a great scandal almost thirty years ago. I cannot quite believe no member of the *ton* has brought it up to you.''

''Actually, no. I did ask Marguerite, but she said only that your mother left when you were young.''

Edward ran a hand through his hair. ''That is true. She left one night when I was seven. She and my father had had a terrible argument. She ran off with an Italian. I never saw her again and my father did not allow her name to be mentioned. She died in Italy.''

''I'm sorry. It must have been very difficult.''

''I hardly remember.''

''I somehow doubt that. My own father died when I was six. I was not overly fond of him, but I will never forget that afternoon.''

Edward frowned. ''What happened?''

''He'd been drinking. He rode his horse into a ravine and broke his neck. The horse was badly injured and had to be shot. I always felt terrible that I was more upset about the poor horse than I was about my father.''

Edward smiled. ''I somehow cannot be much surprised.''

Eliza laughed. ''I suppose that is true. I think that was when I first decided that animals generally had more worth than people. My father had no business even being on a horse that day. Many days. He wasn't much good at being a father, so I did not miss him overmuch, but I will always remember the sight of him being carried into the kitchen on a litter and the look on my mother's face. I was playing in a corner. They didn't know I was there.''

''Eliza, what was your life like?'' Edward asked, surprising himself. He had never thought about it before.

''Oh, it was fairly quiet. We lived in Sussex. My mother married again quite soon after that, but she had no more children, so it was just myself and her. My stepfather was not much interested in farming the land. He was a London sort and spent much of his time there, so my mother and I were left very much on our own.''

''You liked it that way?''

''Yes. I did not care for my stepfather. It did not much matter until my mother died.''

''What happened then?''

''My stepfather did not wish to support me, and as I'd had a Season with no suitable offer at the end of it, he decided I was a liability unless I was prepared—'' She stopped abruptly and went red, and her eyes fell to her needlework. ''I thought I'd be better off in another household.''

''Good God,'' Edward said, shocked to his core.

Eliza shrugged. ''Not too much after that he lost the place, so it was just as well I'd found a position.''

''So you became a companion.''

''Yes. It was not so bad as it might have been, and then Lady Westerfield left me Sackville. But you have very adroitly turned the subject, my lord. I was asking you about your own youth.''

''Which I have made a habit of forgetting as much as possible.''

''Yes, so I had gathered. That only leads me to conclude it must have been quite unhappy.''

''It was not the most exhilarating of times.''

''And your tutor? Were you fond of him?''

Edward laughed bitterly. ''Fond? I would not describe our relationship in such a way, no. He had a perverse fondness for a switch. Actually, I discovered later that he had a number of perversities, but the switch was the only one I would tolerate, and that barely. It was a pleasure to be sent away to school and do battle there. It was a greater pleasure to leave England altogether. It was ironic; I was already making plans to leave, my father be damned. He never would have suffered the defection of his heir, and he made sure I had no funds of my own. Peter was going to lend me the money to get on my feet, having already inherited a small fortune of his own. And then my father's heart gave up before I had a chance to tell him my plans. In one day my life had changed. I had money and freedom. I left anyway.'' He shook his head, his eyes dark with memory.

Eliza had the feeling that he had quite forgotten her presence.

It broke her heart to think what kind of life it must have been for him, a little boy abandoned by his mother, ignored and manipulated by his bully of a father, abused by his tutor. It was little wonder he found it so difficult to show any feeling. Edward had learned that the world was a cold place, rejection and betrayal the norm.

It was odd. Hadn't she learned exactly the same thing?

"Eliza, you're crying," Edward said, a note of surprise in his voice. "What is it?"

She quickly wiped the hot tears from her cheeks. She'd been oblivious to them. "Nothing. I'm sorry. I was just thinking of Matthew. He lost his mother so young."

"But he is lucky," Edward said gently, more gently than she'd ever heard him speak. "He was too young when it happened to remember for long. And now he has you."

"Yes. He does. I do love him, Edward."

"I can see that. I am glad for it." He looked up as Wyatt announced dinner, and then grinned when he saw what Wyatt had on his gloved hand. It was Archie, and Archie was looking very pleased with himself indeed. Wyatt wasn't looking too unhappy himself.

Edward rose, giving Eliza his arm. "Lead on, Wyatt," he said in his most lordly tone, greatly amused and not slightly relieved to leave the subjects they had been discussing behind.

They ate a quiet dinner and then Eliza excused herself, saying that she was tired and wished an early bed. Edward went back to the library, intending to read. But he found that his attention was not with his book. He kept thinking of Eliza, of how she had looked sitting by the fire, the glow catching in her hair as she had softly spoken about her childhood, her voice holding little inflection.

It had sounded like a terrible time, and he could hardly imagine how dreadful it must have been for her when her stepfather had made his intentions clear. Had he not known for certain that Eliza had been a virgin when he married her, he might have wondered just had badly she'd been used.

He could only be thankful that things had not progressed that far. But perhaps it was the shock of her stepfather's suggestion that had altered Eliza's brain, he thought. Poor Eliza. It was no wonder she was odd. And yet . . . over the last few days she had seen more or less normal. Well, perhaps not normal, but not quite as bird-witted, either. She was very good with Matthew, and the staff seemed to like her very much, for it was all he heard: her ladyship this and her ladyship that. It was actually growing tedious, all this blind adoration. She even had Archie mesmerized, and Edward could not help but be slightly annoyed. After all, Archie was his bird, and now Archie all but ignored him in favor of Eliza, who seemed to have an uncommon communication with him. He'd never seen Archie so biddable, nor so affectionate. His child, his bird, his staff, it was all the same. And this adoration wasn't limited to the house.

As he had made the slow rounds of his property, he found that the outdoor staff had a tendency to speak of precisely the same thing: their mistress. He could not help but notice that the staff seemed uncommonly content, so he could not complain. In fact, he was quite surprised to find that everything was running smoothly with much less waste and far more organization than when Seaton had been under Nash's command. From this he surmised that Nash had taught the staff more than he had realized, and now that the skimming of funds had stopped, money was being properly channeled. But he could not understand how the staff could do such a fine job without any central direction. Where he'd expected chaos, he'd discovered order, and he knew that things simply didn't work that way, certainly not with a place the size of Seaton.

Edward brought his attention back to Coleridge, telling himself it was sheer luck and the slow season.

But then there was also Eliza. Eliza couldn't possibly comprehend one-tenth of what was involved in Seaton, given that she could scarcely comprehend the most basic of things. But perhaps she inspired loyalty in the staff . . . Yes, that must be what it was. They liked having the mistress going about admiring their efforts, having the young master trailing at her skirts. It had been a long time since they had had anyone to please, and Eliza could be quite sweet when she chose. He had seen that for himself. That must have been what Peter had meant. She did have a gentle and caring nature when one came to know her a bit. Very well, he conceded, Eliza had a few redeeming qualities when she wasn't trying to impress: he was willing to go that far.

Edward sighed, content to have solved two mysteries at once.

He now knew what Peter had been referring to, and he also knew why Seaton was performing so much better. Really, it was amazing what a touch of loyalty could do.

He settled down to Coleridge, his mind at ease.

"Eliza . . ." Edward stopped dead on the threshold of the morning room as he took in the scene before him. Eliza was once against bent over a book of some sort, but now Archie sat atop her head, tenderly grooming her hair. He really was married to a madwoman.

She looked up at him. "Oh, Edward, it's you. Thank goodness. Would you please remove this confounded bird from my head? I've quite given up persuading him to stay on his perch, for he just climbs down again and climbs up on me. I think it must be mating season."

Archie blinked his long lashes and crooned deep in his throat.

Edward strode across the room and disentangled a very reluctant Archie from Eliza's hair, setting him back on his perch. "Eliza," he said, "I have come to remind you that we are expected at the Clarkes' for Christmas dinner in two hours. I didn't want you to forget."

Eliza shut her ledger. "Yes, of course. I hadn't realized how late it had become. Happy Christmas, Edward."

"Happy Christmas," he said, slightly disconcerted. Eliza might be mad, but when she smiled at him so, she looked uncommonly attractive. Edward was not accustomed to thinking of his wife as attractive in any way, so he turned on his heel and removed himself before he caught the contagion that seemed to be running rampant around Seaton.

It didn't help to discover that Eliza had spread her disease all the way to Keble Park, for she was embraced not only by Marguerite and George, but also by the other guests.

"Edward?" Marguerite said at his shoulder, distracting him from watching Eliza's reception.

"It is pleasant enough being home," Edward said in answer to her question, accepting a glass of sherry. "Tell me how you have been keeping."

"We are well, as are the children," Marguerite replied equitably. "We have so enjoyed Matthew. Eliza has brought him to visit quite often. He is a lovely child, Edward. You are very fortunate."

"Thank you," he said, feeling slightly uncomfortable.

"Oh, do not thank me. He reminds me very much of you, and Eliza, too. How clever of you to have chosen her as your wife. I always knew you were more intelligent than the average man. You must be making her very happy. She is looking decidedly well."

"Yes, she is," Edward said smoothly. "You were most kind to her in town. I am very appreciative."

"Nonsense! I adore Eliza, you know that. We all do. She is a most interesting woman, as well as being possessed of a generous spirit. But I do not need to wax on about your own wife to you. No doubt you appreciate Eliza even more than we do."

Edward agreed and edged away, wondering whether everyone in the whole world had gone insane, save for him. He was stretching so hard to keep an open mind that it felt as if the wind were blowing through his skull.

He kept a close eye on Eliza throughout the afternoon, but found nothing in her behavior to censure. Indeed, he could not help but be surprised that his quiet wife was always at the center of a conversation. She exhibited neither the shyness nor the silliness he had previously seen in her, but what she did have to say, he could not hear, for he was seated a fair way down from her at the table. She did seem to have a gentle dignity about her as she conversed; he had never really noticed what fine posture she had, nor what an attractively slim figure. He had noticed before the curve of her breasts—far too often over the last few days for comfort. And he had often before noticed the slender column of her neck, for he had wished to put his hands around it and choke her on numerous occasions. Oddly, he had not once had the impulse to do so since he had come to Seaton. Indeed, she had become a welcome companion.

A welcome companion? Now he was losing his mind. Seaton always had a strange effect on him, and he supposed that having Eliza there dispensing domesticity counteracted the feeling of rattling around a mausoleum. If only Eliza had had an iota of intelligence, for he would have easily settled for the usual mediocrity, then they might have had a chance at something. She could be amusing and warm, and she was a good listener even if she didn't understand half of what he said. It was hardly her fault, after all.

She really was an attractive woman in her own unique way. He'd have bedded her in an instant if he'd thought she'd have had any ability to respond, for his loins had been ridiculously and constantly on fire for a week. But his prior experience with Eliza did not lead him to believe it would be a satisfactory encounter. It was a shame. The glimpses of thigh he'd had through the material of her skirt showed him that they were long and slender, and, oh, those breasts . . .

"You are distracted today, Edward," Marguerite said, leaning toward him with a light laugh. "Perhaps I should have broken all the rules and seated you next to your wife, for you do not seem to be able to take your eyes from her. And here I had thought to favor myself with an amusing dinner partner."

Edward's eyes snapped from Eliza to Marguerite. "I beg your pardon. I was only wondering how my wife would manage in a gathering such as this. It is the first time we have attended a function in the country."

"Eliza has been to a few, but you are doing very well, Edward." Marguerite was delighted with his startled expression. Edward was not behaving at all like himself, Eliza was no longer playing the fool, and it seemed that the marriage was finally progressing as it ought—or was just on the brink, for Edward did not yet have the look of a man satisfied in love. Indeed, he looked like a man consumed by frustration. Really, it was most gratifying to see the rake who had always had any women he wanted with a snap of his fingers in such a condition. Eliza would bring him to his knees yet, and Edward, the foolish man, could not see it coming. She well remembered her George when he had been in this dazed state.

"Do you know, Edward, marriage has wrought such a change in you," she said mischievously. "It pleases me to see it. Tell me, how do you find Seaton? We think it so improved overall. The house is much more comfortable. I do like what Eliza has done with the library. It was always rather austere in nature before this, but with the changes she has made, it is positively friendly, do you not think? Of course, hothouse flowers do make such a difference, and with Eliza's greenhouse you can have as many as you choose. Your dear wife always brings me armfuls now that she's no longer running it as a business."

"A business?" Edward said, not paying much attention.

"Oh, did you not know? Eliza is very clever about botany.

She had a flourishing flower business at Sackville, but now, of course, she hasn't the time, with all of her other responsibilities. I'm terribly glad you've come, for she was telling me just last week how much needed doing."

"Was she?" he said, his eyes traveling down the table again.

"Yes, George and she have spent much time in discussion, but it is all over my head, I'm afraid. I do know that she is eager to have a steward."

Edward's attention settled fully on Marguerite. "I have told her I will engage one as soon as possible. I hadn't realized she was anxious over the matter."

"Oh, Eliza has a tendency to overwork, I've found, although she won't admit it. Sackville was bad enough, but Seaton—nine thousand acres and that enormous house. It is quite a lot."

"Eliza seems happy enough. She keeps busy with her cows and chickens and the running of the house, but she hasn't complained to me about overwork."

Marguerite stared at him in disbelief. "Her cows and chickens?" she asked weakly.

"Yes," he said blithely. "She transferred her livestock from Sackville. You must be aware that Eliza has an unusual fondness for animals."

"Edward . . ." Marguerite began, then snapped her mouth firmly shut.

"Yes?" He speared a forkful of turbot and looked at her inquiringly.

"Nothing. Absolutely nothing. I only wonder how you manage to run your Caribbean plantations so successfully when you cannot see the forest for the trees, or the jungle for the trees, I suppose it would be."

Edward frowned. "If you are referring to Mr. Nash's mismanagement of Seaton, I do take full responsibility, Marguerite. I hope to correct the matter shortly, as I told you."

"I am not referring to Mr. Nash at all. I simply do not wish to see you make the same mistake twice, and it seems to me as if you are well on your way. But it is up to you to find your own way through the tangle you have made of your affairs. I will say no more on the matter, for I can see I have annoyed you in the extreme." She turned and addressed the person on her left, leaving Edward to ponder her cryptic statement, angry and baffled and miserable all at once, and not knowing why.

The party eventually retired to the drawing room, by which time Eliza noticed that Edward was in a thoroughly withdrawn mood. She wondered if he might not be feeling a bit out of sorts, given that it was Christmas. After what he had told her the night before, she could well imagine how Christmas at Seaton might affect him. He had been unusually quiet all afternoon, even pre-occupied, most unlike himself.

She was about to approach him when he moved from his position near the windows and went over to one wall, peering at something with interest. Eliza's eyes followed, and she froze. She had quite forgotten that Marguerite had hung her sketches. They had been a harmless present at the time, but now . . . Oh, dear God. Edward was no fool. He'd be sure to recognize the one she had deliberately given away.

"Look, Eliza," he said, glancing over and seeing her standing rooted to the floor a few feet away. "Marguerite has three of Mr. Babcock's original sketches, if I'm not mistaken."

"Oh," she said, not meeting his eyes, "how nice."

"I know you do not care for the pen-and-inks, but I thought you might at least enjoy seeing these. I don't believe any of them are in the book."

"Actually, Edward, if you don't mind, I think I'd like to go home. I am feeling tired all of a sudden."

"Certainly," he said, noting that she did suddenly look quite pale. Perhaps it was the strain of being with so many people all afternoon. He felt a sudden pull of concern. "Perhaps you should sit down. I'll call for the carriage directly."

"I see you have discovered my treasure." Marguerite approached them with a smile, ignoring Eliza's pleading look. "I hope you are still not out of temper with me, Edward."

"Not in the least," he replied equitably, forgetting his annoyance with her in his pleasure over the sketches. "How curious you should have these. How ever did you manage to find originals? I'd give my eyeteeth to have them." He walked along the wall, admiring each of the three sketches in turn.

"Mr. Babcock has become a friend. Perhaps one day we can introduce you," Marguerite replied, smiling at Eliza, who wanted nothing more than to murder her good friend.

"Yes, I would like that." Edward's voice trailed off as he looked particularly closely at one etching. "But how peculiar," he said, curiously sharp in his voice.

"What is that, Edward?"

"This scene . . . it seems so familiar."

Eliza's heart sank lower than she'd thought possible.

"Yes, I am particularly fond of this one," Marguerite said. "I wish it had been included in the book. There is something about the mother and her newborn babies that is very appealing, isn't there? I don't usually have a fondness for mice, but the depiction is rather tender, is it not?"

Edward glanced over at her, his eyes puzzled. "Yes. I cannot help but wonder if I have not met Mr. Babcock. I am sure I would have remembered, but perhaps not. And yet this scene . . . I observed something exactly like it. It would be extraordinary if there had been another such occurrence in exactly these surroundings. One would think that the artist would have had to come along at that exact moment, but I was quite alone. Ah, well." He smiled ruefully at Marguerite's look of curiosity. "These days I find that very little in my life bears explanation."

"I think you must have it, then," Marguerite said, lifting it from the wall. "I am sure Mr. Babcock would not mind in the least."

"I couldn't possibly accept such a present, Marguerite," Edward said with surprise.

"But naturally you can," Marguerite replied. "It is Christmas, after all, and the Duchess of York insists on giving presents to all her guests, so it is *comme il faut* for me to do so. Please, Edward, take it and know it will give me great happiness for you to have it. You did introduce us to A.E. Babcock in a roundabout fashion, after all."

"Then, since I do not wish to be churlish, I thank you very much. I will certainly cherish your gift, although I shall have to be very careful in the future not to admire anything else in your house, or I shall find Seaton furnished with Keble belongings, and Eliza is bound to object." He glanced over a her with a smile, but it faded as he saw again her drawn look. "Will you excuse us, Marguerite?" he said quickly. "Eliza is tired from all the festivities, and I should take her home. Thank you so much for a pleasant Christmas, and for the picture."

The snow was now falling in earnest. Edward was silent on the drive back, and Eliza did not interrupt his thoughts. She felt too shaken to speak to him. He sat next to her on the seat, the picture on his lap, his thumb absently tracing the gilded wood grain of the frame. It was extraordinary to her that he held in his lap the very scene that they had both observed, a depiction of the moment she had fallen in love with him. It was even more extraordinary that he was completely oblivious to both facts.

An unfamiliar tension radiated from him. It was not the irritation she had become accustomed to in London, nor the cold, terse manner with which he had treated her before that. This was different. It emanated almost palpably from his body, as if he were consciously holding himself in check. She scanned her mind to see if there was something she had done to anger him, but could think of nothing concrete. It had to be the season, she told herself again. Perhaps over dinner she could find a way to cheer him up.

She went upstairs to see to Matthew, for it was by now his bedtime. And then, since she hadn't checked on the cows earlier, and the cowman, being a Roman Catholic and a good son, had gone home to visit his mother for Christmas, she decided to change her dress and visit the barn. They were to have a late supper so there was plenty of time.

Immediately she slid open the heavy door she knew something was wrong. The animals were restless, and as she brought her lantern around, she saw that Clementine was lying in her stall, her head low.

"Clementine," she said, hanging the lantern on a hook and going to kneel beside the cow, running her hands over its abdomen.

It was taut, too taut. It looked as if Clementine might be in labor, and it was far too early for her to have her calf—five or six weeks too early. Eliza had been concerned about her being due in early February, as it was. But a premature calf in late December? It was not a good thing. She gathered up some blankets from the little room adjacent and settled down in the hay to watch, praying she was wrong.

Edward had seen Eliza hurrying off to the barn and had almost gone to stop her, for the snow was picking up in force, promising to build into a fierce winter storm. But Eliza was Eliza, he reckoned, and would probably not sleep if she didn't kiss her livestock good night, no matter how tired she was. He pulled out a folder of invoices that needed attention before the new year and turned his concentration to them. His attention kept slipping. Eliza had not returned, as far as he had heard, and when the chime on the clock went on the half-hour and then eight times on the hour, and then again on the half-hour, he decided he really ought to see if she had come in the back way. He hadn't been happy with her pale complexion, nor with how silent she'd been on the drive home. He hoped she wasn't ill from something . . . Marguerite's comment about overwork flashed into his mind, although he couldn't see how she could be.

He knocked on her bedroom door but there was no answer, so he pushed it open. The handle had been fixed, he saw. His father had had it tampered with so that his mother could not leave her chambers; she'd escaped by way of the window instead. He had gleaned that information by pressing his ear against the housekeeper's door shortly after the event. He had not been back in it since, not until he'd discovered Eliza locked inside.

The bed was turned down and candles burned. A night rail had been laid out and a book lay open on the bedside table, but there was no sign of Eliza.

She had changed the room. The fabric against the windows and hanging from the bed was a rich, earthy green with a fine golden stripe running through it. There were none of the odds and ends scattered about that he would have expected in a lady's bedroom—indeed, that he was accustomed to seeing. Instead, he noted a pile of leather-bound journals at the desk and a number of sharpened quills. Curious, he went over. For someone who had little brain, Eliza had a disproportionate number of books and writing materials. He looked around him. There was a table near the window that held a drawing pad, pens, and inks. Pens and inks? He thought she disliked them. He casually flipped open the sketch pad and his hand paused as he looked down.

Eliza had done this?

Edward picked up the pad and examined it more closely. It was a view of the main street of the village as seen from the hill behind Seaton, delicately but accurately depicted and well-executed. The road curved past the church and the few shops, the river winding in the background. A cat sat in the foreground, observing the street, its back to the artist. He knew the view well, but there was something else that seemed familiar about it.

He slowly placed the pad down and his eyes traveled carefully over the room. There were stacks of books everywhere, neat stacks, certainly, but from their spines he could see that they were not gothic romances. Kneeling down to examine them, they seemed to deal primarily with agriculture and natural history.

A nasty suspicion began to form in his mind and grew larger and nastier by the moment.

He stood. Marguerite's odd words that afternoon came back to him. It wasn't like her to criticize, nor to involve herself in his affairs. But she had looked mightily surprised and then guarded for some reason when they had been discussing Eliza in the context of Seaton.

Nine thousand acres and an enormous house. He couldn't see the forest for the trees, she'd said.

He noticed an open book on the bedside table. Walking over, he discovered it to be the Seaton ledger, columns of neat figures with notes jotted in the margins—not in Nash's writing—and updated as to yesterday. And he'd thought Eliza spent her mornings scribbling nonsense in the morning room.

Overworked? Edward felt his blood begin to boil as all sorts of pieces fell crashing into place. Hopelessly stupid? Unable to concentrate? A mind like Swiss cheese?

Eliza.

She had hoodwinked him, damn her, flummoxed him with her vacant stares and idiotic conversation. The woman had been running Seaton single-handedly for the last six weeks, and doing it well. It was no bloody wonder the staff sang her praises. She'd given them much-needed direction and no doubt had been paying their wages out of the money he'd given her.

"Damn you, Eliza," he roared, throwing the ledger onto the bed. Here he'd been, making a complete fool out of himself. Peter obviously had known the truth, Marguerite certainly did, probably everyone but him had been aware that Eliza's brain resembled anything but Swiss cheese.

Why? Why had she sought to deceive him so? It made no sense. Wait until he got his hands on her! He'd make her regret every last *non sequitur*, every vapid word, every moment of pretense.

Looking around him one last time, Edward softly closed the door, feeling he had somehow invaded her private realm, and returned downstairs. Where was she? Surely she couldn't still be out at the barn, not with a storm raging?

He went back to his papers, but now he was completely unable to concentrate. Finally throwing his quill down in frustration, he stormed up to his bedchamber, changing into buckskin breeches, top boots, and a warm jacket. He went downstairs again, cursing Eliza. The woman might try to have some semblance of common sense, he told himself as he pulled on his greatcoat, picked up a lantern, and went trudging off in the direction of the barn, battling the wind and blowing snow as he went. She was probably down having a nice coze with the new housekeeper she'd brought from Sackville, but he'd be damned if he'd descend that far to find her.

His mind worked furiously over the last three months, from the time he had first approached Eliza, trying to see everything she'd said and done in a different context. And then his step slowed and stopped as he arrived at the last few hours.

He ducked his head inside his greatcoat as a blast of snow came up into his face. He trudged on, becoming more furious with Eliza by the moment, swearing that if she wasn't in the barn he would do her murder when he did find her. If she was in the barn, he would do her murder that much faster. The wool pulled over his eyes? It was a far greater skein than he'd ever imagined.

He had just realized why the drawing in her pad looked so familiar. Marguerite had given him one very like it only a few hours ago. A different subject matter, to be sure; an entirely different country, for that matter. Apparently Mr. Babcock had removed to England and was now sketching the English countryside. Apparently Mr. Babcock was living in his house, residing in the upstairs bedroom next to his own. Apparently, Mr. Babcock was his wife.

Eliza had a great deal of explaining to do.

12

> "I cannot fix on the hour, or the spot, or
> the look, or the words, which laid the
> foundation . . . I was in the middle before I
> knew that I *had* begun."
>
> Jane Austen, *Pride and Prejudice*

Edward was rewarded for his struggle with the elements
when he saw a crack of light through the barn door. He
pushed it aside and quickly slid it across again, looking
around the dim recesses.

He stopped in his steps. There was Eliza, cradling a cow who
was down and hunched up on its side. She was stroking its
swollen belly, crooning softly. He watched her for a moment,
knowing that she was oblivious to his presence, completely concentrated on her task.

Eliza. A.E. Babcock herself, naturalist, writer and illustrator
of one of the more exceptional chronicles he had ever read,
flummoxer *extraordinaire*.

He found himself smiling, his anger suddenly gone. She did
look rather adorable draped around a cow, he had to admit. His
heart tightened in an unfamiliar but not unpleasant fashion.

Eliza, as if she sensed herself being observed, looked up with
a start. "Edward! What are you doing here?"

"I came to find you, silly woman. Don't you know there's
a blizzard raging outside?"

"Yes, I heard the wind. It's warm enough in here, though.
But why—I mean, why did you come to find me?"

She looked truly bewildered, he thought as he approached.

"I don't suppose it occurred to you that I might wonder where you were and worry about you?"

"No. Why should it have? You've never wondered or worried before."

Edward couldn't think of a reasonable reply to this entirely accurate statement. "What's wrong with the cow?"

"She's gone into premature labor. Edward, I don't know what to do. The cowman's not here, and the veterinarian's too far away to summon in this weather. He'd never arrive in time. I don't suppose you've ever birthed a calf?" she asked in a small voice. "Clementine's had some experience, but I haven't, not under these conditions."

"I take it Clementine is the mother and Matthew's favorite Clemmy of story fame?"

"Yes. I don't know what I'd do if anything happened to her, but Matthew—he'd never forgive me. Do you know anything about difficult births? I think she's in trouble and I don't think I'm strong enough to help her."

Edward pulled off his greatcoat and removed his jacket, then his shirt. It seemed foolish to start railing at her under these particular circumstances. The cow was clearly in trouble from the look of it. "How long has she been going?"

"I don't know exactly," Eliza said gratefully. "When I found her, she was already down and I think she must have been for some time. There hasn't been any bleeding, but her water broke some time ago and she'd been straining ever since, at least an hour now, with no results. I examined her a few minutes ago and the calf's not presenting properly, Edward—it's breech. I found a swelling on Clemmy's leg that indicates she might have had a fall. I think her labor might have been brought on by that."

Edward gave Eliza an incisive look as he sluiced his arms in the bucket of water she had standing nearby. "For someone who knew nothing about conception, much less birth three months ago, you seem to have acquired a good bit of knowledge, my lady. You certainly seem to be up on dystocia."

Eliza had the good grace to blush. "I have been reading."

"I saw. Your room is littered with books. You have an interesting selection, including the current ledger."

"You went into my room?" She looked horrified.

"I was looking for you, Eliza. I did not deliberately invade your personal property, if that's what you are thinking."

"No. Of course you wouldn't."

"I do, however, have a number of questions to ask you."

"Yes, whatever you wish," she said, distracted from his words. Her arms went around Clementine's neck as another contraction shook the cow and she strained to no avail. "Oh, please, Edward, help her. I don't think she can go on much longer like this."

"Hold her head," Edward said curtly, thankful he'd watched the process before, although it had been a horse with a mal-presentation. He eased his arm into the birth canal, feeling for the calf. His hand found only a soft rump, not the tiny hooves he had hoped for. Eliza was right; it was a breech presentation. "Listen to me, Eliza. This is not going to be easy. The last time I saw this, the foal had to be pushed back into the mother so that the feet could be pulled out. They get hooked on the pelvis. She'll never get the calf out like this."

"Do whatever you have to, Edward. At least the shoulders should be small enough that they shouldn't get stuck."

Edward laughed as he started to push the calf back. "Easy enough for you to say," he grunted. "You're not down at this end. It's a bull calf, by the by. Come on, Clementine, try to help out here." Already his arm felt as if it was about to be broken with the force of the cow's contraction, pushing in the opposite direction.

"She's exhausted. I think her contractions are becoming weaker. That should help."

Edward nodded, sweat beading on his body. He waited until the contraction subsided, then pushed again. For an hour it went on like this, Edward nearly as exhausted as Clementine as he used all of his strength trying to get the calf far enough up in the birth canal to get hold of the legs. Eliza spoke softly, a constant stream of encouragement, and his respect for her steadily grew. She was not the least bit repelled by the sight of blood and various other fluids, which by now Edward was covered in. Every now and then she'd come down to him and wipe his face with a towel.

"You're doing beautifully," she said. "How does it feel now?"

"Close, I hope," he said with an effort. "I have a hold on the feet. It's hell trying to get these damned hock joints over the pelvis. Wait—there we go. Good. Good girl, Clementine. Now you can push for all you're worth.''

He pulled with all of his weight behind him, praying the shoulders wouldn't stick. And then he felt the body suddenly release. It came slipping out into his hands as Clementine gave one last push and a moan of relief.

The calf was very small and nearly hairless, but it was full of life, kicking its little legs frantically. Eliza was instantly at Edward's side, a blanket in her hands. ''Edward,' she said in a whisper. ''Oh, Edward, thank you.'' She rested her forehead on his slick shoulder for a moment.

He smiled at her in reply, and Eliza colored and moved away. She pushed the newborn calf up toward his mother, already beginning to rub him down with the blanket, just in case Clementine was too weak to stimulate the calf herself. But Clementine looked around with heavy eyes, then saw her baby. She made a low noise and her fat nose went out, nudging her calf closer as her great tongue began to wash him.

''Let's get Clementine up on her feet. If she stays down, she won't have a chance,'' Edward said after a few minutes when the calf was clean and dry. Together they pushed and pulled until Clementine struggled to her feet. Eliza sat back on her heels and watched. Within five minutes Clementine had the calf also on its feet and nursing, and its suckling was strong, she was delighted to note. The afterbirth was delivered without a problem, and Eliza felt a profound sense of relief that everything was going to be all right, after all. She washed, then turned to Edward, half-expecting him to be gone. Instead, he was leaning back against the stall wall, his arms folded across his chest. He'd cleaned himself up and put his shirt back on. His eyes bore into hers, deep blue into deep brown. There was no question that he had other things on his mind than the birth of a calf.

''Edward? What is it?''

''I think it's time we had a talk,'' he said. ''Perhaps another stall would do? There's no leaving the barn in this weather, and I think Clementine and her calf should be left in peace. I'm sure they'll be fine.''

Eliza nodded, swallowing hard. ''I made a fire next door. There's a proper room—it's for the cowman when things like this come up.''

Edward pushed away from the wall and followed her, picking up his jacket and greatcoat from the hay. Eliza felt a terrible sinking in her stomach. There was a reckoning coming, and although she knew she should welcome it, it was not a pleasant prospect. She held open the door to the small sleeping quarters, wondering just how she was going to manage to explain herself.

"You must think me very stupid, Eliza," Edward said as an opening comment.

"I do not think you stupid in the least, my lord. I imagined it was the other way around. You have always thought me stupid."

Edward crossed the room to put some more wood on the fire. He pushed at it until it caught flame, then turned to look at her. "I'm delighted that you're prepared to be direct, Eliza, although I now know that your tongue is capable of giving a very effective lashing when you so desire. You have been indirectly using it on me for three months. It takes someone of a very astute intelligence to succeed at the sort of game you've been playing. Tell me. Why would you want to deceive me in such a way?"

She dropped her gaze. "It seemed the only defense." Her voice was very quiet.

"The only defense? For pity's sake, Eliza, why would you have to defend yourself from me? Why would you want to make yourself appear to have an affliction of the brain?"

"Because I knew it would disgust you."

"I see. It was important that you disgust me?"

"Yes."

"Do you mind if I ask why?"

Eliza looked into the fire. "I mind, but you deserve an answer, given what I have done." She took a deep breath. "In the beginning I felt uncomfortable around you. I have never been very adept at social conversation, and I knew you already thought me stupid, so it was easy enough to behave that way. It gave me satisfaction to annoy you."

Edward nodded. "I suppose I can understand that. You thought I wanted Sackville, and you thought that if I did not like dealing with you, then I would go away."

"Yes."

"An interesting tactic. But why continue such an absurd pretense after we were married?" He leaned his shoulder against the rough wall and watched her intently.

"I was very angry with you, Edward. I thought to make you regret your action."

"You did an excellent job. You had me in a constant state of fury and regret. I cannot think it was easy for you, though. I imagine it was quite exhausting, in fact."

"Yes, so it became. But in the beginning it truly was easier, for I felt less vulnerable in a very upsetting position. Despite what you thought, I did not want to be a marchioness at all, nor go about in society. That sort of thing is painful to a person with my looks and disposition."

"Whatever's the matter with the way you look?" he said in confusion, forgetting he had ever had a low opinion of her.

She spun around. "Oh, for the love of God, Edward! At least do me the courtesy of returning honesty for honesty. It is difficult enough as it is without having to deal with some belated effort at kindness." She furiously wiped at her eyes.

"Eliza . . . Eliza, please don't cry. I'm afraid I don't know what to do with tears."

"I'm not crying," she said, sniffing hard. "I never cry."

Edward smiled. "Of course you don't. Invincible Eliza. Listen, my dear, I have no experience with belated kindness, and I certainly have no argument with the way you look, if that is what you think. I think you are very attractive, truly I do. Why would you think otherwise?"

"Dear heaven, Edward, you really must think me a sapscull," she said with exasperation.

"But that's the point: I thought you a sapscull because you led me to believe that was the case. I cannot be pleased that you made a fool out of me, Eliza, but I haven't much of a leg to stand on, have I? I haven't treated you very well, I know. But much of that came because I didn't think you had two thoughts to rub together, so you cannot blame me entirely. You played your part exceedingly well."

Eliza wrapped her arms around her waist. "I did, didn't I?"

"Yes." He moved away from the wall and took her lightly by the shoulders, turning her to face him. "I do know that you have been running Seaton. I should thank you, although it wounds my considerable pride."

"Thank you."

"But there are some other, larger questions that I have. You still haven't adequately explained to me your reasons for playing me the fool. Why did I make you so uncomfortable? Looking back, all I did was to appear at Sackville unexpectedly, and I can't think why that would immediately launch you on a campaign to mislead me. Surely you couldn't have thought in the first five minutes that I wanted to take Sackville from you?''

Eliza could not meet his eyes. "No. I only came to that conclusion later.''

"Then why, Eliza? We had barely met before that. I cannot think that I had given you any reason to feel uncomfortable or to dislike me. I suppose in Jamaica you thought me a conscience-less rake, intent on nothing but the pursuit of pleasure.''

"I did not initially think that, no. I thought you quite different from the others. I certainly thought you different from the person you chose to have others assume you were.''

Edward sighed. "You are astute, aren't you? And I suppose that the entire time I was playing, you were watching in your careful way?''

Eliza blushed furiously and Edward suddenly hit his forehead with his fist. "Dear heaven. You really were watching carefully, weren't you? Ah, Eliza mine, what a true fool I feel. The mice. You must have been there. I can think of no other explanation.''

The red stain spread to her neck and chest. "You know?'' she said in a whisper.

"Yes, I worked it out on the way over here. I worked a great many things out, while alternately cursing you and then myself. Babcock was your mother's maiden name, was it not?''

Eliza nodded.

"I should have remembered long before, but I wasn't exactly thinking in those directions. Clever Eliza. You've been pulling wool right and left. Marguerite knows, doesn't she?''

"And George. But only them. They figured it out on their own.''

"Having the advantage of knowing you properly, they would. And the A?''

"Alice. My Christian name.''

"Yes. Now I remember. I saw it on the marriage certificate. Eliza suits you better. Alice Eliza Babcock Austerleigh March, Marchioness of Seaton. You do have rather a lot of names, haven't you? I suppose they go well with a diversity of per-sonalities.''

"Edward, I wish you would not make light of me. I feel quite foolish enough as it is."

He laughed. "No, no. Foolish is no longer in your vocabulary, remember—only in mine. So, you crept up on me unawares as I was secretly indulging in a spot of mouse-watching, waited for me to leave, and immediately recorded the incident. You then had the discretion to keep my sentimental tendencies to yourself, for you knew that my reputation would have been irredeemably compromised had it become public knowledge that the urbane Marquess of Seaton had a habit of watching rodents giving birth. Disgraceful."

Eliza smiled. "Utterly. Certainly far too human for the cold and haughty Edward March. I was very taken."

"Then, why, my dear naturalist, knowing and appreciating my deepest weakness, did you decide to alter your opinion of me? What did I do between then and our next meeting here in Oxfordshire? You have made it very clear that I must have committed a grave error."

"Not a grave error, Edward. You merely spoke your mind and I happened to overhear you. It's the sort of thing that can happen to anyone."

Edward gave her a curious, questioning look and then paled as comprehension dawned. "Oh, dear God. Not the night of that deadly Denigham ball? Lowdry. He issued a challenge and I turned it down. Eliza, I'm so sorry. I honestly had no idea you were anywhere about."

"I didn't think you would be quite that cruel. It was enough to hear."

Edward groaned, cursing himself for his thoughtless tongue. "Listen to me, Eliza. I hardly remember what I said now, but I know it was probably not considerate. I assure you, I meant nothing. Lowdry was always issuing absurd challenges, and it became a game. This time it involved a seduction, I remember that much. Whatever it was I said, I swear to you that I meant nothing by it. How could I? I did not know you."

"Perhaps not, my lord, but your words were nevertheless barbed and so they wounded."

"I've gone through my life barbing my words, Eliza. Perhaps, like you, it provides me with a defense. And I had a reputation to uphold at the time. That, too, offered me protective coloring." He smiled ruefully. "My carefully nurtured reputation seems to have gone completely by the wayside since I have married you. I have become respectable. Not a single mama has grabbed up her daughter and fled.''

"I cannot be sorry, although I hope you have not allowed a simple marriage of convenience to stand in your way.''

"Eliza, you can be most disconcerting. And, no, I have not let it stand in my way, but neither have I found a reason to go elsewhere.''

Eliza blushed furiously.

Edward smiled lazily. "How interesting you look when you color like that. I cannot help but wonder how far down such a blush spreads.''

"Edward! Do not start playing the rakehell with me now. It is a bit late for that, and I cannot be amused.''

"Amusement was not what I intended. Do you know, Eliza, since you began leaking your true personality over the last week, I have come to see you in quite a new light. What made you decide to give up your game?''

"I was tired of fabrication. Somehow it did not any longer seem appropriate. Seaton has become home to me and, in any case, in all conscience I could not behave like an imbecile in front of Matthew, for he would have been most surprised. Children tend to be so much more perceptive than their adult counterparts.''

"So I am beginning to see. It is a good thing you have revealed these parts of yourself in small doses, or I might have been completely overwhelmed by tonight's revelations.''

"I doubt much can overwhelm you, Edward. You seem to deal with life with astonishing *sangfroid*.''

"When it suits, yes I do. But I have recently noticed my blood boiling on a number of different occasions, almost all of which have had you either directly or indirectly involved.''

"I can hardly apologize.''

"I do not expect you to, although I think some of the reasons it has been set to boiling might surprise you. But I would ask you to tell me something, and tell me honestly. Do you hate me, Eliza?''

Eliza stared at him. "H-hate you!''

"Yes, hate me.'' Edward regarded her with an intensity she had never seen in him. "You have every right. I have treated you abysmally; I have been every kind of fool; I have, in fact, been a huge lout. I have most certainly not given you the credit that is your due. In short, I have been incredibly stupid.''

''I am also at fault,'' Eliza said, unable to resist a smile. ''Although you are quite right. You have been very stupid.''

Edward gave her a long look. ''I suppose I deserved that. I will take it to mean that you accept my apology. It's never much mattered to me before what people think, but for some reason it matters tremendously that you do not hate me.''

Eliza had never thought to see Edward look so humble. He was sincere, that much was very clear. She stepped toward him and rested her hands on his chest. ''Edward, I do not hate you. Far from it.''

He sighed and reached a hand out to stroke her hair. ''That's good. It's a bloody miracle, but it's good.''

She looked at him, perplexed. ''Why does it matter so much?''

''Ah. That's not quite so easy. In fact, it's extraordinarily difficult.''

''Please, Edward, whatever it is, I think we have established that honesty is best. I would rather you tell me than leave me to wonder.''

He smiled. ''You have the mind of a true adventurer. Very well, I can hardly thwart you in your pursuit of my inner recesses, which are most unfamiliar to me, I might caution you. It seems, my dear Eliza, that I've become extremely fond of you.'' His voice was very low.

''You have?'' Eliza's heart had begun to pound in an alarming fashion, for it felt as if it might not stay in her chest much longer.

''I have. I realized it at some point after wanting to pull all of your teeth out by the roots when I was coming down here, and at some point before that cow of yours was about to crush my arm into a useless pulp. When is not really important, although I do believe it might have been seeing you lovingly entwined with Clementine that first brought it into my mind.''

''Oh.''

''I can see now why Peter spent so much of his time in incipient hysteria. You made good sport of me, Eliza. It really does take a very clever person to be able to pull off something like that on such a grand scale.''

''I'm sorry, I truly am, Edward.''

''Don't be. I am very glad to know that Mr. Babcock has

changed his sex, for it makes it so much easier to express my appreciation for his fine mind. Forgive the way I must smell, but I owe you this. For my sins, sweetheart.'' He put a hand under her chin and lifted it, gently lowering his mouth onto hers.

Eliza felt her blood leap and rage through her veins at his touch, and her mouth softened under his, opening quite without any conscious thought. Her arms seemed to have the same will of their own as they moved around his back and tightened, and she pressed herself full-length against him.

"Dear God," Edward said on a wondering note, raising his head and looking down into her eyes, "I was wrong about a great many things, wasn't I?''

"I don't know,'' she whispered, reaching her mouth up to his again. "I don't care.''

Edward pushed his hands through her hair and captured her face. "Eliza, look at me. Look at me—this is important. I will not take advantage of you, not ever again. But if I kiss you now, then I shall make love to you, right here where we stand, for I won't be able to help myself, despite how filthy I am. Is that what you want?''

"I wish you'd stop explaining things to me, Edward," she said, her cheeks flushed. "I thought you had realized that I have a perfectly clear understanding. Perhaps I should explain to you instead. If you don't kiss me, then I shall have to kiss you and make love to you right where we stand, for I shall not be able to help myself. And I smell just as much of Clementine as you do, and I couldn't care less.''

Edward laughed, his face alight with an unexpected passion. "What have I been missing?'' he murmured. "You do amaze me, Eliza.''

"Good. I feel that I amaze myself also. Show me, Edward, how lovemaking is really meant to be, for I find that I want to know most dreadfully.''

He stroked her face, thinking that he had never seen anything quite so precious. Her eyes were luminous as she gazed up at him, and he felt as if she were handing her soul into his keeping, a terrifying prospect. "I'm not sure I know myself,'' he said gently. "I have never embarked on lovemaking and love at the same time. I think it will be a new experience.''

Eliza drew in a sharp little breath, and he laughed and ran his hands down her arms. "Is that so shocking? I suppose it is. I think I have finally succeeded in shocking myself. Show me too, Eliza, how it is really meant to be, for up until now I think I have only been playing at it.''

He drew her close and kissed her again, but this time there was no restraint. His mouth possessed hers hungrily, his tongue seeking hers and tangling with it in a fierce and demanding dance. He heard her moan, and it only inflamed his senses further. Picking her up, he moved her onto the low straw pallet, caressing her throat, kissing her ear, seeking out the little crevices with the tip of his tongue until she was shaking beneath him.

"Eliza," he murmured, pushing her dress from her shoulders and exposing the white skin to his hands, thinking that his blood would surely sear his veins. "Eliza," he said again, freeing her breasts and gazing at them, drinking in the sight of her naked flesh. He lowered his mouth, licking and nuzzling the peaks until she moaned and her hands tightened in his hair. She thrust her hips against him in reckless, uninhibited desire, and he raised his head to drink in the sight of Eliza in her first foray into passion. Her head was thrown back, her eyes shut, her breathing rapid, her lips slightly parted. Her eyes slowly opened and he smiled to see what they held.

"You are beautiful," he whispered, and took her mouth in a deep kiss, and she wrapped her arms around his neck and kissed him fiercely in return, her mouth tasting like honey and mead and Eliza's own special sweetness.

"I'm not beautiful," she said against his lips, determined to have nothing but the truth between them, despite the fact that she felt she was swimming underwater and couldn't quite breathe. "I have freckles and a dent in my chin," she managed to say.

"A dent?" he replied with amusement, slowly stroking her throat. "No. A lovely, enticing cleft. And as for freckles, your skin is smooth and soft and quite as unique as you are. I have become fond of your freckles also. Do not let Jeanette completely eradicate them, for I fear I should not know you."

"Not know your bran-face? Oh, Edward, how appalling!"

"And your nose . . . How could I not appreciate a little nose that turns up just so in the most frivolous manner?" He kissed it.

"I abhor my nose."

"Ridiculous. Do you question my excellent taste?"

"I have hideous red hair. You said I was a carrot-top."

"And so you are. I adore carrots. I find I have become unreasonably enamored of carrots. I will have carrots for breakfast, lunch, and dinner."

"Edward, you called me a scarecrow." She nuzzled her nose in his neck, drinking in his scent.

"No. Now, that I must deny. You have a most appealing form, that I can swear to, for it has made the sweat break out on my brow a number of times."

Eliza raised her head. "The sweat, my lord?"

"From the effort of controlling my baser masculine instincts. Your body is beautifully shaped, what I have been able to see of it, but your breasts, Eliza . . . I have suffered agonies over the sight of your glorious breasts." He lowered his head to them again.

"Oh," Eliza gasped. He was pulling on her nipple in a manner that threatened to completely undo her, and at the same time his hand was stroking over her abdomen in a very enticing fashion, causing her to wish for him to do the most shockingly erotic things to her.

"Would you make love with me on a cowman's pallet?" he asked, his tongue stroking up her throat to the hollow beneath her ear as he removed all of her clothing, his eyes wandering up and down her long, beautifully formed body, conditioned into sleekness by constant exercise.

"What better place than a cowman's pallet?" she said, shivering uncontrollably. "Truly, Edward, your orchestration is most impressive. Oh!"

"My orchestration, sweetheart, is entirely accidental and born from a desperation that has been building for longer than I had realized. But I want this to be right for you, not like the last time. What I did I have been ashamed of ever since."

Eliza took his face between her hands. "Do not think of it, Edward. Things were different then. I might have told you how I felt rather than teasing you so terribly and pretending to be ignorant and indifferent."

"How you felt?" he asked slowly, looking down at her. "I thought you despised me."

"No. I loved you, you see."

"You loved me?" He looked truly shocked.

"Yes. That was what made everything so much more difficult.

I had tried to convince myself that I didn't care at all, but it simply wasn't true."

Edward dropped his head onto her shoulder. "Oh, Eliza, I had no idea, none at all. My God, I used you badly."

"No," Eliza said, running her hands through his thick hair. "I don't want to think of it that way. I want to think we were both ignorant. And I want you to show me how it can be."

"I will show you, sweet Eliza. I will show you all I can. And then I have no doubt you will take over from there and show me things I have never dreamt of." His hand moved up her thighs, slowly, seductively, stroking up and down, lightly tracing the long muscle beneath her velvet skin, knowing she was as aroused as he was. He waited until her long legs fell apart, begging for his touch. Then and only then did he touch her, gently, generously, as she writhed underneath him, gasping as he slowly and intimately stroked her with sensitive, exploring fingers.

"Ah, Edward, that feels so good," she whispered, quite out of her mind with pleasure. "Don't stop. Please don't ever, ever stop."

"Eliza," he said, "I have to stop just for a moment, or I won't be able to go on." He quickly removed his breeches and came back to her, relishing the feel of her hands and mouth wandering over his flaming skin, smoothing, kneading, caressing, kissing until he thought he could bear no more. "I want you." His voice was rough with his need. "God, how I want you."

"I want you too—all of you, right now, for I do not think I can wait any longer."

Eliza raised her knees and welcomed him as he guided himself to her, and he knew she did it freely and from the depths of her soul. He slid into her, thinking that it was the most natural thing in the world, the most incredibly right thing he had ever felt, this sheathing in Eliza as if they had been made for each other. He waited for a long moment before beginning to move in her, and then he was careful, very careful to be sure that she was comfortable.

"It is wonderful, Edward," Eliza murmured against his shoulder. "But I do not think you are usually this tame. I am not made of glass, you know."

He looked down at her, seeing the laughter in her eyes. "Wanton," he said with a grin. "Then I shall show you, my lady, what it is you are made of." He thrust deeply into her, and Eliza answered him, calling him to her in a rhythm that was as old as time and just as familiar to him. But now all familiarity fled as he was taken beyond simple physical pleasure and into a place of heat and light and love and union. He felt himself drowning in Eliza, in her love, for that was unmistakable, in her uninhibited giving, in her simple acceptance that raised them both out of the ordinary. It was Eliza, he realized, who was teaching him what it was he was made of.

He gathered her up in his arms and drove into her one more time, feeling himself shatter and feeling her shatter with him in a physical communion unlike any he had ever experienced.

"Dear heaven," he eventually managed to say, smoothing the hair off her brow and pulling her over onto her side next to him. "That was remarkable."

"Mmm," Eliza answered, and stroked his mouth with a finger. "I don't believe it's anything like the bull covering the cow, after all."

Edward laughed. "Nothing like." He pressed a kiss to her breast. "Bulls pay absolutely no attention to a cow's udder, none at all. You really do have the most beautiful, delectable twin udders I have ever come across."

"I am happy they please you, Edward," she said, grinning.

"Please me? I have been dreaming about your breasts for the longest time. I swear they have grown more delectable by the week, for I haven't been able to keep my mind off them."

Eliza cradled his head. "I never knew breasts had a purpose other than the obvious," she said. "Had I known they were going to have such an effect on you, I should have bared them years ago. I would have stripped my dress from my body when I saw you that day by the river, and walked toward you quite naked, knowing you would be inflamed by the sight and would take me right there on the riverbank, mice forgotten. History would have turned out quite differently."

Edward, whose imagination had been captured by this tantalizing image of Eliza naked on the bank of the Rio Grande, rolled over onto his back. "I think," he said slowly, pulling her over on top of him, "that I am exceedingly glad that A.E. Babcock turned out to be a woman, or what I have done and am about to do again would not be at all the thing. However, as it stands, A.E. Babcock is about to have another and most enlightening lesson in natural history. Pay close attention, Eliza. You might want to record the enormous ingenuity and variety that *homo sapiens* is capable of bringing to the sexual act.''

Eliza smiled. ''I have found field experience invaluable. Come, my intrepid husband, and show me how these things are properly done.''

A few hours later she woke. The fire had died down, now only glowing embers in the hearth. Edward lay sprawled next to her, his arm thrown over his head, his breathing deep and even. His body was curved slightly toward her, one leg bent at the knee, the rough blanket covering only his hip and thigh.

She admired the broad span of his chest, the strong, cleanly developed muscles, the lean, ridged abdomen. He was a fine figure of a man, indeed, but much more important, he was Edward. She could scarcely believe he was hers: her husband, her lover, her friend. He had given her his inner self and there was no greater gift. Had he had no hair, no muscle, no flashing blue eyes, she could not have loved him more.

Dear Edward, so vulnerable, so afraid of showing it, so proud. How much better she understood him now, how her heart went out to him, how her body embraced him

She smiled softly. Edward was a wonderful lover, careful to give her pleasure, sure to see that it was as great as his own, waiting, controlling his release until he was certain that he would bring her along with him. Eliza sighed, drinking in the scent of fresh hay, relishing the warmth of Edward's body next to hers, listening to the wind howl around the barn, all of her senses heightened. How had she ever become so lucky, she, homely Eliza Austerleigh, whose husband had just made her feel like the most beautiful, desirable woman on the face of the earth?

She carefully slipped out of bed and went to stir the fire into life, shivering a little in the cold air, for she wore no clothes.

''There is something, isn't there, about spending Christmas night in a cow barn?''

Eliza looked down to see Edward's eyes open and watching her. ''Actually, there is,'' she said. ''I wouldn't be surprised to find the Three Kings outside the door and a newborn child in a manger just about now.''

''I think we've had enough miracles for one night. We have a newborn calf in the stall, and each other. Let's not be greedy.''

"I'm too full to be greedy about anything."

"You, my darling wife, were born to fill the senses and soul all at the same time. Standing there without a stitch on, you put me in mind of a druid priestess, Christmas notwithstanding. You're tall and noble and all aflame."

"Yes, and my modesty is screaming at me while my pride will not allow me to cower."

"Come here, then, my valiant druid, and let me show you again why it is that your pride is for once correct." He moved to make room for her, and the blanket shifted off his hip. "Anyway, the pagans celebrated the winter solstice with all sorts of earthy delights long before the Christians came along, so we have them to thank—"

"Edward," Eliza exclaimed with delight as the leaping fire caught his flesh in its shimmering light.

"Was it the mention of earthly delights?" he asked dryly as she bent over his hip.

"You have a mark just like Matthew's!"

"Yes, I do know. Mavis pointed it out to me first thing. Not mine, you'll be happy to know. Matthew's."

"But how would she have known . . . Oh! Martha."

"Exactly. I'm surprised your own eagle eye didn't spot it earlier. We Marches have a tendency to pass it on the way we do arms and legs and all the rest of the odds and ends children are born with."

"So that's how you knew Matthew was yours," she said, tracing the crescent with a finger. "How very wonderful."

"Mmm. That feels very wonderful, indeed. And, yes, it was a useful way of identifying him. But right now I do not want to think about Matthew, or Martha, and I most certainly do not want to think about Mavis. I want only to think about you, Eliza, and how glorious you look and feel and taste." He reached his hand out and captured her around her waist. "My very own pagan priestess. It really is quite a coup. There aren't very many around these days, especially ones that can draw. I do believe I might enshrine you, Eliza," he said, pulling her down next to him. "Or at very least write an ode to you: 'her breasts lush as ripe melons, her limbs as long and slender as a unicorn's . . .' "

Eliza burst into laughter. "I think you had better leave off the ode, for I do not think you have a talent for it. In any case, you have a mark on your hip, my lord, that is a sure sign of favor from the gods. If you must compose bad poetry, then I shall draw an enormous picture of you and hang it in the front hall: his lordship in all his glory, with one crescent moon on his left buttock. The servants will be thrilled. No doubt they will see it as a favorable omen.''

Edward grinned. ''Yes, most favorable. I might have panting serving girls lined up outside my bedroom door, begging for a peek.''

''To find me just inside, hatchet in hand.''

''Ah, Eliza, you must love me greatly to want to protect my honor.'' He kissed the palm of her hand. ''Will you marry me?''

''I thought I had.'' She moved slightly away from him, the laughter going out of her eyes. ''But if you asked me tonight whether I would marry you of my own free will, I would not hesitate.''

He went very still. Then before she could comprehend what he was doing, he sat her up and took her hand in his, working the heavy gold band off her finger, while Eliza watched him, mystified.

He held the ring up between them, the gold leaping in the firelight. ''Eliza,'' he said, his voice strained, ''I know our wedding was not a happy time for either of us. There was too much that was wrong between us—suffice it to say I behaved very badly. But I know now that I love you. The words are new to me, so I don't speak them very well, or very romantically, or whatever it is one is meant to do. I honestly don't know if I can make you happy, as you so greatly deserve, but I would like to try. Will you let me?''

Eliza's eyes sparkled with tears, but she smiled. ''You really are such an idiot.''

Edward gave a short laugh. ''I know. I'm not very good at sentimentality, am I? I just wanted to be sure that this time when I put this blasted ring on your finger it will be with your sanction.''

''To tell you the truth, I feel quite odd without it. Do put it on quickly, Edward; my finger's growing cold.''

''Dreadful woman, will you be my wife?''

''Naturally I will be your wife. I have been your wife three times over already, four if you count the beginning of October.''

Edward put the ring back on her finger with a very broad

smile. "Then, in that case, you shall be the most married woman in history by the time you reach your fortieth year. And imagine what people will think when you're seventy—you'll be a proper scandal. Now, stop your chattering and come here."

He pulled her down and came over her, lowering his mouth onto hers and effectively silencing any further comment Eliza might have wished to make.

13

She was a woman of mean understanding,
little information, and uncertain temper.
Jane Austen, *Pride and Prejudice*

Edward and Eliza went back to the house in the very early hours of the morning, just as dawn was breaking over the eastern sky. The snow had stopped, but great drifts were piled up against the side of the house, and the fields were covered in a thick layer of white.

They walked hand in hand, not speaking, each content in a personal solitude, wrapped in a mutual peace. There was not a sound. Eliza felt as if the whole world had gone into a magic sleep that night and only they had been left awake to discover each other. Now, with the pale sun pushing up over the horizon, the spell would soon disperse and they would be back in the realm of everyday reality. She could not help but wonder what sort of an effect that would have on Edward. She was not foolish enough to think that love was so simple as to be acknowledged in a blazing night of shared passion and ever thereafter maintained in that condition. Edward was a complex man with many flaws. She was equally difficult. They had many things in common, including a stubborn streak, vile tempers, and an overabundance of pride. It would be an interesting marriage, however it worked. She, at least, had had the advantage of loving and being loved by her mother. For Edward, given everything he'd told her, this was his first experience with that uneasy emotion.

The house was still. They climbed the stairs, still without speaking. Edward paused on the landing with an odd look on his face.

Eliza stepped away. "I'll be in my room should you need me," she said softly, and he nodded, then walked off in the direction of his own chambers.

Eliza gave herself a thorough wash and changed into her night rail, wondering whether Edward would come to her or choose to stay on his own. It was an important decision, and it would tell much. She had already promised herself not to expect emotional intimacy from him, to accept what he was prepared to give, as difficult for her as that might be. But Edward had a great deal of healing to do, and she had learned long ago with animals that sometimes the thing they needed most when healing was distance.

She would leave the choices up to him.

Eliza slid under the cool sheets and curled on her side, tucking her hands under her cheek, wondering at how different she felt since the last time she had lain there. She was the same Eliza, but not. She had been indoctrinated into a new aspect of her womanhood, had learned much about her body and her capacity for sexual passion. She no longer felt homely, for Edward had looked at her with desire and had very clearly expressed that desire to her. She knew perfectly well she was not beautiful, but if she was beautiful in Edward's eyes, she was more than content. She had had the very satisfying feeling that he had been looking as much into her as at her. It was strange: it was the first time since her stepfather had made his outrageous proposal that she had felt comfortable about her body, that it was a thing of joy and not something to be disgusted by. For years she had lamented her generous breasts and tried to hide them, and now she took pride in them because they gave Edward pleasure—not to mention the pleasure she'd discovered they could give her.

On that happy thought, Eliza sighed and settled down to sleep, her mind drifting in drowsy wisps and fragments of dream. And then she felt the weight of the bed shift and Edward's arms come around her. He smelled freshly washed and his skin was still slightly damp but warm as he pulled her close against him. She smiled as sleep overtook her.

* * *

"Eliza, now where the devil did you put the ledger?" Edward demanded, poking his head into the upstairs linen room, where Eliza was counting linens with Annie.

"Did you look on your desk, Edward?" she replied, looking over her shoulder with a smile. "I have not seen it since then. If it is not there, you might look—let's see that's ten, eleven, twelve, Annie—you might look in the bedroom, for you might have brought it up last night after your discussion with Peter. I don't think you were concentrating when you came to bed."

"That's true," Edward said with a grin. "It must have been the excitement of seeing Peter again. We must engage a steward, Eliza. It's absurd having to hunt down the ledger every time one needs to make a note. Matthew, do cease this hanging on my leg."

"Let's go, Papa. You said we would go."

"Matthew, please be patient. I'm speaking with your father. Whenever you decide, Edward. There's still plenty of time before the spring planting. Sixteen, seventeen, eighteen."

Edward smiled. "I think we should leave your mama in peace, Matthew. She's far too busy counting pillowcases to pay any attention to us. Let's go see to that pony now."

Matthew hopped up and down. "Hurrah!"

Edward swung him up on his shoulders and headed down the stairs. There were times he could hardly believe how ordered his life had become. He made a quick stop in his bedroom, now a medley of his things and Eliza's, for she used her own room only for dressing and to hold her books. Sure enough, the ledger was exactly where Eliza had predicted. He scooped it up and proceeded downstairs, pausing only to make a note of the latest feed bill before bearing Matthew off out the door.

"Good God!" He halted in his step to find Pamela Chandler and an unknown female descending from a hired carriage.

"Oh, Lord Seaton," Pamela exclaimed. "What good fortune to find you at home! I had so hoped . . . Oh, you must think me utterly without manners, but my abigail and I have met with disaster, and we thought we'd prevail upon darling Eliza to shelter us for a few days."

"Disaster, Miss Chandler?" Edward asked coolly, removing Matthew from his shoulders. "What sort of disaster?"

"Oh, is this your little boy? How delightful, to be sure. You

see, we were on our way up to Lincolnshire when our carriage
had a mishap. The weather has been so dreadful and the ruts
in the road . . . well, our carriage went over and now they say
it will take days to mend, and since we were so close, I thought
it would be better to ask for hospitality here than to have to
stay at some dreadful inn for all that time. I do hope it is not
an inconvenience,'' she finished uncertainly, not at all sure she
liked the menacing look on his lordship's face.

"You will have to speak with my wife," Edward said shortly.
"I am sure she will tell you whether it is an inconvenience or
not. Matthew and I have a previous engagement. Wyatt," he
called over his shoulder, only to find that Wyatt was already
standing behind him.

"My lord?"

"Show Miss Chandler into the drawing room and have her
ladyship summoned. Tell her it is entirely up to her own
discretion what she chooses to do about the matter. Come along,
Matthew."

He took him by the hand and walked past Pamela and her
abigail without another look.

"Well," said Pamela, thoroughly put out, then picked up her
skirts and followed Wyatt into the house.

"You are so terribly kind, Eliza," Pamela said, sipping her
tea. "I knew you would not hesitate to extend your hospitality,
given all the time we shared together."

The implication was clear enough to Eliza, but she chose to
ignore it. It was bad enough to have Pamela there; to respond
to her barbs would only make things worse. "I am sure we can
make you comfortable for the few days it will take to mend your
conveyance."

"How nice that will be. I do so look forward to growing better
acquainted with your husband and child. What a very comfortable home you have here."

"Thank you. We find it so. Perhaps you would like to be
shown up to your bedchamber?" Eliza said, rising and going
out into the hallway.

Pamela inclined her head and followed.

Eliza saw Pamela safely put away, then picked up her cloak
and went for a very long, vigorous walk.

Edward found her some time later standing in the middle of

their bedroom, her back turned away from him and very stiff, her arms straight down by her sides, the fists clenched. It was by now a familiar stance and a certain sign of temper, and he paused just inside the room, carefully shutting the door.

"Eliza?" he ventured cautiously.

She spun around. "Edward, it really is too much! I don't mind Peter in the least, for he is perfectly charming; he may stay as long as he wishes. But she is a scheming miss and I cannot bear to have her in this house, chattering on, sure to flutter her eyes at you, and generally being disruptive, and how you could allow her to carry on in such a way—"

Edward had crossed the room and gathered her into his arms by the time she had reached this last remark. "You are quite correct, sweetheart, on all counts. But see here, it is a perfect opportunity to put paid to all Pamela's foolishness while allowing her an opportunity to see how well we suit each other. We can make all sorts of allusions to an intimate past that did not exist, and we can make all sorts of allusions as to an intimate present that does exist. Most happily," he added, gently nipping her earlobe.

"It is no good thinking you can soften me by nuzzling my ear, Edward, for you know I cannot resist it. But it does not change my mind about Pamela. It was hard enough living with her for two long years and suffering all sorts of humiliations at her hand, but to have her invade us here at home, I simply cannot like it. Anyway, she is stupid," she added uncharitably. "Who do you think was my model?"

Edward chuckled. "I had thought as much all on my own. Now, cease your temper and let me love you before dinner, or I shall not eat a morsel."

He bent his head to her neck, and Eliza thought it was to her credit that she let him open her wrapper and cup her full breasts in his hands, that she let him pick her up in his arms and fall onto the bed with her, that she let him do delightful things to her and slake his thirst in her as if he had not done the very same only that morning, for, really, she had every reason to be out of temper with him.

"Oh, Edward," she cried, forgetting all about Pamela as she wrapped her hungry arms around his back and her legs about his hips. "Oh, Edward," she cried more softly, feeling him empty himself with a moan, and found herself lost in her own intense pleasure yet again.

Really, she thought as Jeanette quietly dressed her only a half-hour later, Edward made it very difficult to stay cross with him for very long.

"What a marvelous chef you have, Lord Seaton," Pamela trilled as if Eliza was not present at the dinner table. "I have seldom had a such fine Cumberland sauce, and the mutton! It is a marvel."

"Thank you, although you must direct your praise toward Eliza, for she trained our cook herself."

"Oh, really?" Pamela said with ill-disguised surprise. "I was not aware that you knew anything about cooking, Eliza, dear."

"Didn't you? There was never a reason to go into the kitchens. I learned from my mother."

"Oh, yes. Your mother," Pamela said as if the subject of Eliza's mother was most unsuitable. "My own mother believes such things best left to the cook. Will you be coming back to London, my lord, now that Parliament is open?"

"No. I have never taken my seat and have no intention of doing so now."

"Oh! My papa says—"

"I am sure your papa is a highly esteemed gentleman, Miss Chandler, and an exemplary servant of the crown. I, however, am not. Nor is Eliza. We find that we like to pursue different pleasures." He smiled at Eliza with such warmth in his eyes that it brought a rosy blush to her cheeks. "Country life suits us very well. Which reminds me. We have a winter calf, did Eliza tell you? Out of Clementine."

"Clementine?" Pamela repeated, completely confused and rather shaken by the look Lord Seaton and Eliza had just exchanged.

"Yes, Clementine," Eliza said, picking up on Edward's cue. "She's a fine breeder, although the calf was early. Edward named him Bottom. From Shakespeare," she added, trying not to laugh.

"No point prevaricating, Eliza. It was the first thing I felt of him," Edward explained. "There's nothing more invigorating than delivering a calf. We often did it together in Jamaica, didn't we, sweetheart?''

"Calfing, do you mean?" Eliza said, delighted by the laughter in Edward's eyes. "Oh, yes! And when Matthew was born," she said, adding to the fiction, "Edward was right there, telling the midwife just what to do. She became most annoyed. Edward threw her out.''

"Good heavens!" Pamela looked genuinely shocked as she grasped the meaning of this statement.

"I cannot tolerate overbearing females. I have always held to the policy that if you want to see something done right, do it yourself.''

"I am sure Edward would have borne Matthew himself if he could have. He kept telling I was being dreadfully inefficient.''

"Well, really, Eliza, all those faces and peculiar noises you insisted on making. I've never seen anything like it.''

Edward glanced up to see Wyatt's face going through contortions. "But I suppose it is most improper to be discussing birth in front of the servants.''

Eliza had to bite the inside of her cheek to keep from laughing, and she gave Wyatt an apologetic look. They had long ago agreed that Edward could be a most difficult master, and now was clearly one of those times, judging by Wyatt's now stony expression. Wyatt had recently been most elucidating about the truth of Edward's childhood, but there were some things even Wyatt would not forgive, even though he knew Edward was making an effort, and she could hardly blame him if he censured them both for his evening's work. "Tomorrow I shall take you to visit Bottom in the barn, Pamela," she said, trying to change the direction of the conversation. "He is terribly sweet, only four weeks old.''

"The barn? Oh, but I really don't know if I want to visit a barn.''

"Nonsense, Pamela," Edward said heartily. "It's a particularly good barn. Why, Eliza and I spend a great of time there mucking it out. We're saving the manure for the fields.''

Pamela had gone completely pale. She put her fork down with a shaking hand. "M-manure?''

"It makes the most marvelous fertilizer. Did you not know?''

"I did not, no." She shuddered.

"Ah, well," Edward said on a sigh, "I can't expect everyone to share my interests, I suppose. It is enough that Eliza does. We have come to realize how well we suit, and we have only you to thank, Miss Chandler, for bringing us together in the beginning. We had quite forgotten until recently how very much we did have in common other than Matthew. Good evening, Peter," he said, having seen him standing in the dining-room door for the last few minutes, unsuccessfully trying to keep a straight face. "Do look who's come directly on your heels."

Peter came into the room and bowed. "Miss Chandler. What a surprise. I had thought you were on your way to Lincolnshire. Or at least so you told me when we met in London only three days ago. You said nothing about stopping here."

She colored hotly. "It was unexpected. My—my carriage met with an accident."

"Did it? You chose an interesting route. Aren't you slightly out of your way for Heckington?"

"I have friends in Coventry," Pamela said defensively. "I was to stop there."

"I see." Peter accepted the chair that Wyatt had pulled out for him. "Where is Archie this evening?"

"We thought he might be happier having his dinner in peace," said Eliza. "He doesn't respond well to high-pitched noises when he's eating. Would you care for some dinner, Peter?"

"I would, thank you. Please excuse my tardiness. I was delayed in Oxford. I do believe I might have finally found you a steward."

"Really?" Edward and Eliza said in unison. "Who?"

"A gentleman named James Trevor."

"James Trevor?" Edward said with astonishment. "Not James Trevor from Cambridge?"

"The same. He has recently left a job in Hampshire and is seeking a new post. We came across each other quite accidentally. His references are excellent and his experience is everything you could ask for. If you and Eliza plan to divide your time between England and Jamaica, he might be exactly the person to have in place."

"A more honest man could not exist. What astonishing luck!"

"I asked him to come around first thing tomorrow morning.

I hope you don't mind, but as he was in the area, it only seemed practical. And I remembered what good friends you were at university."

"That suits admirably. You must be there for the interview, Eliza. Trevor is a Scotsman with a frugal streak but a generous nature, and he does love the land, so you need have no fears on that score. You don't mind, do you, sweetheart?"

"I'm terribly pleased," she said quietly. "I know you have been delaying making a decision because of what Graham Nash did. If this a man you can trust, then we must have him. I know you have come to care a great deal for Seaton."

She smiled at Edward, and he reached out and took her hand. "Gentle warrior," he said. "You've fought for that, haven't you? And you're quite right, I have, although part of my heart still lies in Jamaica, as I told you last night."

"As does mine, so it suits very well."

"Good. So we will leave directly the spring planting has been seen to?"

"Oh! I had thought not until later next autumn, Edward. Wouldn't it be nice to see the first harvest brought in? We have been working so hard to plan it."

"But with Trevor here . . . Oh, well, I suppose I can wait. It would be foolish to rush back and arrive just in time for the rainy season, and I do have perfectly competent people in place."

"Thank you," she said with relief. "I hope a year will not be too long for you to be away."

Edward laughed. "I am sure my people are delighted by my protracted absence. And I really would rather be here with you, bringing in the harvest. Sheaves of wheat always did make my heart beat faster."

"You know they do, Edward, so it's foolish of you to pretend differently."

"How did your business go in Oxford, Peter?" Edward asked.

"It was interesting. I hadn't wanted to say anything until I had the facts from the buyer, but apparently I am in direct line for an earldom. A cousin very recently died in a drowning accident and his elder brother was killed in Spain some years ago. The present earl is not well. He heard I was in England

and wished me to be informed." Peter took a spoonful of the soup that had just been placed before him.

"Which earl?" Edward asked impatiently. "There are not all that many in England, but neither are there so few as to be immediately apparent."

"Blakesford," he said, taking another mouthful.

Pamela sat up.

"Good God," Edward said, astonished. "I had no idea you were related."

"It was a sore point in the family. My father would not have anything to do with the man. It's a long story, but my father ended up poor as a church mouse. What money I have I derived from my mother. Theirs was a very unfashionable love match at the time. So it stayed, you'll be happy to know."

"How encouraging," Edward said wryly. "I imagine this will probably change our business situation."

"Yes. Unlike you, I think I would rather live on the estate full-time. I have no appreciable land in Jamaica, only my Kingston house and the shipping concerns we share, and I believe it would suit us both well to have me here to oversee them when you're not here. It's been a bit wearing going back and forth all these years."

"It is a shame, but I suppose my own situation has changed much. We will still see each other quite often."

"Yes. I cannot say I am pleased by the change. It will take time to adjust. My cousin is not expected to live much longer and I'll have to go and visit, I suppose. He's meant to be a cantankerous old fool but desirous of seeing his newest heir."

"Oh, but he would be, Lord—I mean, Mr. Frazier," Pamela said brightly. "After all, a man on his deathbed . . . Well!"

Peter only looked at her, then shifted his attention back to Edward. "I think next week I shall take myself to Leicestershire and introduce myself. He will no doubt prod me with a bony finger to see if I have any meat on my bones. I shall no doubt prod him to see how long I have left to my freedom."

"Before thinking about wife and children?"

"Exactly. Duty and all of that."

"It's not such a terribly bad thing," Eliza said, looking at Edward with amusement. "Actually, it can be quite pleasant."

Edward raised an eyebrow. "Pleasant, my lady? You do the

situation an injustice. I would say, maddening, delightful, at times fraught with torment, at other times fraught with joy. But certainly nothing so spiritless as pleasant.''

Peter burst into laughter. "Oh, dear. I hardly think that sounds relaxing. But then, you are married to Eliza. I cannot think there is more than one like her.''

"Do you not think a family of your own the most delightful thing, Mr. Frazier? I am sure I do.''

"How nice for you, Miss Chandler. I think you must find yourself a husband to give you the happiness you deserve.''

Pamela, misunderstanding him, sighed ecstatically. "I shall do my very best, sir, to make my husband very happy. I desire nothing but the satisfaction of seeing him so.''

"Let us leave the men to their conversation, Pamela.'' Eliza, knowing Pamela's deep desire to be married to a wealthy and titled gentleman, could see there was nothing positive in the direction Pamela was springing off in. Edward had very effectively accomplished the desired result of putting Pamela off him that evening, but now it appeared it was to be Peter's turn. Eliza could not relish spending the next half-hour or so alone with the woman, but there was little choice. She accepted Pamela's very uncharitable look in her direction as she rose and led her away.

The next day, Eliza went off to pay a visit to Marguerite. There was nothing for it but to bring Pamela along with her, for Edward and Peter were otherwise engaged. Eliza was most distracted. She had liked James Trevor tremendously and had been instantly assured that Seaton would be put into the best of hands. Edward had felt the same way, for he had hired Mr. Trevor on the spot. It would be interesting handing over management to him, albeit a bit wrenching, but she was beginning to tire more easily and needed to think of herself for a change. That was the second distraction and the reason she needed to speak to Marguerite, but she couldn't think how to divest herself of Pamela, who had suddenly ceased her hostile behavior and become positively cloying.

"Eliza, my dear,'' Marguerite exclaimed, happily accepting an armful of Eliza and the hothouse flowers at the same time. "It seems an age, although it was only last week, I know. Tell me how you have been keeping. Miss Chandler, how delightful," she said, slightly bewildered as Pamela appeared behind Eliza. She instantly took in Eliza's look of entreaty. "Now that you are here I should so like for you to see our house, Miss Chandler, although sadly I cannot conduct you myself, for I have business with Lady Seaton. There is a most interesting gallery. Perhaps you will go with my housekeeper, Mrs. Harper. She is very knowledgeable. Roberts, do take Miss Chandler to Mrs. Harper. You don't mind, do you, Miss Chandler? We will be so boring for you to have to listen to. Do join us for tea when you are finished."

Roberts bore Pamela off before she could say much by way of protest.

"Now, Eliza, tell me everything, for I cannot wait another moment," Marguerite said. "The last time I saw you, you and Edward were dealing famously. How does it go?"

"Very well, although Pamela's precipitous arrival has put me very out of sorts. She is the most annoying creature, and I find I cannot be charitable. At least she is no longer ogling Edward, but has turned instead to Peter, who also just arrived and is soon to become a rich earl. When will she learn?"

"Probably never, for she has no sense. You mustn't let it trouble you, for men can be much more sensible than we give them credit for. It is a pity that Pamela has not married, for it would steady her. I think all she really wants is a house of her own and to be away from her domineering mother."

"Maybe, but Pamela believes that she must marry better than anyone."

"But only because that is what is she has been told, and because her mother has absurd ambitions for her. She hasn't the brain to be able to think for herself, Eliza. I know she was a tyrant while you were in her employ, but she has been for many years at the mercy of her mother."

"I know. She felt better to be able to treat me exactly as her mother treated her. It was nevertheless very difficult to accept."

"Eliza, my dear, I imagine she was a little bit jealous of you. She has superficial beauty and very little brain, and she could hardly miss the fact that you have a great deal of intelligence and the kind of beauty she could never aspire to, for it comes from within. Now, tell me. How are you feeling? Have you told Edward yet?"

"Told Edward? Told him what?"

"About the coming baby."

Eliza stared at her friend. "How did you know? Did Jeanette tell you?"

Marguerite laughed. "She would never say anything. Jeanette is completely loyal and devoted to you. But I could see for myself."

Eliza's hands went to her abdomen, only very slightly rounded. "There is no real change. How could you know?"

"You forget I have had three children of my own. You have that certain look about you. And with the way you and Edward have been behaving, I can hardly be surprised. When is your child due, Eliza?"

"Sometime in late July."

"Ah! I think I see. Your letter told me that you were concerned about something. Is it Edward? I gather you haven't said anything to him?"

"No, I haven't. Edward teases me that I have put on some weight, but I cannot keep it from him much longer. I don't want to keep it from him. I just am not quite sure how to tell him."

"So. If I am correct, this child was not conceived at a happy time for either of you. I am not surprised at your reluctance to tell him."

Eliza shook her head. "I can hide very little from you, Marguerite. You are quite right. Edward feels very badly about that particular night, and as it is the only night it could have happened, he will know that, too. How can he be happy?"

"I completely understand your concern. But women are so much more sensitive about that kind of thing. It will not matter, Eliza. Does it matter to you?"

"No, of course not. I love Edward. I look forward to having his child."

"And I am sure that when he knows, Edward will also embrace the idea. He seems to love you greatly. Please, do not put off informing him much longer, for he is bound to see it for himself. He might feel that you do not trust him or his love for you enough."

"Jeanette has said much of the same thing to me," Eliza admitted. "But Edward . . . he can be difficult, Marguerite. Difficult about a variety of things, most of which I can accept, but in this instance I am very concerned. Edward is proud. I am not sure I quite know how to tell him that a child is to come out of an encounter about which he feels ashamed.''

"But you conceived Matthew under many of the same circumstances. From Edward's behavior, it is clear he adores him. Now that Edward knows he loves you, why would he not welcome another? It hardly matters if you were disgruntled with each other at the time. You will have a child in—let me see—in less than six months. Edward will be as happy as you are, believe me.''

"He really is dear with Matthew, isn't he? Quite besotted, although he'd never admit it. He swears he hates children, but he's actually a very good father. Matthew worships him. Maybe you are right and I am worrying overmuch.''

"But it is wonderful news, Eliza! Perhaps this time you will have a little girl. I am sure Edward will love having a daughter to spoil. Can you not see him now? Really, I am so pleased for both of you. There is nothing like having a baby in the house. I am almost jealous of you. I have always enjoyed my pregnancies, especially when the child begins to move and kick. Most people think it terrible, but me, I feel wonderful. And then, after they are born, each time I tumble in love all over again. Ah, you have given me something to look forward to, Eliza. July will be a joy for us all.''

Eliza smiled, considering. Edward might deeply regret the occasion of their wedding night, but he might after all welcome the fact that something positive had come from it. That possibility had not occurred to her. And he did adore Matthew, despite the circumstances surrounding his birth, it was true.

She resolved to tell Edward immediately. It would be a blessing to have it out in the open.

She would have resolved to tell him even more immediately if she'd known that Pamela had been about to enter the room and had overheard the tail end of their conversation.

14

> "My idea of good company . . . is the
> company of clever, well-informed people,
> who have a great deal of conversation; that
> is what I call good company."
> "You are mistaken," said he gently, "that is
> not good company, that is the best."
>
> Jane Austen, *Persuasion*

E dward had just finished his business with Peter and was
headed out of the house to take a long walk and clear his
head. The ship was about to be loaded with cargo brought
by barge from various places in England, and it was now almost
ready to return to Jamaica. They had been poring over the
various lists, always a tedious and time-consuming task.

He had decided to go to Southampton and see that everything
went smoothly. It was a valuable cargo and he wished to make
sure that everything was loaded exactly to his liking, for
although he trusted the captain, it never hurt to check for oneself.

He didn't think Eliza would mind his absence too much; he
didn't plan to be gone over a week, and now that he had hired
Trevor, Eliza would no doubt be kept busy explaining her
concept of estate management to him. He had already told
Trevor that whatever Eliza had to say, Trevor was to listen to
as if it came directly from him, for she knew as much, if not
more, about Seaton. He was just on his way out the door when
Eliza and Pamela returned in the carriage.

"Did you have a nice visit with Marguerite?" Edward asked,
his mind preoccupied with his plans.

"Very nice, thank you, Edward. She sent her love."

"Hmm. I need to speak with you when you have a few minutes."

"Is there a problem, Edward?" Eliza asked with a smile, seeing he was off in another world.

"No problem. The *Kestrel* is scheduled to sail on Wednesday, and I . . . Never mind. I'll tell you all about it later."

"I'll be upstairs. I'm going to lie down for a while," Eliza went inside.

Edward was just turning away when Pamela said, "It is so exhausting when one is increasing, isn't it? I wonder that Eliza is able to keep up with all that she does. She really ought to get more rest, Lord Seaton. My mama says—"

"What?" Edward slowly turned to face her. "What did you say?" His tone was glacial.

"That Eliza needs more rest in her condition rather than gallivanting off all over the countryside. She was always head-strong, but I should think you'd be most annoyed—"

"What gives you the notion that Eliza is increasing, you idiotic woman, or makes you think you have the place to speak at all?" he said with extreme annoyance, having had more than enough of Pamela Chandler.

"Well," said Pamela, her dignity sorely wounded. "She did just say so to Marguerite quite plainly. I couldn't help the fact that I was about to enter the room, and if she hasn't told you about it, you cannot hold me responsible. She's having a child in July, and I hardly thought she'd hide the fact from you, although I can now see that it was very foolish of me to express my natural concern. I feel quite like a megrim is coming on." With a dainty little sob she put the back of her hand to her mouth and fled indoors.

Edward could not move. He felt as if he had just been cleaved in half by an ax. Eliza, pregnant? It wasn't possible. It simply wasn't possible. But just as he was firmly asserting that fact to himself, flashes came to him of Eliza recently. Her breasts, which he had laughingly sworn were larger from all the attention they had received, were now run through with delicate blue veins beneath the pale skin; and her abdomen, once flat, now had the slightest of swells. And there was her fatigue. On top of that, to his certain knowledge she had not had her menses any time in the last month. And she had definitely not wanted to leave the country until the autumn.

He raked both his hands through his hair as if that could erase the treacherous thoughts that were racing through his head. A child in July? If it was true, that would put conception sometime in October. Oh, dear God, in October, when he had wondered whether Eliza and Peter had been together.

He spun on his heel and strode off in the direction of the fields, walking faster and faster, hoping that would somehow erase his torment and the agonizing images racing through his mind. He remembered all the time Peter and Eliza had spent together in London, their tender departure, their happy reunion only two nights before, the conversation he had interrupted in the library before dinner, when Eliza had looked embarrassed and Peter uncomfortable.

So. It had to be true, then. They had both been lying to him. This last unbelievable month with Eliza had been just that—unbelievable. It had all been based on a lie. Her heated passion, her surprising lack of inhibition had been born of experience with another man. Edward groaned, feeling a pain far greater than any he could ever remember experiencing. Eliza, to whom he had given his love, his trust, his very soul, had been betraying him, had been carrying another man's child all the time he had been making love to her. It all meant nothing. Had she truly loved him, she would have told him the truth.

He laughed derisively. No doubt she thought she could inform him with the greatest of joy that she was pregnant, not having any idea that he could not be the father. No doubt she thought it was the luckiest thing in the world that he had taken her that one night in the beginning of October. And if he had not known about his condition, surely he would have believed her? If anyone felt guilty, it would be Peter, for he was the only other person who knew about his sterility. It was so damned ironic. The one man he had trusted with his secret had gone and put his own child in his wife's belly. How kind of Peter to make up for what Edward was lacking.

It was finished. He'd been taken for a fool. He'd let down his defenses, allowed himself to believe that maybe there was some good in the world, after all, and where had it led him?

Nowhere. The world was still the same rotten place it had always been.

Edward realized that tears were streaming down his cheeks. He wiped them away with his sleeve, disgusted with himself.

His course of action was very simple. He would go home. It would be easy enough to dissolve his partnership with Peter, who was already planning on leaving Jamaica. He would not have to see him again. As for Eliza, he needn't see her again, either. Matthew—Matthew he would miss, he thought with a painful tug, but Matthew could always come to visit when he was older. But he'd be damned if he left Archie behind.

Eliza would look after Seaton. No doubt it would prosper in her capable hands. No doubt she would raise Matthew well. No doubt she would raise both her children well, damn her to perdition. She wasn't worth suffering over. He had learned long ago that it was a waste of time to suffer. He clearly hadn't learned well enough, but he was damned if he'd lose another moment.

Edward turned with determination and walked back to the house.

Eliza sat up in bed, rubbing her eyes. "Edward, what is it?" she said, suddenly frightened. She had not seen him look at her in this cold fashion for months. "Has something happened?"

"Yes. I am leaving directly for Southampton. From there I will take the *Kestrel*, which is bound for Jamaica. The carriage is waiting outside, my bags are already on it. I did not want to leave without telling you my intentions."

"What? Edward! What are you saying? You are going to Jamaica immediately? Have you had bad news?"

"Of a sort."

"Oh, no! I'm sorry. But how long will you be away? Wait, let me dress and pack, and I'll come with you; at least I can stay with you until you have to sail," she said, throwing off the covers and swinging her legs over the side of the bed. "You can explain everything on the way, for I can see you're in a fearful rush. It will only take me a moment."

"No. You will stay here, Eliza. I might as well be plain. I do not plan on returning any time soon. I have left instructions for Trevor. He will answer to you. Seaton funds will pay for Seaton's upkeep, not you, Eliza. He has instructions as to that as well."

"But, Edward . . . I don't understand."

"You don't need to understand any more than that."

"But—but you sound so angry."

"I am not angry. I am simply leaving, Eliza. I doubt very much if I'll be back. I am sure you will cope very well without me."

"You won't be back?" Eliza could hardly speak, her mouth was so dry. Fear made her heart hammer in her chest, until she felt that she couldn't think at all, for it was now clear that Edward was leaving her and she had no idea why. "Have I—have I done something?"

"Have you, Eliza? I could hardly say." He turned to leave.

"Edward," she said, catching at his sleeve, "please, talk to me! You cannot leave like this, with no word, no explanation. Is it the money that arrived from the publisher for the reprinting? Is that upsetting you?"

"Please, Eliza, you are being absurd. Let go of my arm."

Her numb fingers unclasped his coat. "Please," she said with as much dignity as she could summon. "Please don't leave without talking to me. I love you, Edward. I thought you loved me—I know you did. Something must have happened. Whatever it is, I am sure I can explain."

"I am sure you can, but I am not interested in explanations. I must be on my way."

"I see. You really do mean to go, without talking, without any explanation at all." She bowed her head. "I suppose I should have expected it was too good to be true, that something so wonderful couldn't last, but I cannot quite believe this is happening. It is like a dream. All the happiness we have had together, all the love—it is gone, just like that?"

"Just like that. Life is whimsical, is it not?"

Eliza's entire being was rocking with shock, but one thing resonated clearly in her brain, the fact that Edward must know about his child to come. "Edward." She took a deep breath and raised her eyes to him. "I do not know what has happened, and you will not tell me. Very well. There is nothing I can do to change your mind, and I will not grovel at your feet. But there is something you must know before you go, something very important. I had not wanted to tell you like this. I had wanted to wait for a peaceful time, but you leave me no time but this. I—I am going to have a baby."

"Are you? How nice for you. I am sure it will keep you amused. Good-bye, Eliza." He left her standing in the middle of the room, feeling as if the bottom had just dropped out of her world.

"Peter!" Eliza burst through his bedroom door, having only just taken the time to knock. Her face was white and streaked with tear stains.

He took one look at her and jumped up from the writing table. "Eliza! What's happened? Is it Matthew?"

"No, it's Edward. He's gone, Peter. He's left without a word of explanation, gone for good." She bent her face into her hands, trying not to cry.

"Gone? Why? He was perfectly content a few hours ago—disgustingly happy with his lot, in fact. Don't upset yourself so, Eliza. I am sure we can untangle it. Edward's forever doing something starkly dramatic. Nothing's arrived by mail, has it?"

"No," she said, pulling herself together and blowing her nose into her handkerchief. "I asked Jeanette to inquire, and she says nothing has come—no message and no person."

"Did you have an argument?"

"Don't be ridiculous, Peter," she said, sniffing. "I wouldn't be so upset if we'd only had an argument. You know me better than that."

"Yes, I suppose I do. What is the last thing that happened between you and Edward?"

"Nothing the least bit interesting. When I returned from seeing Marguerite, Edward told me he wanted to speak to me. He seemed the same as ever, on his way out of the house. He mentioned something about the *Kestrel*, but he was very relaxed—just distracted, as he often is. Then, an hour later, he was waking me from my sleep, saying that he was going to Jamaica, and he would not give me a reason. I asked and I asked, but he was very angry and distant. He said only that he has made arrangements for Seaton and left instructions and that sort of thing as if he were talking to the housekeeper. He said he's not coming back."

"This is very strange. It is not unlike Edward to fly into the boughs, but to leave in such a manner when I know how much he loves you! Something must have happened to upset him terribly."

"But what? What, Peter? There is nothing I can think of,

nothing at all. When I left him this morning, he was quite himself, and just now I have never seen him quite so cold and forbidding.''

"Pamela," Peter said, his eyes suddenly keen. "What about Pamela? She's a conniving little nuisance. Perhaps she told him some piece of nonsense. She's been pestering him for an age.''

"Oh, Peter, she quite gave up on Edward and his talk of manure last night in favor of you and an incipient earldom. She has no more use for Edward now than for me, except as a way to get to you.''

"I thought I had felt the wind abruptly shifting in that direction. Still, she might have said something utterly stupid to him. I don't suppose you had any sort of conversation at Marguerite's that she might have gotten hold of?''

"No, virtually none,'' Eliza said, frantically trying to remember. "We sent her away while I talked to Marguerite privately, and she did not return until after we had finished.''

"May I ask what the conversation was about? It might be important.''

Eliza flushed crimson. "I—I was telling Marguerite that I am with child, and that I was not sure how Edward would receive the news, given the fact that it happened when we were were first—when we reconciled unhappily.''

"Oh, dear Lord. Oh, dear, sweet Lord in heaven.'' He took her by the shoulders and looked intently into her face. "Are you sure you're pregnant, Eliza? Quite sure?''

"Of course I'm sure, and I think your reaction is most peculiar. It isn't as if I announced I was growing another head.''

"Forgive me, but there's no possibility that the child is anyone's other than Edward's?''

"I should slap you for that remark,'' Eliza said very softly, cold fury flashing in her eyes.

"Indeed. Indeed you should. Please do. No, don't, for I abhor physical violence, really I do.'' He put his face in his hands, having to overcome a most terrible desire to burst into laughter. "Eliza,'' he said, sobering successfully, "I believe I begin to understand what has happened, and I think we both need to sit down. This is not easy to explain to you.''

Eliza gave him a puzzled and highly suspicious look, but obediently sat in one of the chairs facing the fire. "I wish you would try, Peter. Surely it cannot be that complicated.''

"It is, rather, but the bigger problem is having to betray a trust Edward placed in me. However, it seems that it has become such a complex situation that I can think of no other way of explaining it, save for the truth."

"What truth?" Eliza said impatiently.

"I know that Matthew is not your natural child, Eliza. I also know that Edward only married you recently, because he needed a mother for Matthew."

"You do?" she said, horrified. "Why did you never say . . . Oh, I could do Edward murder!"

"Please, do not be upset. He explained it all to me very clearly. He could hardly avoid telling me the truth, given that I was not about to be taken in. I know how he coerced you, I know the entire unfortunate story. But that brings me to the point. Why, my dear Eliza, do you think a man like Edward would feel compelled to do such a drastic thing?"

"Edward is eminently fair," she said defensively. "He did not want Matthew to suffer the consequences of illegitimacy."

"Edward did not even know Matthew, Eliza, nor pay any attention to him before he returned to Seaton in December."

"But he's been everything a father could be since then—"

"So you told me the other night, and I've seen it for myself. I couldn't be happier, but Edward took these measures long before."

"He felt responsible, Peter."

"It is not many men who would risk the kind of illegal action that Edward has taken."

"I don't know why, then. How should I know? Maybe he didn't want the world to know he'd had a bastard child."

"Think of this. As his legally married wife, had you become pregnant, what of your own child, Eliza? Do you think he would have risked that? Your child—the child you are, in fact, now going to have—will be Edward's true legitimate heir if it is male."

"Don't be absurd, Peter. I could hardly care about that, Matthew is as much my own as if I had given birth to him, as well as being Edward's firstborn son. No child I have now or in the future will displace him."

"I am delighted to hear it, but that is not the point. Please use your eminently sound brain, Eliza, and think. Do you really think Edward would have consummated the marriage had he thought there was any chance that a pregnancy might result? The risk would have been extreme."

"He said it had to be consummated. I understood his insistence quite well, once I discovered the circumstances. Matthew could not appear to be an immaculate conception."

"My dear Eliza, forgive me, but there are very simple precautions that can be taken to prevent pregnancy. Did Edward take them?"

"No," Eliza said bluntly.

"Don't you think he would have done, given the circumstances, if he'd thought he might get a rightful heir?"

"Oh, dear God," Eliza said as the full weight of comprehension bore in. "Do you mean that Edward thought he could not have children and so did not bother?"

"Yes. That is exactly what I mean. He had some illness after Matthew had been conceived, and that is what he had been told. I am overjoyed you have proved him wrong, Eliza, but Edward would find it hard to believe. I think that Pamela must have overheard you and Marguerite talking and said something to Matthew about your condition. He would only draw one conclusion, would he not?"

"That the child was not his?"

"It is not as if we have not been previously accused of consorting together."

Eliza stared at him, and then a laugh escaped, and another, and soon her shoulders were shaking quite helplessly. "Oh, Edward. Oh, poor Edward. It is the most stupid conclusion he could have drawn, and the very idea is ridiculous. But what else could he think? I'm sorry, Peter," she said, looking up to see his averted back. "I didn't mean to offend you, but you must see—"

Peter turned around and she saw that he had tears pouring down his face, which was twitching quite uncontrollably. "I—I know. I'm not at all—at all the thing. Terribly sorry, Eliza." He went off into unrestrained laughter.

"Now, see here," Eliza said with an attempt at severity. "It is not amusing in the least when you look at it from Edward's point of view. He loves me very much, and he must be very hurt indeed. I know I was only minutes ago, before I understood. So I must go and find him before he does anything stupid. He is not used to trusting people, you know, and to think that the two closest people to him have been . . . Well, it must make him feel quite dreadful, especially if he thinks a child has resulted. Even more especially if he thought he could not give me that child himself. Oh, poor Edward. He is not the sort of man to take that sort of thing easily.''

"Yes, you're quite right," Peter said, wiping his eyes with his handkerchief. "It's been a terrible thing. You must go directly, Eliza. He's bound to put up for the night at the White Hart, for it's the only sensible place to stop. I stayed myself before coming here. He'll have only an hour or so on you. Shall I go with you?''

"I think that would be a very serious mistake. I shall take Jeanette, for she is most sensible and she will keep me in one piece on the way. You might, however, give a resounding lecture to Miss Chandler and see to it that she is not here upon my return, for I shall not take it kindly if she is. Where exactly is this inn?''

Peter gave her explicit directions, went down to order a carriage, gave the groom equally explicit directions, and saw Eliza off. He then went to hunt down Pamela.

Peter eventually sent a message to Pamela's room, saying that he wished to see her privately in the library, and found that she appeared with alacrity.

"My dear Miss Chandler," he said, indicating that she take a seat on the sofa, "have you been hiding? I have been looking for you everywhere.''

"I wished to be alone, sir. Lord Seaton most upset me with harsh words he spoke.''

"Did you not have the temerity to inform him of his wife's pregnancy?" Peter asked bluntly.

"Oh! He told you? It was quite by mistake, I assure you, and I only said anything at all because dear Eliza has been so tired of late.''

"It was also absolutely not your place to repeat a conversation you overheard.''

"But—but I didn't. I only said Eliza should be more careful of her health in her condition.''

"Miss Chandler, I suggest you listen to me very closely. You seem to have made a practice of alienating the affections of a great many people because of your desire to meddle. I had an opportunity to observe you in Kingston, and also in London, as well as here at Seaton. I do not think you deliberately mean to hurt or to anger in most cases, although I would sorely question your motives in this instance. You were no doubt annoyed with Eliza and felt yourself ill-used. I think your tactic to attempt to engage her husband's attentions was foolish in the extreme. Please, let me finish. I also think that you need to consider what it is you are doing, and why, for people do not often appreciate interference in their affairs. You are a very pretty young woman, and I am sure you will soon find a husband if you would forget your foolish airs and desire to be in the middle of everything around you.''

"Mr. Frazier, I cannot credit that you can speak to me so. It is most forward as well as rude.''

"It is not forward, although it might well be rude. Actually, I speak mostly from a desire to see you take yourself home, where you belong, at least for the moment. It is not a very kind thing to come to Seaton and attempt to lure Lord Seaton away from his wife as you attempted to do all of the autumn. It is also not very clever, for as anyone can see, they are deeply attached. But I do not wish to demean you. It must have been difficult to see your companion win the man every woman wished for her own, however ill-advised that desire, for Edward would have made just about anyone but Eliza quite miserable. Please trust me, Miss Chandler, and look beyond the prize to the person beneath, or you might find yourself deeply unhappy. Once such a thing is done, it is nearly impossible to undo.''

Pamela burst into tears. "Nobody wants me," she sobbed. "I have tried and tried to be everything right, to say all the correct things and be friends with everyone, but it never works. My mama is quite despairing I will ever take with someone of import, and I do not know what is to become of me.''

"It might help," Peter said gently, "if you were to be yourself. I am sure that person is very nice. It does become so exhausting always to be what you think other people expect, does it not?''

Pamela nodded miserably.

"It is not so bad as all that. It might take some practice, but I think you will find yourself much happier to be content with being Pamela. I think it would be a good thing if I summoned your perfectly adequate carriage, which has been waiting quite in one piece at the Swan, first thing tomorrow so that you can go home. Don't you agree?''

Pamela nodded. ''Yes, I suppose. I think I would prefer to take supper in my room,'' she said on a gulp. ''My head is throbbing.''

''I quite understand. Good night, Miss Chandler. I wish you the best of luck with your future. I truly do.''

Really, Peter thought as he settled back with a glass of sherry, life was never dull.

Eliza descended from the carriage and gave Jeanette a nervous look.

''Go, madame, and find your husband,'' Jeanette whispered. ''I am confident that with your love you will bring him back to your side. I will bespeak us rooms. You cannot travel any farther tonight. You must think of the child.''

Eliza squeezed her hand. ''Thank you, Jeanette. You have been all that is good to me.'' She took a steadying breath and marched inside.

In two minutes Eliza, who had learned to be imperious when necessary, was standing in front of a closed parlor door. She bit her lip, then opened it.

''I told you I don't want anything else, damn you!'' Edward's voice came from a wing-backed chair, and she could only just see the top of his head.

''Not even the truth, Edward?'' she asked softly.

Edward jumped to his feet. ''Eliza, what the devil are you doing here? I thought I told you—''

''I chose not to listen to what you told me, Edward. I discovered the cause of your anger, and seeing that you were completely misguided, I thought it would be best to come to you and put you in the correct way of things.''

''You have a great deal of nerve,'' he said coldly, leaning one shoulder against the mantelpiece and crossing his arms.

Eliza, much used to this characteristic pose, felt slightly more comfortable, for at least she knew he was listening.

''I do have a great deal of nerve. I also love you very much. It's a good thing, for how else was I to face you?''

''Eliza, this is pointless. You have gone out of your way for nothing at all. What we had between us is finished. It was foolish of us to delude ourselves into thinking that it could possibly work.''

"Actually, Edward, it is you who has been deluding yourself. I think your considerable pride prevented you from telling me the reason for your anger. Pamela told you about the baby, did she not?''

He frowned. "She did. Inadvertently.''

"Nearly everything Pamela does is inadvertent, Edward. And you immediately assumed that I had, in fact, been sleeping with Peter.''

"Enough, Eliza," he roared. "I will not speak of it. You might have had the courage to tell me the truth, but it is of no consequence now. How dare you come here and confront me?''

"I dare because you are very wrong. Peter told me of your condition.''

Edward spun around and crashed his fist on the mantelshelf. "Damn you both! It was not his place.''

Eliza steeled herself. "He did so to salvage whatever we might have between us. Your doctor was mistaken. I do not know the details of your illness, but I am most definitely carrying your child, Edward. There is no other possibility. I was a virgin when you married me, and the only man I have ever been with is you. Peter is my friend. I do not find him the least bit desirable.''

Edward turned and fixed her with an incredulous eye. "You expect me to believe that? Eliza, I know I am sterile, for the love of God! Do not think I didn't devote a great deal of energy to making sure of that. I tried to get a hundred women with child. Why on earth do you think I engaged in this scheme? I needed an heir, and I knew I couldn't produce one for myself, not any longer, not legitimately. Dear God, woman, do you think I would have gone to these lengths for any other reason?''

"I understand exactly why you did. I am happy for Matthew that you did, for we both have him as our own. We have each other because of it. But the fact remains, I am carrying your child, Edward. Your rapidly growing child, who just had the sense to move inside me on my way here and remind me that there was hope when there was love. I am not sure when you think I would have had the opportunity to conceive a child with Peter, not that I would have ever considered such a thing. But if you do think back, there was a night in the beginning of October, most specifically when you took me to bed after we'd been married, when I did conceive."

"Then tell me, Eliza dear, amid all this earnest talk, why you did not tell me earlier? You are well into your fourth month, if that is the case, nearly into your fifth. I do not see the signs of a pregnancy quite so advanced."

"Oh," Eliza said with relief, "is that what makes you doubt me? I asked Jeanette and she said that women who are tall and fit often do not show for some time. I did not notice myself, not for the longest time, for I did not think one night would be enough. But Jeanette pointed it out to me, thinking it was most odd that a woman who had already had a child would not have realized sooner. I felt quite stupid for not having thought of it myself."

"That is a very pretty statement, Eliza, but then why did you not tell me? You must have known for the last month at least. It seems rather strange that an event over which you should have been so happy instead made you so reticent."

Eliza colored. "I have known for a good month. I knew before you returned. This is why I spoke to Marguerite today. She can be very wise, and I did not know how you would feel."

"How I would feel? You had no reason to think I would be anything but delighted, my dear."

"How you would feel, knowing it had come out of that particular night. I thought you might be very upset. You have told me often enough how you have regretted that occasion. I did not want to cause you to regret it further by presenting you with an unwelcome reminder. Although I gave Marguerite no details, she suggested that she thought you would be very happy and my reticence was foolish. Neither of us had any idea of the other factor at work."

Edward looked at Eliza long and deeply, for this rang of the truth. "You are saying this in all honesty."

"My dear love, I understand why you would doubt me. I cannot think that a child who was abandoned by his mother so early in life would have reason to believe any woman would stay by his side and be loyal to him. And as for me, when you left me today, the first thing that occurred to me in my confusion was that I was unworthy of you, that you had tired of me. But somewhere inside of myself I knew that both of us were mistaken. We have been injured, Edward, by people and events beyond our control, but we have been given a wonderful chance to repair those injuries. I would never lie to you, nor harm you in any conscious way. You mean too much to me, have meant too much from the first. Perhaps then I recognized in you a kindred soul, complete with all the hurt, all the defenses, all the raw edges. I don't know. I only know that I have grown to love you far beyond any expectation I ever had. I feel incredibly fortunate. I also feel incredibly fortunate to be carrying your child, Edward. My greatest wish has been that you would be there at the birth, commandeering the midwife, just as I described last night.''

She swallowed and wiped away the tears that were blinding her. ''If you cannot believe me, then I will find a way to carry on. I will love Matthew, I will bring this dear child into the world and do my very best for them both, for they are yours, and I cannot help but love what is of you. I cannot make up for what was lost to you, Edward, but I cannot carry the blame for your mother's defection, nor can I carry the blame for your father's brutality. I can only be what I am. If that is not enough for you, then I will have to accept the fact.''

She finally stopped, unable to continue. The words had come pouring out without volition. Now she could only turn away, for there was nothing else to do, nothing else to say.

''Eliza.'' Edward's strong hands were on her shoulders, and she turned to look at him, her vision blurred. But what she saw made her heart constrict. He was crying, his face contorted as he pulled her against him. She slipped her arms around his back and held him close to her, pressing her face against his chest as his shoulders shook helplessly with a pain too intolerable to speak aloud. Eliza did not attempt to comfort him. She knew he was struggling with his own demons, and all she could do was be a solid physical presence.

''My Eliza, my sweet Eliza, forgive me,'' he finally said in a choked voice, wiping his eyes and nose with the back of his hand. ''I have been most foolish. You are right. I have let other, older things come between us.'' He released her and sank down into the chair, looking away as he pulled out a handkerchief and blew his nose.

Eliza sat down opposite, waiting, her heart so filled with love

for him that it felt as if it would break with his pain as well
as her own.

"Eliza," he said, having composed himself, "I have been
a damned fool. I have judged you unfairly, accused you falsely.
I wonder if you will ever forgive me."

Eliza slipped off her chair and settled at his feet, resting
her cheek on his knee. "I love you. It is that simple. You had
your reasons to doubt me. Know now that there will never be
any reason to doubt me again."

"How could I, sweetheart?" He leaned down and scooped
her onto his lap, kissing her hair. "You are irresistibly sincere.
But it is hard releasing this canker that has eaten away at me
for so long. I suppose I have never really learned how to trust."

"I know. I do understand. I have had my own canker,
Edward, which my stepfather put there, first when he told me
that I was ugly and worthless, and then when he made his
proposition that I become his mistress. I never quite felt the
same about myself after. I felt ashamed, that I surely must be
ugly and worthless, good for nothing but—but that. That is why
it hurt so much when I heard what you said at the Denigham
ball that night. I had fallen in love with you and so was
vulnerable to what you thought of me. It only confirmed what
I already believed about myself, although you thought I was
not even worth bedding."

"You are beautiful, Eliza, inside and out. I cannot forgive
myself for speaking so thoughtlessly and hurting you." He
hugged her to him.

"It no longer hurts me. I realize that I purposely hid behind
dowdiness and shyness, hoping no one would notice me. But
you have shown me what I can be, Edward. That is a great gift.
All I can do is give that gift back to you by loving you for all
that you are."

"You have done that. And you have shown me what I can
be, sweetheart. I have surprised myself greatly in the last month.
Among other things, I find I quite like being a father."

"You are a very good father, Edward. And now you are to
be a father again."

"Yes. It is hard to absorb. I find it difficult to believe that
my manhood has not been so crippled as I thought it."

"It was never crippled, my darling. You have always made
me the happiest of women. But nor was it affected in the way

you had thought. What was it that brought you to believing it, Edward?''

"Mumps," he said.

"Mumps?" she repeated, looking up at him with laughter in her eyes. "You contracted mumps? I hardly dare think where."

"My throat was also inflamed. It was damned uncomfortable in both areas, so you needn't look so amused."

"Oh—oh, I am truly sorry, for I am sure that it must have been dreadful. But fortunately you were only temporarily impaired."

"I'm not quite sure how such a thing is possible."

"I don't know myself, although it seems perfectly possible that such an illness weakened you for a time—no, *not* your ability, Edward, although I cannot quite believe you tried to impregnate every woman on the island. Really!"

"Not every woman. I did use some discretion."

Eliza smiled. "I beg your pardon. In any case, it is possible that the women you were bedding used some discretion also to avoid pregnancy, and you weren't aware of the fact. Or, as I said, perhaps it took time for your internal mechanisms to correct themselves."

"I can hear you about to launch off on the bulls again, Eliza, my love. Don't, I beg you. This is humiliating enough."

"Why? I am sure you can now sire as many children as you choose."

"Are you? I feel most encouraged. Beware, Eliza. You might be smitten with a dynasty."

"A dynasty of March offspring might just be enough to keep me busy. If I wasn't already carrying one of them, I should immediately insist you give me another." She buried her face in his neck with a laugh.

"I will give you precisely what you need, whenever I feel you need it. Eliza—you really do not mind about the child? There are some ramifications we need to consider. After all, I did go to rather a lot of trouble to see that Matthew would succeed me, but now—"

"I am terribly happy, and I'm not the least interested in ramifications. Matthew will have a brother or sister, which will do him good, I will learn what is it to give birth, no doubt a most interesting experience, and something very wonderful and unexpected has come from our wedding night. You don't mind, do you?"

"An onus or two has been removed, and, no, I don't mind. As you have so rightly said, something miraculous has come out of that night. I am truly very happy, sweetheart." He placed his hand on her abdomen. "It's definitely in there, isn't it? I cannot believe I didn't notice."

"You were not expecting it. I think I had better tell Mavis, though, and reassure her that her darling Matthew will remain Lord Glouston, or she might not look so favorably on this pregnancy."

He gave her a long look. "You truly mean that, don't you."

"Isn't that what you want?"

"Yes, naturally, but I thought that with our own child, you might—"

"Edward, Matthew is our own child. I would never think to consider him anything else. He is also your rightful heir, no matter which side of the blanket he was originally born on. In any case, it would create quite a scandal if the truth came out now, and it would be extremely difficult to explain away, even if I didn't feel this way about Matthew—which I do, absolutely and without reservation. And you're not to worry about it. For all you know, I'll present you with a stable of carrot-topped daughters. There has been hardly a male in the Austerleighs or Babcocks for generations, not that I wouldn't mind another son or two."

Edward smiled softly. "Thank you for that. You are very generous."

"Don't be ridiculous. Would you declare Bottom worthless if Clementine took with another calf by a different father?"

Edward rubbed his forehead with one finger. "I knew it would creep in. I was certain you would not be able to keep the cows out of it for long."

"I'm terribly sorry, really I am," Eliza replied, well-pleased by his amused expression. They had had enough of gravity for one evening. "It just seemed to be the best analogy at the moment. And as for Mavis, she can be slightly overprotective, but she's utterly loyal and devoted."

Edward rolled his eyes. "Mavis. I suppose we have to keep her?"

"I'm rather fond of her, Edward, and she is good with

children, which is fortunate, considering the dynasty you are planning. She's even coming around to you, believe it or not, for although she might consider you a callous lout, you are Matthew's father, and you have been behaving rather better recently. All the staff think so, according to Annie and Jeanette. Even Wyatt has come around to you."

"You have bewitched the household, madam, both my households, and I imagine I shall feel very disgruntled when you do the same to my ornery servants in Jamaica. You have also bewitched my bird, who spent the journey crooning your name, not good for my frame of mind at the time. Now let me take you home, Lady Seaton, before the devoted staff go into a frenzy."

"No, my autocratic lord. We go on to Southampton. You have a cargo to see to. I have Jeanette and appropriate clothes, for I had it quite in mind, wanting to see how this side of the business works. I left a message for Mr. Trevor, who will no doubt be thankful for a week in which to see for himself how things go without our interference. Annie has been advised, as has Wyatt."

"Let it never be said I was bullied by my wife," Edward said with a smile.

"Let it never be said you did not give your wife everything she required. And I do so want to experience what it is like to be properly bedded in an inn. Pallets and featherbeds and linen closets are all well and fine, never mind the wine cellar, but it is my fondest desire to add a progress of inns to the list."

Edward burst into laughter. "Then let me love you into silence, wife, for it seems the only way for either of us to achieve any peace." He stood, setting her on her feet; then, taking her hand, he led her through to his bedchamber.

"Just one thing, Edward," Eliza said as Archie drew his head out from under his wing and gave a great shriek of delight when he saw her. "Archie will have to sleep next door, for I must draw the line there. He takes far too much interest in my activities as it is."

Edward grinned. "For a naturalist you have a prudish mind, my love."

"I don't have a prudish mind in the least, as you know perfectly well. But I will not be watched by that little orange eye as I demonstrate that fact to you, nor will I have whatever I choose to say to you repeated to the servants tomorrow morning at breakfast and for a long time thereafter.''

Edward's shoulders shook with laughter. ''What a shame! It would make breakfast an unusually stimulating occasion. But very well, sweetheart,'' he said, picking up the small traveling cage. ''Say good night, Archie.'' He bore off a very disappointed and loudly protesting bird and was back in a moment.

''Now, my dear wife,'' he said, drawing her to him and beginning to unbutton her dress, ''let me see firsthand how the pregnant female of the human species behaves when performing the mating ritual.''

Eliza smiled. ''Pregnancy is going to be so very stimulating. I cannot imagine just how ingenious you are going to have to become, my lord, but I certainly intend to find out.''

''If you ever stop talking, you will,'' he murmured from the recesses of her neck. ''I do believe I know just where to start.''

''Edward,'' Eliza cried. ''Whatever are you doing?''

''Loving you!'' Eliza,'' Edward said with a muffled laugh. ''Simply loving you.''